KELLIE HAILES dec .... oing
to write books when .... get
there, with a career a ....ance copywriter
and beauty editor filling the dream-hole, until now. Kellie lives
in Auckland, New Zealand with her patient husband and delightful
daughter. When the characters in her head aren't dictating their
story to her, she can be found taking short walks, eating good
cheese and hanging out for her next coffee fix.

You can follow Kellie on Twitter: @KellieHailes

The Little Bookshop at Herring Cove

KELLIE HAILES

ONE PLACE. MANY STORIES

HQ
An imprint of HarperCollins*Publishers* Ltd
1 London Bridge Street
London SE1 9GF

This edition 2019

1
First published in Great Britain by
HQ, an imprint of HarperCollins*Publishers* Ltd 2019

ISBN: PB: 978-0-00-834784-0
EB: 978-0-00-833613-4

MIX
Paper from
responsible sources
FSC
www.fsc.org **FSC® C007454**

This book is produced from independently certified FSC™ paper
to ensure responsible forest management.

For more information visit: www.harpercollins.co.uk/green

Typeset by Palimpsest Book Production Ltd, Falkirk, Stirlingshire

Printed and bound in Great Britain by
CPI Group (UK) Ltd, Melksham, SN12 6TR

For my little fur face, Alfred. I miss you every day, but you live on in my heart... and now in the pages of this book.

CHAPTER ONE

She just had to survive for a few more months. Six months, to be exact. Then the Christmas rush would see enough money in her bookshop's bank account to scrape through for another year. Maybe. Hopefully.

Sophie sucked in her lower lip as she tightened her grip on the hammer's wooden handle, slowly practising lowering the head to the nail before raising it again.

She forced herself to put aside all mental images of the spreadsheet she'd been looking at earlier that morning. It told a terrible story. Of loss. Lacklustre book sales. And looming financial disaster. She could tell herself things would get better but the numbers didn't lie. Sales were getting worse. Year on year, even during the festive season, she'd seen a fall in profit. People weren't buying books the way they used to, at least they weren't buying them from her little bookshop.

She held her breath as she raised the hammer a little before bringing it down on the display case she was trying to fix.

'Ow!'

The pained word filled the room as she pressed her lips together, dropped the hammer onto the ground, doubled over, and gripped her thumb and forefinger, hoping the pressure on them would ease the throbbing that was building second by second.

'Are you okay there? Should I call an ambulance? Perhaps a funeral parlour?'

Sophie forced her eyes open, ready to give the owner of the bemused voice the kind of glare that would make him think twice before being cheeky to a woman in distress.

Except no glare came forth.

And her racing heart, which had only just begun to slow down to a canter, picked up once more.

Cripes. The smart-arse was a babe. Dark brown hair, shorn short at the sides with a touch more length on top, made way for a face that no doubt spelled trouble. Green eyes, dancing with good humour, twinkled down at her. Lips that were all hard-edged on the outside and plump in the middle twitched to one side. Cheekbones, sharp enough a model would be envious, were raised high.

He was laughing? At her? Well, he could take his babealiciousness and bugger off.

Taking a step back, Sophie folded her arms over her chest, lifted her chin and adopted her most professional tone. 'I'm fine, thank you. Just a little mishap between my finger and a hammer. Now, what can I do for you? Are you after a book?'

The smirk straightened out as his eyes ceased twinkling. 'Actually, I'm looking for Sophie Jones. Is she about?'

Sophie Jones. Her name rolled off his tongue. Smooth, sweet. With a hint of seduction. And the way he was staring at her. Penetrating. Lingering. Like he could see past her red A-line knee-length skirt and simple white T-shirt all the way into her soul, where worry and loneliness huddled together as uncomfortable bedmates.

'That would be me. And you are?' She raised an eyebrow and tightened her grip on herself. There was no way he knew who she was, not really. She was crazy to even consider it.

'Alexander Fletcher.' He offered her his hand to shake.

Manicured nails. He had manicured nails. She shouldn't have

been surprised. It matched his outfit: a tailored, form-fitting navy suit, which gave way to a lighter blue shirt, accented with a tie the same shade of the suit with a white geometric pattern running through it.

An outfit that was completely at odds with the fashion of Herring Cove, where the dress code was strictly T-shirt and shorts in summer and jeans and chunky sweaters in winter. Even the village clerk avoided suits – said they didn't suit the blink-and-you'll-miss-it Cornish fishing village's laid-back image.

And what was it about his name that was ringing a bell? And not the tinkly, light ding-once-for-service ring that told her when she was out back that a customer was ready to be attended to, but a clanging alarm-that-gave-you-a-migraine kind of bell.

She glanced out the window at a poster that had been taped to a pole. 'Stand up for Herring Cove' was emblazoned on top of a picture of a fancy hotel with a big X struck across it.

'Fletcher. As in the resort builders.' The words escaped before she could stop them. Before she could pretend she had no idea who he was in order to find out what exactly he wanted when she'd already made her position to the Fletcher Group crystal-clear.

'Well now that you know who I am, then this will make the visit that much quicker.' He flashed her a boyish grin, then picked up her abandoned hammer, squatted down beside the display stand and gave it an experimental shake that saw it wobble back and forth, in danger of complete collapse. 'She's seen better days.'

Sophie didn't answer. Didn't give him anything. She knew why he was here. What he wanted. And he wasn't going to get it, no matter how polite he was, how nice he seemed… or how much money he was offering.

An unwanted image arose of emails with 'Urgent – payment due' in the subject line, and old-fashioned paper bills stamped with 'Overdue'. The most terrifying of the lot was the council tax. If she didn't pay that, and soon, they could force her to sell.

Not going to happen. She gritted her teeth and shoved the image into the darkest corner of her mind where it held less power. Where it couldn't freeze her with fear, unable to make solid decisions.

She just had to figure out a way to boost sales. To change the downward trend that had come with the shrinking of Herring Cove's population. That's all. No big deal.

Except it was. A huge deal. Massive. The bookshop was her livelihood and the flat above was her home. The place she'd been born and raised. The living memory of her parents who'd passed away when she was five. She wouldn't let that go. Couldn't.

Alexander picked up the nail that had fallen to the floor, repositioned it, then with one quick movement knocked it into place. 'Got another? We don't want it falling apart in two seconds, do we?'

Sophie shook her head. 'No, there's not another.' She felt a slight blush at the fib. 'Besides, I didn't ask you to help, and I don't have the time for small talk. I'm busy.'

Alexander's gaze roamed over the empty shop. Bare of customers. And, if Sophie were honest, a touch too bare of books.

'Busy? Doing what? Trying to break your fingers?'

His tone was gentle, teasing, which only set Sophie further on edge.

'I have to ready the shop for the Herring Cove Book Appreciators' Club.' Which consisted of two people: Natalie and Ginny. Also known as her two best friends. And, if the truth were told, not exactly massive book appreciators. So much so that they'd cancelled the meeting for that week, both citing family obligations. But Alexander didn't need to know that. 'The kettle needs to go on. Biscuits need to be arranged. I can't let my customers down.'

'Well then, I'll help. Where's the kettle? Out the back?' Alexander took a step towards the doorway that led to the small storeroom and office.

4

Sophie shot an arm out, blocking him. 'It is out the back but you're not to go there. Staff only.'

'Well I'm not leaving until we've had a proper chat. I understand that you declined our offer.'

Sophie widened her stance, squared her shoulders and crossed her arms over her chest, hoping it would perform a dual purpose: as a blockade should Alexander try and head out back again and to show him that she meant business when she said no.

'You understand right. I did decline your offer. I have no desire to sell this place.'

'Can I ask why?' Alexander's head tipped to the side, a small furrow appearing between his brows as they drew together.

If she didn't know better, if she hadn't figured out he was one of *the* Fletchers – a family whose fortune was built on taking small villages and transforming them into tourist hotspots – she'd have thought he might genuinely care. Except she knew better. He was here for one reason and one reason only: to get her to sell.

'You can ask, but I'm not going to tell you. It's none of your business.' Sophie inwardly cringed at the curtness of her tone. It wasn't like her to be so sharp, but then again it wasn't every day that a big business tried to buy your land and that surrounding you in order to build a towering monstrosity that could only be a blight to the quaint charm of the little village she called home.

'Well if you're not going to tell me why, then could you at least hear me out? Let me explain our vision for Herring Cove? Maybe we could take a seat over there?' Alexander indicated to the vintage bobbled-fabric turquoise sofa.

Bathed in the summer sun, it was the perfect spot to curl up with a book. Something Sophie did regularly. A way to pass the time when the shop was quiet. Which was a lot of the time.

She breathed out low and slow. The irritation that had her shoulders hitched up towards her ears disappeared with the whoosh of expelled air. 'If I listen, will you leave me alone? Never talk to me again?'

Alexander shrugged, the too-hot-for-its-own-good smile was back. 'Can't promise that. I have a few more people to see and it's a small village. There's always a chance we'll bump into each other.'

He had a point. Although if he hoped bumping into her would see her change her mind, he was mistaken. There was no number of pennies pretty enough to make her sell. And the pennies the Fletcher Group initially offered had been exceptionally pretty. More than the place was worth. But not enough for her to see her home, her place in the world, reduced to rubble.

'Fine. You can talk.' Sophie flicked her hand, hustling him towards the sofa and the two armchairs that flanked it. 'You go first.'

'No, you go. Ladies first.' Alexander stood his ground.

'I never said I was a lady.' Sophie brought her hands to her hips.

'Only calling it like I see it. Besides, if I don't let you go first my mother will be disappointed in me. She worked hard on my manners. It's a point of great pride for her.'

Sophie's lips twitched to the side. *Do not smile.* Too late.

Seeing a man in a suit worrying about his manners because he didn't want to disappoint his mother was… well… adorable. Even if said adorability was coming from a man she was sure was a wolf in sheep's clothing.

'Fine. I wouldn't want to be responsible for undoing all her good work.' She crossed the room and settled into the burnt-orange armchair and indicated for Alexander to sit on the sofa. 'So, talk.'

'I know you've got the book club coming so I'll keep it quick.' Alexander leaned forward, his forearms flat upon his thighs, his hands clasped loosely together. His voice calm, collected.

Like what he was wanting to do was no big deal. Like he made visits to people who weren't playing ball regularly. Which, maybe he did.

6

'The thing is, we think Herring Cove has so much potential. Potential that's not being realised. If we built one of our resorts here, created a proper path down the cliffs to the beach, then the local economy would be revitalised. There'd be more jobs. More people. More money.'

And a whole lot less soul. Sophie kept her thought to herself, there was no point in trying to change Alexander's mind. It would be like trying to change her mind about selling the shop. A waste of time.

'The reason I came here is that I wanted to talk to you in person about what it is you're missing out on by not saying yes.'

Sophie's spine stiffened. This was what he was here for? To give her the hard sell? To guilt her into selling? Good luck with that. She'd long ago learned that listening to men with silken tongues was a bad idea. 'Fool me once' and all that. She wasn't about to be fooled twice.

'I'm not missing out on anything. I have everything I want right here. I don't need anything else.' *Or anyone else.*

'Here. This is for you.' He reached into the concealed pocket of his suit jacket, pulled out a folded square of crisp cream-coloured note paper and slipped it across the teak Scandinavian coffee table. 'We've upped our offer.'

Sophie let it sit there. 'Not interested. I said it to your lackey over the email, then again over the phone, and I shall say it now – my home is not for sale.'

Alexander sat back in the chair, his expression unchanged, unperturbed. 'And why not? In my experience, everything is for sale… as long as the price is right. And, trust me, the price is right.'

Sophie eyed the small square. How much was in there? Crazy money? Her fingers itched to pick it up, unfold it, and see what was on offer.

No. She mustn't. Besides, whatever number was written down wouldn't make her budge. 'All Booked Up' was the last thread of her family. All she had left. It was her home and she loved it. Nothing could make her move.

What if you go broke? Because that could happen. What if you can't afford to pay the rates on the place? You won't be moved out, you'll be chucked out.

Not going to happen. She'd survived all these years – even after her horrid ex, Phillip, had stolen the money she'd saved for lean times, then disappeared to who knows where. She'd find a way to make things work. She'd save 'All Booked Up'. Bring it back from the brink. She just had to figure out how.

'You're not even going to look at the offer?' Alexander's head tipped to one side, as corrugated lines wrinkled his forehead.

'I don't need to. I'm not going to sell. Now if you don't mind, I have work to do.' Sophie stood, strode as purposefully as she knew how to the counter, then opened up her laptop and pretended to be engrossed with what she saw on the screen.

Footfalls on the wooden floor told her Alexander was up and, hopefully, leaving. A shadow fell over the counter.

Wishful thinking, then.

'That piece of paper contains enough money for you to do anything you want in the world. To go anywhere. To start fresh.'

Sophie fixed her most unimpressed look on her face, then looked up. 'But what I want is to stay here in Herring Cove and run the bookshop. I don't want to do any old thing. Go any old where. Or start fresh.'

Despite his tan Alexander's face paled, the hint of colour on his cheeks gone.

She'd rattled him? Interesting. But not interesting enough for her to waste any more time on a man who wanted to take her life away from her.

'Well, I've heard what you've had to say. You can go now.' Beside the laptop, her mobile buzzed and lit up as an email notification came through.

Sophie closed her eyes as she noted another reminder notice.

8

This time for the power. Could she go without power? Could she run the bookshop without it? What did she really need power for? She ran through the list: no till, no cash machine, no kettle for cups of tea, no light to read books by late into the night. Conclusion? Allowing the power to be cut off was not an option.

She glanced up at Alexander to remind him it was time to move on, but his eyes were on her phone, his hand on his chin, fingers stroking its smooth, freshly shaved skin.

Had he seen the bill? Was he going to use it against her?

His eyes met hers and he gave no indication that he'd seen evidence of her finances being in dire straits. Instead he pulled a wallet from the back pocket of his trousers, opened it and produced a nail.

'Before I go, allow me. Please.'

Before she could answer he knelt down, picked up the hammer and hit the nail square into the display shelf. He gave it a nudge and nodded. 'That'll hold.'

'You didn't have to do that.' Sophie shut her laptop and made her way to the door, opened it. A sure sign to Alexander that it was time for him to leave.

'I didn't have to, but I wanted to.' He gave the display shelf a pat that Sophie could almost describe as loving, then made his way to the door. 'Well, thanks for hearing me out.'

'No problem.' Sophie waited for him to leave.

And waited.

Alexander showed no sign of leaving as his gaze flitted around the shop.

'Waiting for me to bow?'

'No, just thinking how great this place would look if the books were displayed in bookshelves like you find at a library. Though you'd need a few more bookshelves knocked up to make that happen.'

Sophie followed his gaze. Saw what he saw. Row after row of bookshelves, the titles in order, neatly shelved, with popular books displayed throughout. One simple change could transform the store, without changing its rustic essence.

One problem. Shelving cost money. And she didn't have that.

'Well, thanks for the advice.' She inclined her head toward the street.

'Anytime. See you round, Sophie.'

'Ah, no you won't. The deal is done, remember? You spoke. I listened.'

A gleam of sparkling white teeth appeared as Alexander smiled, the lines of worry on his forehead disappearing. 'I know that's what I said, but here's the thing. I don't believe in the word "no". I believe "no" is the first step of a business negotiation. It's the first word on the way to a "yes".'

Sophie gripped the door knob, hoping it would hide her hand, which had begun to shake with anger. 'If that's the case, you're about to discover what it feels like to hear a solid, firm, absolute "no" for the first time. I'm not selling All Booked Up. Not now. Not ever.'

Sophie turned away from the door – Alexander could see himself out. Her outrage deepened as she caught his grin broadening. She curled her fingers into her palms, dug the nails in, let the pain focus her as she marched back to the counter.

He had no idea who he was dealing with. Sophie had spent her life treasuring what was left of her family. The bookshop meant everything to her. And she wasn't going to sell it or lose it without a fight.

Alexander wouldn't take no for an answer? He'd have to.

Because Alexander Fletcher had met his match.

CHAPTER TWO

Alexander left the bookshop and Sophie without a backward glance. To do that would show Sophie how unsettled his encounter with her had made him.

He dropped the grin he'd forced to his face and began the walk to the village's only accommodation, a small B&B which, with its tiny rooms decorated with faded blue and yellow anchor-patterned wallpaper and shabby age-worn rugs, was a world away from his spacious mews home in London, where the colour scheme was shades of grey and off-white, and the furniture minimal.

He shoved his hands in his trouser pockets and considered he and Sophie's conversation.

She was the first person he'd dealt with in over a decade of working in the family business to not open an offer letter. Most people couldn't resist the crisp sheets of paper that held the answers to problems, offered the chance to chase one's dreams. And once they saw the numbers written within the small square, couldn't resist saying yes.

He reached the end of the angled lane that led to a road that hugged the clifftops, along which cottages, mostly empty, sat in various stage of decay. He crossed the road, drawn to the view, leaned against the basic wooden railing, and took in the stretch of sapphire water that streaked out to the horizon where the sea and azure-coloured sky kissed.

The rumble of rolling waves crashing upon the golden sand below and the fresh, briny air he breathed in did nothing to soothe him.

His plan had not gone to plan. Not by a long shot.

Get in. Make the offer. Show Sophie the benefits of having a Fletcher resort built in her village. Show Sophie the benefits of taking the deal offered to her. Then leave, and continue with the plan to bulldoze the businesses and create a first-class resort with top-of-the-line amenities and offerings. A day spa. Fine dining restaurant. Coaches on hand to teach everything from tennis to surfing to cake-baking if the person coughing up the money so desired.

The end result being a transformed Herring Cove. Goodbye sleepy fishing village, hello vibrant, exciting place to visit.

The template was there. His father's life's work – and his grandfather's before him – had been to take quiet seaside villages and turn them into tourist hot spots. The rules were simple: first, find a seaside town that might not be worth investing in on the outside. In this case, Herring Cove. Picturesque, with a decent climate in summer, but you had to walk down a hair-raising, heart-thumping track to get to the beach. A track his father's contractors could transform into an easily negotiable path.

Second, buy land that had a view of the sea so visitors would wake up immediately feeling like they were on holiday. He'd have preferred to buy land along the clifftop, but the cottages were protected. The land Sophie's business sat on, along with the two businesses either side of her, was not. And due to the slant of the lane, they had the sea views required. Combined with the fields behind – land that had been secured thanks to a local farmer who was ready to sell up and move to Tenerife – and there would be more than enough room to build the hotel, create a poolside area for those who liked the idea of a beach holiday but preferred to swim in temperature controlled water, with land left over to create a nine-hole golf course.

Finally? Promote the area as the hottest new seaside destination. Bring in the visitors. Empty buildings would soon fill with businesses featuring boutique offerings. The village would flourish. The Fletcher fortune would grow.

Job done. Everyone happy.

Resistance by locals was rare.

Rare?

Unheard of. Until now.

The business beside Sophie's had been a simple sell. His team had researched Solomon Murphy and knew he'd be an easy sign. He'd run his fishing supplies store forever and was well past the age of retirement. As expected, he'd leapt at the offer. Said he was Tuscany-bound where his daughter, son-in-law and grandchildren lived.

The other business beside Sophie was on the fence. The hair-salon owner was taking some persuading. However, it was clear her building was falling apart and with two small children to take care of, and the floor area not being conducive to a growing family, he couldn't see her saying no to the upped offer. To the chance of being able to provide a bigger, more modern home.

Sophie, though?

How did he get things so wrong? How did he get *her* so wrong?

It didn't help that she was virtually an internet recluse. Information had been scarce. She wasn't on social media. Her bookshop didn't even have an online presence. All he'd been able to find were two articles in a local paper. One reporting on the car crash that had taken her parents' lives when she was five, Sophie only saved as she was buckled into her booster seat at the rear of the car. The other announcing Sophie was taking over the family business after her aunt – who he'd gathered had been her guardian after her parents' passing – retired and moved away.

With such a tragic past, he'd assumed Sophie would have

13

jumped at the chance to move on from the bookshop. Instead she'd chosen to remain where she was – doing what was forced upon her because there was no other family to take the bookshop on.

Was it a sense of honour keeping her there? Some misplaced belief that she owed it to those who'd passed to keep their legacy alive? And, if so, how could he make her see sense? What would it take to get her to sell?

The staccato ringtone of his mobile broke his train of thought. He glanced down at the screen. His gut contracted on seeing his father's name. He'd expect to hear everything was signed and sorted. That his son had sorted out what others could not, as he had many times before.

Despite his heart not always being in the job, Alexander knew he was good at it. People warmed to him, trusted him almost without question, believed he had their best interests at heart.

Which he did. Which the family business did. When dealing with competitors they showed no mercy, but when it came to buying land that they would one day profit from, the Fletcher Group ensured they were more than fair. It was one of the reasons Alexander was able to commit to the job. That, and he had no choice. The only child of Frank and Veronika Fletcher meant he had no option. He was the future CEO of the Fletcher Group, whether he liked it or not.

The phone's ringtone pierced his ears once more. His father wasn't going to like what he was about to say, but if Alexander didn't update him now, Frank Fletcher would be down here in a flash, and while he was generous with payouts, his methods of getting people to sell up were nowhere near as kind in their persuasion as Alexander's.

Alexander accepted the call and braced himself for the barrage of questions that were sure to follow. 'Dad, what can I do for you?'

There was no point exchanging pleasantries. His father was no more likely to ask how Alexander was than he was going to

14

wish him a good evening. Such pleasantries were his mother's job. His father's job was to ensure his son was ready to take the reins of the Fletcher Group when the time came.

'Alexander. Are all the contracts signed?' In the background Alexander could hear the tinkle of ice hitting the bottom of the tumbler. He checked his watch. Just gone six. His father would still be at the office, but it was time for his daily gin and tonic. The one he drank as he went over the day's dealings, while barking orders at his secretary, who would then stay as late as necessary to get what needed to be done sorted.

Alexander loosened his tie, hoping doing so would make the constricting piece of material feel less like a noose. No such luck. 'The farmer, and the fishing supplies fellow signed immediately. The hairdresser still needs some convincing, but I'll get her over the line.' He pursed his lips together. This was going to go down like a tonne of lead bricks. 'We have a hold out.'

'What's gone wrong?' Frank's tone was calm, steely. With a hint of condescension. He knew Alexander's methods didn't mirror his own, and he had little time for them, only tolerating them because they brought results.

'Nothing's gone wrong.' Alexander gripped the phone and focused on a lone seagull soaring in the sky. What would it be like to be able to do just that? Soar on one's own. Do whatever one wanted, whenever one wanted to do it? 'It should have been a shoo-in. I researched her. I know her background. I saw an in.'

'Clearly you saw wrong. You know how we do this. We find their weak point and we use it to our advantage.'

'I know. And I thought I'd found it. I still think I have. I saw a bill flash up on her mobile while I was in there. She's in debt. Can't make payments. Where there's one overdue bill, there will be more.' Alexander left it there. Frank's motivation in life was expanding the business in order to make more money, and if he thought Sophie was in financial trouble, that would settle his unease over Alexander not getting her to sign.

'I'm going back to see her tomorrow. I left the offer with her. I can see it piqued her interest.' Alexander crossed his fingers. Sophie had left the offer on the table. Unopened. A move that had astounded him. How could she not be even the remotest bit curious about what kind of money he was offering? She'd been so resolute in her refusal to sell, he was willing to bet a goodly sum of money that the offer was still on the table, unopened. 'If she's in the kind of money trouble I think she's in, one night should give her enough time to realise how much easier her life would be without companies chasing her for money day-in, day-out.'

Except the original offer was enough to take care of debts and then some. If she was going to sell she would have by now.

He pushed the thought out of his head. Sophie would sign on the dotted line. They all did. He just had to find the right angle. Or find another option.

'Get it done, Alexander. And if they still won't sign, explain to them that they are a mere irritation in the grand scheme of things and that if we have to, we'll build around them. We've already spent enough on this project that it can't not go ahead. Do you understand what I'm saying?'

Alexander swallowed a sigh. 'I understand what you're saying, Dad. I know what's riding on it.' The family name. Pride. Respect. Bottom lines. Profits. The future of the family business, which would one day sit squarely on his head, whether he wanted it to or not. 'Talk tomo—'

He tucked the mobile back in his pocket. His father had already hung up. Moved on.

He swore under his breath. How was he going to play this? How was he going to balance his family's expectations over his own way of doing business? Of getting the deals done without compromising his own values?

He slipped his tie over his head and tucked it into his trouser pocket, then released the top two buttons of his shirt.

Approaching Sophie twice in one day was out of the question. She wasn't ready to trust him. Wasn't ready to see his way of thinking.

His mind churned with possibilities as he turned his face towards the sun as it dipped closer to the horizon. He leaned his head back and allowed himself a moment to enjoy its soothing warmth.

His shoulders, bunched towards his ears, dropped. His hands, screwed up tight at his sides, unfurled. Alexander breathed in and took a moment to appreciate the intoxicating scent of the jasmine that wafted over the fence rails of the cottages that lined the street-side of the cliffs. Mixed with the salty aroma of the sea, it was a heady combination. One that made him want to change out of his formal uniform and slip into a pair of cargo shorts and a T-shirt and forego work for a barefoot walk along the beach below, followed by a spot of sand-sitting and sunset-watching.

The shimmering water, bathed in sunset colours of golds and reds, encouraged him to shirk his responsibilities.

There's time enough to figure things out tomorrow. What's a few hours to yourself? The waves shushing back and forth on the sand whispered. *Take a moment. Relax while you can.*

He shook his head clear of the temptation. The Fletchers didn't relax; they made goals and met them. They took ailing communities and improved upon them.

What they achieved in a year did not happen by resting on one's laurels.

He turned back to the tiny township and began to march towards it. He couldn't see Sophie again, but he could drop in and see the hairstylist, Natalie. She was a sure thing, he felt it in his bones.

He reached the bookshop, and was surprised to see a light shining in the front window. He slowed his steps, acted as casual as he could as he side-eyed the window.

Sophie was curled up on the couch, her nose buried in a book. One hand stroking a small black and white cat that had snuggled

17

up beside her. Her petite bow-shaped pink lips moved, as though she was reading the story to the cat.

Cute. Such a Sophie thing to do.

'Such a Sophie thing to do'? What was he thinking? He'd barely spent half an hour in her presence. Sure, he'd researched her past, but that didn't give him the right to believe he had intimate knowledge. That he knew her.

God, he needed to get back to the nitrogen dioxide-filled London air. This ozone was clearly playing with his head. Sending him on random flights of fancy. He no more knew Sophie than he knew the hairstylist, Natalie.

Yet the more he watched her read to the cat, curled up and comfortable on the worn sofa, a mug of tea steaming on the old coffee table, the more his brain whirled.

She was at home in the bookshop. Yet she was in danger of losing it, if his assumption that she was in serious debt was correct. Did that debt extend to council taxes? One call to the local councillor his father kept in his pocket would confirm just how dire the situation was.

And what if she was? Could he use that information to force her to sign? Prickles of discomfort skittled down his neck. No, that was his father's way. So what could he do?

Think, Alexander. Think.

He turned his attention to the empty shop across the road. Though overrun with honeysuckle, it was a handsome building. Perfect for a bookshop. And it had a flat above. All it needed was a good water-blasting to revive the red bricks, and for someone to train the wild tangle of vines. A new sign, fresh paint job inside and it could be a fresh start for Sophie. She'd still have her bookshop, and he'd have the approval of his father. Win/win.

He reached the hair salon's entrance and rang the bell to alert Natalie to his presence.

He felt good about this plan. It could work.

Now he just had to make Sophie see things his way.

CHAPTER THREE

Sophie paced the length of her small lounge, hit the pastel lavender-painted wall. Turned. Paced back. Stared out over the lamp-lit lane below, not seeing the villagers strolling home from the pub, or her cat, Puddles, prowling along the path, hiding behind flower boxes, lamps and the tyres of parked cars as he stalked a mouse.

What the heck was taking Alexander so long at Natalie's? What business did he have with her?

She blew out an exasperated sigh. She knew exactly what business he had with Natalie. The same as he had with her. Except Natalie wouldn't sell. Surely not?

Herring Cove was her home. Her hair salon was her livelihood. Her two kids were her everything; surely she wouldn't rip them away from their home just because some man in a fancy suit flashed some money in her direction?

She heard the click of a door closing and pressed herself to the wall, leaning over just enough that she could look down on the lane without being seen.

Alexander filled her field of vision. Was that a spring in his step? A triumphant smile on his face? Damn it. She couldn't tell through the late evening gloom.

There was only one thing for it.

She snatched up a lightweight sunshine-yellow cardigan from the back of the couch and shrugged it on. Summer may officially be here, but the nights were cool enough that an extra layer was called for. Even if you were only going next door.

She jogged down the stairs, then locked up the shop, even though she didn't have to. Crimes committed were few and far between in Herring Cove, and usually of the petty variety, like kids nicking off with flowers from flower boxes the night before Mother's Day. Still, it was better to be safe than sorry. She didn't have much, but what few trinkets she had were touchstones to her parents, and losing them would mean losing a little more of her heart.

She walked the few steps to her neighbour and friend Natalie's home and business, opened the door, and poked her head over the threshold. 'Nat? You in?'

Miniature elephants running over the wooden floorboards answered her call.

'Muuuuuummmmm!'

'Mummy!'

'Aunsof's here!' Natalie's two children chorused in unison, as they opened the flat above the salon's door and two identical mops of brown curly hair with matching sparkling chestnut brown eyes came into view.

Sophie smiled up at them, the weight on her heart and mind instantly lightening. Joe and Bella, along with Natalie and Ginny, were the closest thing she had to family.

She'd witnessed their christenings and attended all their birthdays. She'd almost been there for Joe's first steps, but had seen his eighth, ninth and tenth as he tottered into her shop. She'd been named Bella's godmother. And from the day Joe could say her name she'd been Aunsof because he couldn't get his wee tongue around Aunty Sophie, a title Natalie had insisted on. A matter of respect, she'd said. But Sophie suspected it was Natalie's way of giving her the family she knew her friend longed for, but didn't see herself ever having.

The shipwreck that was her last relationship had seen her vow to never get involved with a man again. She'd risked her heart once, and as far as she was concerned, when it came to love and falling in it she was all washed up. Even if a tiny, sliver of her heart tried to convince her otherwise. Whispered in her quiet moments that she should let love in, learn to trust again.

She'd let the loneliness win once, and where had that got her? Alone, broke, with no desire for a repeat performance.

Natalie's head appeared around the corner. 'You kids, get out of the doorway. Give Aunty Sophie some room.'

The worry that had tinged Natalie's words in the past few months was gone, Sophie noted as she entered the lounge – an exact replica of hers, but painted in a riotous blaze of yellow and red, instead of the calming purple hue that had been Sophie's mother's colour of choice. There was also a brightness in Natalie's tone that she'd not heard since her husband had left her for another woman.

'Hey.' She squatted down on the floor beside Natalie, who was folding a mountain of laundry, and gave her a half hug and a kiss on the cheek. 'Need a hand?'

'Always.' Natalie rolled her eyes good-naturedly. 'I swear Joe just needs to look at dirt and it's on his clothes. And Bella changes three times a day and refuses to wear anything that hasn't been washed. I try tricking her by putting the clothing all nice and folded back in her drawers – but it's like she knows. Strange child.' She shook her head, affection warming her face as a smile blossomed.

The adoration on her friend's face tugged at Sophie's heart. What would it be like to look at a little person in that way? To feel bemused, frustrated, and absolutely unstoppably in love, all at the same time? Was that how her mother once looked at her, before the crash that had stolen her away?

She faced the window and blinked, refusing to entertain the

tears that threatened. There was no point in pondering the past. Or considering that kind of future.

It had been hard enough for her to commit to a cat, but there was no way she could've left wee Puddles to look after himself when she'd found him wandering the lane, mewling mournfully. No family of his own to be found. He'd been so small, innocent and helpless, and before she could overthink the situation she'd scooped him up in her arms and taken him home with her.

Now he was her constant companion, her little shadow. Her little light.

'You're a million miles away, Soph.' Natalie laid a warm hand upon her shoulder, bringing her back to earth. 'What's up?'

Sophie settled herself into a more comfortable, cross-legged position and tried to brace the subject of Natalie potentially selling to the Fletcher Group as casually as possible. 'Something strange happened today. A man from that company that wants to build the resort in Herring Cove came to the shop. He wants to buy it.'

'Aha…' Natalie's lips mashed together.

'Does that seem weird to you?'

Natalie shifted her gaze from Sophie to the floor. 'Yeah. I mean, no. We've all heard the talk down at the pub. They've bought the farm behind us. Mr Murphy's sold as well. If they want that land it makes sense that they'd want your land… or mine.'

Sophie's suspicion deepened. A knot formed in her stomach. Natalie was acting strange. Off. Like she was hiding something. Keeping something from Sophie.

'Nat? Do you have something to tell me?'

Nat shook her head. 'No.'

The word came out a squeak.

'That "no" sounds like a yes.'

'I don't want to say. I don't want to upset you. So if I say nothing, you can't be upset with me.' Natalie zipped her mouth shut, then turned an invisible key.

22

Sophie's stomach plummeted and nausea swelled. 'Are you trying to not tell me that you've sold the shop? Your business? Your home?' Sophie tried to keep the reproach from her voice. The hurt. She scooted back, up onto the couch. Needing space to get herself together. 'I mean, it's your business to do what you want with. Your flat. But, I don't know… Selling this place is a huge deal. Massive. I just… I can't believe you weren't going to tell me… That you haven't told me that it was even a possibility.'

Natalie shuffled over to sit beside her on the couch, rose up, fished out a naked baby doll, tossed it aside, then sat down again. 'Like I said, Soph, I didn't want to upset you. I love you to bits. And I know how much Herring Cove means to you. How important routine is to you. It keeps you safe, secure.' Natalie opened her arms as Bella ran full tilt towards her wanting a cuddle. She caught her in her arms and brought her close, breathing in the scent of her hair.

Apples and sunshine. Sophie knew. Sophie had taken enough surreptitious sniffs of her own.

Natalie released Bella and turned to face Sophie. 'Have you seen the offer? You must've if he's been to see you.'

Sophie sucked in her lower lip, refused to meet Natalie's gaze.

'You didn't? Oh, Soph.' Natalie shook her head. 'He's not some dodgy dealer trying to get the best deal possible in order to turn a quick buck. It was serious money. Well above what this place is worth. I mean, the roof leaks even when it drizzles. I have to get all the pots, pans and buckets out when it rains proper. To fix this place up?' Her eyes searched the ceiling, as if its peeling paint would provide answers. She shrugged and met Sophie's gaze once again. 'Well, it'd cost more money than I'm likely to have anytime soon. But what he offered me? Offered *us*? It's a game-changer.'

Curiosity loosened the anguish in Sophie's stomach. Not because she'd sell. That would never happen. She'd no more share what few remaining memories she had of her parents for fear she'd lose them. The way her mother's hugs smelled of rose-scented moisturiser. The way her father's jumpers were a mix of his spicy aftershave and the smoke from his pipe he'd enjoy every evening after dinner, while nursing a whisky.

'Would you look at that. I think I see a reduction in that worry wrinkle of yours. Does this mean you're interested in just how rich I'm about to become?'

'No, not at all.' Sophie massaged the line between her brows. 'Not really. Just…'

'You're wondering what you're missing out on? Wondering what it would take for me to leave this leaky old house with a fabulous view of the sea that stretches all the way out to the horizon?' Natalie's knee nudged Sophie. 'Go on, admit it. You want to know.'

Sophie returned the nudge, a smile playing about her lips. She didn't get in a funk often, but on the odd occasion that she did, Natalie always knew how to get her out of it. 'Fine. I'm just a bit… Okay, a lot interested. But not because I'd sell.'

'I know. You never would.' Natalie draped an arm around Sophie's shoulders and brought her into a cuddle.

'Never could. I love that place. It's where I belong. But enough about me, tell me, just how much money is being flung your way?' Sophie glanced out the window. Night had fallen and though she couldn't see the endless stretch of sea, the sound of waves crashing onto sand told her it was still there. As it always would be.

'Enough money that I'm in the mood for a celebratory glass of wine. Just the one though. This lot had me up at the crack of dawn. Any more than one glass and I'm liable to fall asleep on the couch and they'll be putting themselves to bed. Bella and Joe should've been in bed an hour ago as it is, but they're refusing.' Natalie stood and ruffled Bella's hair as she passed her on the way to the kitchen. 'Pinot gris okay?' she called out.

In typical Natalie fashion, she didn't wait for an answer and not twenty seconds later she walked back in with a glass of chilled wine in each hand. 'Here you go.'

Sophie accepted the glass, then raised it in a toast. 'To you, my friend. You've had it hard the last few months. You deserve this bit of luck.'

Natalie settled down onto the floor and began folding washing. 'Indeed. And this money. Oh, it's a glorious amount.' A teasing smile flirted about her lips.

'Enough that I'll be seeing chunky diamonds dripping off those dainty fingers of yours? Or that you'll be swanning round head to toe in designer duds?'

Natalie slid her hand into her jeans pocket and pulled out a perfectly folded square of crisp cream paper. Identical to the one Sophie had been offered and ignored earlier that day. 'I'm not really meant to share how much it is… but you're my best friend, family really, and I know you're not going to blab it all over town if I show you, so, here.'

Sophie took the proffered piece of paper, opened it slowly, as if afraid it would bite. Or worse. Tempt.

'This can't be right.' She glanced up to see Natalie nodding, a giant grin on her face. 'There has to be one too many zeroes on here, surely?'

The nod morphed into a shake. 'That's what he offered. That's what I accepted.'

'Nat, with this kind of money you could…' Sophie didn't know where to start. She could buy a home that the family could grow into. She could build a house from scratch and still have plenty left over. This was life-changing money.

The kind of money that could change *her* life?

Sophie shoved the thought away. Yes, she needed money. But not if it meant selling the one place she loved more than anywhere else in the world.

'So, what are your plans, Miss Moneybags?'

Natalie paused her folding, twisted a small pair of shorts

around her hands, averted her gaze towards the corner of the room. Her smile disappeared as a cloud of concern darkened her features. Natalie was worried? When she may as well have won the lottery? But why?

'I'm going to leave Herring Cove.' The words came out a constrained whisper. Like it hurt her to say them. 'I'm sorry.'

Now she understood. Natalie had been cagey about the deal because Natalie didn't want Sophie to feel abandoned. To feel like she was losing her little family.

A painful lump appeared in Sophie's throat. 'I see.'

She knew she couldn't leave it with just those words. Natalie deserved more. She'd always been so supportive, so *there*. Bringing Sophie home for afternoon tea after school. Inviting her to Christmas dinner leftovers knowing Sophie's aunt would have fallen into a food and heavily-laced-with-sherry trifle coma after lunch that would last until the next morning.

When Sophie turned eighteen and her aunty decided it was time she returned to Manchester, it was Natalie, along with Ginny, who'd spent as many nights as possible at Sophie's. Keeping her company. Keeping her sane. Ensuring she didn't fall into the doldrums.

And how could she when they'd been the bright spots in her life. Her life could have gone in a very opposite direction without the love and strength of her friends. Their gorgeous qualities had reflected on Sophie, infused her. Given her a positivity and determination to keep on going even when loneliness or sadness reared its head.

'It's just… there are too many memories here.' Natalie's knuckles further whitened as she wrung the shorts tighter.

Sophie slid off the sofa and sat beside her friend, so close their knees were touching companionably. 'Give those to me.' She held her hand out for the shorts. 'You're going to tear them in two.'

Natalie relinquished the shorts. 'I mean, there were great times here, but finding my ex cheating on me. In our bed. In this house.

I can't un-see it. It's ruined the place.' Tears welled up in her eyes, and she brushed them away. 'Ugh. I'm not feeling sorry for myself. Not when I have *that*.' She nodded to the paper, held gingerly between Sophie's thumb and forefinger. 'Not when I don't have to give *him* a cent of it because I got that loan to buy him out when he left. A loan I can now easily repay in full.'

'So where will you go?' Sophie fixed a smile on her face, forced a lightness into her voice. 'The sky's the limit.'

'Well, not quite. I don't see myself buying a mansion in the country anytime soon. But we could certainly get a bigger place. In a bigger town. One where people won't whisper about "that poor woman".' Natalie's smile faded quickly.

Sophie rubbed her friend's arm. 'No one ever talked about you like that. What I heard was, "That idiot, what was he thinking?" And they were right.' She picked up her glass and took a long sip. The cool liquid soothed her nerves. Settled her mind. 'You do what you have to do, Nat. You deserve all the good things in the world. And besides, it'll be wonderful to have free accommodation… wherever it is that you end up.'

Natalie took Sophie's hand in her own. 'You're amazing, Soph. The best. What I'd do without you, I wouldn't know.'

'Actually, I think that sentiment needs to be switched round. You've always been there for me. Right from the beginning.' Sophie pulled herself into a crouch, then stood. 'If you need help packing, or if I can look after the kids while you sort house-finding things out, let me know. I'm only one door away.' *For the time being, anyway*.

Natalie hefted a pile of folded laundry into her arms and pushed herself up to stand by Sophie.

'Thanks, lovely. There's no hurry though. Alexander said a few loose ends had to be tied up before the project could go ahead.' Natalie stifled a yawn. 'Right, I've got to get these kids to bed. I'm not long for the sack either.'

Loose ends? Was she a loose end? Could the resort not go

27

ahead without her buy-in? Or should that be sell-out? And if she stuck to her guns, did that mean her friend would lose her chance at happiness?

She stashed the questions away to mull over later. There was no point worrying Natalie now, not when Sophie had no answers.

She fixed a smile to her face and pecked her friend on the cheek. 'Night, Nat. Sweet dreams.'

'I'm rich. Well, by my standards. My dreams will be full of golden paths and fancy cars and four-bedroom houses with solid unleaky rooves.'

Sophie forced out a happy laugh, then traipsed down the stairs. She stepped into the cool night air and scowled at the pro-Fletcher poster someone had placed over the anti-Fletcher poster. A towering building with a bright red tick over the top.

There was no way that offensive piece of propaganda was going to be staring her in the face all day tomorrow. She marched up to the pole and pulled it down, reinstating the anti-Fletcher poster.

Natalie was right. She liked her routine. Thrived on it. She enjoyed knowing everything had its place, and the Fletcher Group had no place in Herring Cove.

They could throw all the money they wanted at her, she wasn't budging.

She unlocked the shop and stepped inside. The musty smell of books mixed with furniture polish washed over her. Reminded her of what was important.

Her home. And she was going to do everything she could to save it. To keep her place in the world.

CHAPTER FOUR

Alexander checked the lay of the land as he reached Sophie's shop window, and readied himself to enter and spell out the reality of what was about to happen to her bookshop if she didn't sell, and how much better her situation would be if she changed her mind and signed her land over to the Fletcher Group.

Sophie was hunched over a notepad, her face covered by her sheet of auburn hair as she scribbled away, while a blonde-haired woman Alexander didn't recognise sat next to her, her lips moving as fast as her hands.

He pushed open the door, his client-ready smile fixed on his face and paused at the threshold as their heads jerked up to see who'd interrupted their gathering.

The silence was broken by an exasperated sigh. Alexander could have had his eyes closed and he'd still have known which of the two women the puff of displeasure had come from.

'If you're not here to buy a book, then you may as well turn around and leave,' muttered Sophie, her gaze returning to the notebook she held in her hand. 'Where were we, Ginny?'

Alexander stepped into the shop and mentally revised his plan. Explaining the reality of Sophie's situation was out, for the moment. He was more interested in what she and her friend were busy discussing. From the screes of writing and the pages flipped over, anyone would think Sophie and her friend were planning to go to war. Which, considering the divide in the village regarding his family's plans, wasn't something he could disregard.

'Charming way to greet a customer.' Alexander kept his tone light, friendly. 'Can you point me in the direction of the autobiography section?' He gazed round the room and tried to figure out Sophie's system.

Hand-painted wooden signs, flaking with age, showed romance novels huddled up against horror. Fantasy sat next to astronomy and astrology. The travel section nuzzled up to books on philosophy. No wonder things weren't going great for her. You'd spend five minutes looking for what you wanted, give up and leave empty-handed.

For someone who professed to love the place so much, he couldn't understand how Sophie had let it go. Hadn't moved on with the times; at the very least placed the book sections in alphabetical order.

'Interesting system you've got going.' He ran his hand along the book spines, noting how dated they were. He'd figured her finances were in bad shape, but to not even update stock? His father had emailed him to say he would talk to his man on the council to see if he could find out anything more about Sophie's financial issues. Alexander suspected he wasn't going to need confirmation. The facts were staring him in the face.

'You'll find autobiographies next to the biographies, which is next to the science fiction. Just behind me.' Sophie waved her hand in a vague direction, then resumed scribbling.

Alexander followed her directions and made his way to the autobiographies. The selection was small, and as he'd suspected, dated.

'Meow?'

A little squeak drew his attention to the floor where the sleek cat he'd seen snuggled up to Sophie the previous evening sat on its haunches, its eyes pleading for attention.

'Hey little one.' He squatted down and patted its soft fur and marvelled at its dignified markings. Its jet-black body and face contrasted with a white bib, long white boots on its hind legs and shorter white gloves on its front paws, giving it the look of an old-fashioned butler. 'Aren't you adorable.'

The cat meowed its agreement and leaned into his touch as he scratched its cheek.

'Puddles, don't engage with the enemy,' hissed Sophie in a low whisper.

The comment was terse but not hurtful. Simply a way for Sophie to remind Alexander he wasn't welcome.

'Puddles.' Alexander ran his thumb from the top of the cat's nose to the back of his head and was rewarded with a deep, vibrating purr. 'You look more like an Alfred to me.'

He gave the cat one final stroke, then turned his attention back to the books.

'So, I was thinking I could organise a market for this Friday night. A Midsummer's Night Market.'

Sophie's hushed tone caught Alexander's attention. He pulled out a book about an old has-been television actor, flipped through to the first chapter and pretended to be absorbed in the old fella's words.

'Get some locals to sell their wares. Have music. Food. Advertise through social media to the surrounding areas. Bring the village together. Remind them what we're capable of if we stick together.'

'Sophie, that's a brilliant idea. We should have done it ages ago. Why didn't we do it ages ago? I'll be able to sell my home-made skincare products. The local dressmaker could set up a stall. I'll spread the word down at the pub tonight. We'll have the lane filled with goodies and punters and hopefully lots of lovely money.' She clapped her hands and bounced up and down in her seat.

'Excellent. I'll need to get some sort of permission, but I'll figure that out later on tonight. I was also thinking it's high time I set up profiles for All Booked Up on all the main social media sites.'

'Another excellent idea. Sophie, you're on fire.'

Sophie chuckled. 'I don't know about that, but a spark's been ignited, that's for sure. Will you show me how to run the social media?'

'Absolutely. It's not hard. You just need to keep people amused, engaged and interested. Then when they need a book you'll be top of their minds. We'll need to find someone who can build you a website but won't charge you the earth. Don't suppose you know anyone?'

Alexander waited for Sophie to say her neighbour's name, Natalie. When he'd researched her and taken a look at the salon's website, he'd been so impressed with its clean, contemporary design that he'd searched for the business who'd created it should their services be needed one day. That's when he'd noticed her salon's website had been self-designed. She'd even created a business name 'Cut to Fit' and a basic landing page, which led him to believe Natalie harboured a desire to start up her own web-design business one day but wasn't ready to make the leap.

With that knowledge in mind, he'd made a point of including it in his sales pitch. New home, money to start a business, a chance to follow her passion, enjoy a fresh start.

Natalie's eyes had lit up, and he'd known that particular deal was done.

He turned to face Sophie and the other woman, Ginny. 'What about Natalie from the salon?' He reached his hand out to Ginny. 'I'm Alexander, by the way.'

Ginny automatically brought his hand to hers and shook it with a welcoming smile.

'Nice to meet you. I'm Ginny. And I think you've got your wires crossed. Natalie cuts hair, she doesn't create websites.'

'No, I think you'll find she's quite accomplished at website building. She did her own, and it's easy to navigate and intuitive. She's set it up so if you go to buy one product, other suggestions are made. Checkout is easy. The design is simple, modern, stylish.

I was very impressed. Look for yourself. There's a link at the bottom of the page that takes you to a business landing page. Her name's right there.'

'I don't believe you.' Sophie pushed herself up and strode over to the counter where her laptop was open, then tapped on the keys. 'You've got your wires cross—'

Alexander raised an eyebrow. Waited for an apology.

'He's right. She did do it herself.' Sophie's lower lip slackened as her brows furrowed together. 'I'm going to have to have a chat with her about doing mine. It looks great. I can't believe she didn't tell me she could do that. Did she tell you, Ginny?'

Ginny shook her head. 'No, but then she's been quieter than usual lately. I put it down to the stress and strain of the past year.'

'Must be that. Anyway, she's got herself a client, if she wants one.' Sophie clapped her hands, her eyes sparkling with excitement.

No apology then. And no thank you either. Alexander turned back to the books and faked interest in an autobiography by a marine biologist.

'I've also been looking into writers who might come here to give talks. I saw that romance author, Lucille Devine, was touring the area and figured I'd see if she could fit us in. No harm asking, right? And a spruce up of this place is well and truly in order.'

So that's what the scribbling and serious looks were for. Sophie was trying to drum up interest in the bookshop to save it from closing down.

'Love it, on both fronts. Writer talks would be amazing – especially Lucille. She seems like a right character. And can you imagine this place painted sunshine yellow?'

'I'd like to stick to the same décor.'

Alexander caught a hint of steel in Sophie's voice. Interesting. Why wouldn't she want to change things up?

'But before you start going on about what a stuck-in-my-ways-stick-in-the-mud I am, I've been thinking I'd love to create a library feel to the shop, with bookshelves placed in the middle, as well as round the edges, of the room.'

Alexander twisted round and caught Sophie's eye. Her cheeks burned red, but she held his gaze, her chin lifting ever so slightly, as if daring him to take the mickey out of her for using his idea.

The temptation to do so was there, but it would have been too easy a wind-up. He winked at Sophie, then went back to his book, but not before her eyes widened in what he swore was irritation. She'd wanted him to call her out? Was she looking for a fight? A reason to throw him out?

Good luck with that. He'd been trained to negotiate, to deal with all sorts of situations and personality types. If he'd learned one thing it was never to be drawn into a petty scrap.

'Actually, it was Alexander's idea.'

The fight had gone from Sophie's tone, replaced with the seriousness of someone who had plans and wanted to make them happen.

'Don't suppose you know anyone with basic carpentry skills, Ginny? Someone who knows their way around a bit of timber and a few nails?'

Alexander's heart abandoned its steady pace and began to thump against his ribcage. Not caused by the realisation that Sophie was trying to invigorate her business, to make it viable. But because he knew someone who was good – no, great – with nails and timber and building and creating. Except that person had been told in explicit terms he was not to indulge in that pastime. That there were not enough hours in the day for hobbies – for something that made his soul sing – when there were deals to be done and connections to be made. Yet his fingers automatically curled into a loose fist, as if the hammer was already in his hand. The satisfying whack on metal as he landed its head straight into the bullseye of the nail, sending it clean into the wood with one thunk, stirred a satisfaction in

34

his gut that no amount of getting people to give up their lives for inordinate amounts of cash ever did. Ever would do.

'I'd love to say that husband of mine could help, but he's shocking. I still have a half-built outdoor bench cluttering up our yard. I love Mike, but he really needs to stick to fishing.'

'Maybe there's a local handyman who'd do it in exchange for books?' Sophie's fingers tapped out an erratic tune on the counter.

Alexander glanced at her out of the corner of his eye. Her teeth were sunk into her bottom lip, her gaze distant, a tiny line marred the smooth area between her brows. Beneath the strain he saw a brightness to her rich, chocolatey eyes. Burning intensity. Passion. The kind he wanted to bask in. To be part of.

It was one thing to build an empire, another to build something that mattered to someone so much they'd go into battle to fight for it.

He wasn't meant to care. To get involved. To focus on anything except expansion and returns on investment, but his heart wasn't satisfied living that way. His heart wanted to do more. To help. To reinvigorate. And Sophie's need for someone who had the skills that he possessed was like a sign from the universe, giving him one last chance at happiness – even for a few days – before surrendering to his destiny.

'I can help.' The words escaped his lips before the thought was fully formed. His stomach clenched. What the hell had just happened? What was he doing offering to help someone build the business he intended to buy in order to pull down?

'What's that now?' Sophie's eyes narrowed in suspicion. 'Did I just hear you offer to lend a hand? You? The guy who wants to buy my home so he can destroy it?' She stood and strode towards him, her arms folded tight over her chest. Her jaw as tense as her frown. 'Is this how you plan to get me to sign my business over to you? By helping me out, while what? Buying the most expensive timbers and nails and glue, or whatever it is you need to hold a set of shelves together. Spend what money I have so the business goes bust and I have no choice but to sell?' She tilted her chin, held his gaze. Dared him to deny what she was saying was the truth.

So, what are you going to do, Fletcher? You've just gone and created a fork in what was meant to be a very straightforward road.

He could back out. Back off. Let Sophie try to save her shop. And probably fail if the rundown look of the place and lack of customers was anything to go by.

Or he could step up, help out. Give her what she needed to make her business work. Whether that business was in her current spot, surrounded on three sides by a five-storey resort, or somewhere else. Somewhere bigger. Better.

Like the empty shop across the road.

This was the moment he'd been looking for. The chance to explain what would happen to her village and how selling up and moving would benefit her, and what the ramifications of refusing to do so would be.

'I'm going to be honest with you, Sophie, because I get the feeling you prefer a straight-up relationship to one that's filled with layers of machinations. The Fletcher Group will build a resort here. We have the council's backing. The support of the village.'

'*Some* of the village,' Sophie interjected. 'And once they see how this market idea of mine can save the town, they'll all want you gone.'

'No, they won't. It'll just show them a taste of the success they'll experience once the resort is built, the facilities are improved and people are here not just for one day, but all year round. Speaking of which, if you're going to hold a market you'll need a licence.'

'I know that.' Sophie smiled, tight and determined. 'I'm planning on getting permission.'

'It takes around three months.'

Alexander watched Sophie's triumphant smile fall. Remorse

squirmed low in his gut. He didn't mean to burst her bubble, but Sophie had no idea what she was taking on, and he didn't want her to get in trouble. Not when he was bringing enough distress to her door as it was. 'Let me hurry the process up. We're in the council's good books. They need us more than we need them at the moment. I can sort it.'

Sophie's smile didn't return. A good thing considering the truth bomb he was about to lay on her.

'Look, the reason I'm here is to spell out the reality of what's going to happen in the coming months. Simply put, if you don't sell we will build around you. It's not our ideal situation, but we can make it work.'

'You wouldn't.' Sophie's jaw dropped, her eyes widened in horror.

'I wouldn't, but the Fletcher Group would.' He rubbed his hand over the layer of stubble that had sprouted since he'd arrived in Herring Cove and tried to remember the last time he'd forgotten to shave, let alone allow it to grow that long. It was like the village's laid-back vibe was getting to him. 'I hate to be the one to tell you this, but I have to. It's the truth. I've been thinking about a solution to the problem and I think there's a way we can make this work. The empty shop across the road had plenty of potential and oozes charm. It would be the perfect spot for your bookshop. With the money we'd give you, you could have it done up and looking brilliant. Best of all, you'll have all the money you need and you won't have to worry about being in debt to anyone.'

Anger shimmered off Sophie. 'You saw the email notification. That wasn't yours to see.'

Alexander shrugged. 'It wasn't, but I saw it and I'm offering you a chance to be financially stable, or to put up with the consequences.'

Sophie's lips pressed together in a way that took the wind out of his sails. His pitch seemed rock-solid, yet she didn't look to be buying it.

'I'm not taking the deal.'

'You understand what I'm saying, right? This is going to happen whether you want it to or not. We will build around you. Three-quarters of your building will be in shadow. You'll have tourists peering into your flat upstairs as they go about their business. Day in. Day out.'

'I don't care.' Sophie folded her arms, her eyes not leaving his.

Alexander's heart began to thunder in his chest. This was the worst-case scenario. His father wouldn't care about building around a small business. Making their life untenable, but he did. Very much so.

He cupped the back of his neck and worked through the options to make things better for Sophie.

'Take me up on my offer. Let me help you build the shelves. I'll make a new sign for outside since the old one's looking like it'll fall apart in a gentle breeze. I can repaint the walls the same shade if you want me to.'

Sophie shook her head. Her lip in a stubborn line.

'Please, Sophie. Let me work with you. Let me help build you up. Don't let your determination to stay in your home be in vain.'

Ginny came to stand beside Sophie and laid her hand on her forearm. 'Soph, I hate to say it, but can you afford to say no? Don't let pride get in the way of your business succeeding. Not when you've got so many excellent ideas on the boil. Alexander's offering free labour, even though he doesn't have to. What's in it for him?'

What was in it for him? He'd be able to walk away from Herring Cove knowing he'd done right by all concerned. Those who'd sold would have enough money to make their lives infinitely easier. With his help, Sophie's business would have a chance at survival. And his values would be intact. All the while, as far as his father was concerned, he'd have done right by the family.

He massaged a knot in his neck as he realised his mistake. His father. He'd left him out of the equation. Helping Sophie meant needing time. Time he did not have. He was expected back in the office any day now. Offers signed. Job done.

The fluttering poster on the pole caught his attention.

That was it. He'd use the rising tension in Herring Cove as his cover. He'd stay for the week to smooth things over with people. Slap some backs. Shake some hands. His father would understand that. The last thing he'd want was negative press coverage due to villagers holding protests when building was due to begin.

'Will you let me help? No strings attached?' Alexander pressed his palms together and gave his best big-eyed pleading look.

Sophie's chest rose then fell as she exhaled a long, loud breath. 'I'm going to regret this. I already think I'm an idiot for considering it, but... Fine. I have conditions though.' She held her fisted hand up and began listing off her rules, a finger rising for every statute. 'You will work here only when I'm here. You will work out the back, away from customers. You will only interact with me. And you will only use the materials I provide you with. If you cannot or will not agree to those terms, then we have no deal.'

Without hesitation Alexander stretched out his hand, kept his face devoid of emotion. Wanted Sophie to see he was serious. That he genuinely wanted to help. 'Deal.' Her palm met his as they shook hands in agreement.

Sophie's eyes widened, as if she'd been zapped by an electric fence. Her hand jerked out of his. She took a step back. Another. A flush of pink bloomed on her cheeks.

Alexander swallowed hard as he tried to figure out what had just happened, what he'd just done. He'd just agreed to do something magnificently stupid. It went against everything he'd had drilled into him by his father. Yet, he didn't say no to Sophie's conditions. Couldn't have. He shoved his hands into his trouser pockets, the warmth of Sophie's hand still making its presence known.

He couldn't have said no because it was the right thing to do.

And good could come of it. What kind of good he didn't entirely know.

But for the first time in a long time, he couldn't wait to find out.

CHAPTER FIVE

Sophie massaged her temples in an attempt to fight off the nagging headache that had pulsed, low and painful, since she'd woken that morning. The cause of said headache wasn't hard to pinpoint.

It fell squarely at the feet of a man who wore a suit far too well, whose smile came too readily, and whose offer to help her rebuild her shop couldn't be trusted.

Yet she'd agreed to let him help. Fool that she was.

A good-looking face and a bit of encouragement from Ginny and she'd been thrust into a déjà vu spiral. She'd made the mistake of trusting a handsome face before and look how that had turned out. Her heart well and truly dented, and her business in danger of being taken from her.

At least this time she wasn't going to be fooled by a pretty face and charming ways. She was simply going to let him do the work, then send him on his way. No chit-chat. No case of the friendlies. No letting her guard down.

'Morning. Alexander Fletcher, reporting for work.'

Sophie dragged her gaze up to see Alexander saluting her, a wide grin on his face, emphasising the twinkle in his eyes and the straight, white perfection of his teeth.

Fooled by his pretty face she would not be, but it didn't mean she couldn't appreciate it. Herring Cove wasn't exactly teeming with men you'd call a good catch. Not that she wanted to catch a man. Her hook was firmly reeled in. There was no law against looking though.

Alexander released his salute. 'So, what have you got for me to do?'

Sophie dragged her hand across her eyes and stifled a yawn. 'Are you always so perky at this time of day?' She pushed the home button on her phone. 'It's only just after nine.'

'I wake at five sharp. Go for a run. Check emails. Deal with whatever needs dealing with.'

'Like destroying people's lifestyles.' Sophie mentally zipped her lips. Alexander had offered to help for free. It wasn't right to be rude to him. And she couldn't afford to look this gift horse in the mouth. 'Sorry, Alexander. I know you think you're doing something good here by building the resort, and even though I'm vehemently against it, I shouldn't be rude, not when I'm taking blatant advantage of your kind but misguided offer.'

Alexander shrugged. 'At least we know where we stand with each other.' He rubbed his hands together. 'So, where are the materials? I'm ready to go.'

Sophie waved her hand towards the storeroom, which led to the storage area behind the shops. 'Follow me.'

'I'm glad you liked my library idea. It's pretty cool, if I do say so myself. And I really like your idea of writer talks, and setting up a website. E-commerce is a must in this day and age.'

The thrumming in Sophie's temples intensified. 'How about you just start with the shelving and we'll see how that goes, shall we?' She unlocked the door and pushed it open. 'Here we go.' She swept her arm over the 'materials' he had to work with.

'Pallets. That's what you've got for me?' Alexander knelt down and ran his hand over the pale gold, streaked with colours of honey timber. 'Because a hammer and some nails would be good. Maybe a bit of sandpaper so I can smooth off the edges?'

42

'Not enough nails in your wallet?' She waited for him to rise to the bait.

'Nope. Just keep the one in there. It's kind of like a good-luck charm.'

Okay, so he wasn't catching. She bit the soft inner flesh of her cheek, torn between wanting him to give up and go and knowing she needed the help.

'Sophie? Are you alright? You're looking a bit dazed.' Alexander stood and before she could say no, he'd placed his hand on her forehead. 'Are you coming down with something?'

Sophie swiped the hand away, his kindness adding to the squirming in her stomach. 'I'm fine. Just got a headache. The hammer and nails are by the door there. I'll get you some sandpaper. I'm sure Ginny's husband, Mike, will have some we can use.'

'Great, thanks.' Alexander bent over and scooped them up. His hand confidently grasped the hammer like it was second nature to him.

Which made no sense. What kind of businessman was as at home in a suit as he was with handling a tool?

'Right, I'll get started then.' Without another word, he turned his back on her and began pulling out nails from the pallets using the claw-end of the hammer.

He made it look so easy. Like pulling a thorn from your skin.

If only she could remove the financial problems of the bookshop as easily, in a way that didn't mean selling up.

'If there's enough wood left over I'll make some new display cases.' Alexander didn't look up from his work. Didn't look for confirmation.

Sophie backed towards the door. 'Okay. Thank you.'

What else could she say? 'No' would be churlish, and questioning why he was helping her out was a waste of words since he'd made his position and reasoning clear.

She shut the door behind her and pressed her forehead to the door. The pressure of the hard, cool wood against her forehead eased her headache a little, but not enough to erase the pain altogether. For that she needed all her problems solved, and the only person she could trust and rely on to do that was herself.

***

'Here.' A plain, white mug was thrust before Alexander. 'I thought you might like a cup of tea since you've been out here for hours. And I made you a sandwich too.'

Alexander's stomach rumbled as loud as the thunder that had grumbled off-shore for the past hour as he took in the glistening slabs of bright red tomato, crisp green lettuce and generous slices of cheese and ham, held together by two hunks of crusty brown bread. A summer storm was brewing and he was trying not to see it as an omen.

Loyalty to his family warred with loyalty to his self-respect and his ethics, and no matter how hard he tried to find a common ground between the two, he always came to the same conclusion. He'd either end up disappointing his family or losing himself. Neither option was appetising.

Another rumble bounced around the sky, followed by a smaller version coming from inside him.

'Sounds like I should've brought you this earlier. Sorry.'

Alexander set his hammer aside, wiped his forearm across his sweaty brow and forced himself not to look surprised. Sophie sounded sorry. And the way she was gnawing on her lower lip indicated she felt sorry too.

'It's okay, I was so busy being head down bum up working on this shelving that I didn't notice how hungry I was until I saw that beast of a sandwich.' He took the plate from her with a nod of thanks. 'The bread looks amazing. Is there a secret local bakery that makes it?' He took a bite and closed his eyes as the sweet acidity of the tomato mixed with the freshness of the lettuce and the richness of the ham and cheese. 'Tastes amazing too.'

The sandwich couldn't hide the grin that came out of nowhere. His father and mother would both be having hernias if they could see their son right now. His business suit cast aside for a simple T-shirt and shorts. Dirt had made its way under his fingernails. And the fact that he'd just spoken while his mouth was full? A Fletcher family no-no. All manners all the time.

'Why are you smiling like that? You look like you're up to something.' Sophie sank down onto the paving stones beside him. Her look of suspicion was back, but it was nowhere near full strength. Instead it was mixed with curiosity.

Alexander swallowed his mouthful and ran his thumb over his lips, removing any traces of crumbs. 'Not up to anything. I'm just really enjoying this…' *This everything.* 'This sandwich. It's honestly one of the best I've ever had.'

Sophie's cheeks bloomed a pretty pink. 'I make the bread myself. It's my mother's recipe. And the lettuce and tomatoes come from the farmer next door. He has a small roadside stall, and his produce is always picked-that-day fresh.'

Guilt threatened to steal the joy that came from enjoying a simple sandwich and an honest day's work. He knew the exact roadside stall Sophie was speaking of. A handcrafted rectangular box, painted red with blue trim, its shelves filled with fruit and veg. A charming addition to the countryside, and one that would soon be taken away and replaced by a stone wall running the length of the land designed to keep non-paying guests out.

'Though I guess since you've bought the farm, we won't be enjoying produce from there for much longer.' Sophie picked up the pile of bent, rusty nails that he'd pulled from the pallets and jiggled them in her hand.

'No, I suppose not.' Where the vegetable plots currently sat were earmarked for part of the golf course.

Sophie humphed her disapproval, then crossed her legs and

wiggled back and forth, getting comfortable, like she was settling in for a serious chat.

'So, I saw how much you offered Natalie next door. It's a lot of money for a building that run down.'

Alexander nearly spat out his mouthful. The agreements between the Fletcher Group and their vendors were meant to be confidential. Monetary arrangements were not to be disclosed.

Sophie pointed a finger in his direction and waggled it back and forth. 'And before you get all grumpy that Nat told me, we're like sisters. We tell each other everything.'

Alexander thought back to Natalie's website and the surprise on Sophie and Ginny's face. Not everything, apparently, but he wasn't going to bring that up and risk shaking the barely even ground he and Sophie were currently on.

'Well, it's what the land is worth. And I'm not here to play games.'

'Yet you're here, building me shelves, talking about building a new sign, painting walls. It feels a lot to me like some kind of game is being played.' The edge was back in Sophie's tone.

Of course it was. All the shelving in the world wasn't going to give her reason to trust him. And he had the distinct feeling that it would take a lot more than just words and promises to allow Sophie to trust him. Only time and consistency could do that.

The former he didn't have a lot of. As for the latter, he'd said he was going to help her out, and he was a man of his word.

'There's no game-playing here, Sophie. You know our plans. We're going to build a resort here. We believe more good will come from a Fletcher resort than from letting this village continue its descent into a ghost town.' Alexander picked up the hammer and gripped it. Embraced its solidity, its ability to create, to help. 'The thing is, I hate the idea of destroying someone's livelihood in order for me to get what I want.'

Sophie turned to face him, her eyes steely. 'Is that how you see it? You think stamping a fancy resort in the middle of a beautiful

46

village is a good thing? A way to change people's fortunes? Their lives?' She dropped the nails on the ground and fisted her hands, her knuckles blooming white. 'What that tells me is that you don't really see this place at all. You see pound signs. You see your family name on another building. You see a chance to expand *your* fortunes, not ours. Not everyone in this village is motivated by money. Not even Nat. She has her reasons for selling that aren't money-oriented at all. And if those reasons weren't there, she'd have told you to bugger off, that I'm certain of.'

Sophie picked up the plate and pushed herself up. 'The thing is, Alexander, you weren't born here, you weren't raised here, you can't see how special this place is. You'll do what you think needs doing to make your goals happen. You'll take Herring Cove, our home with its beautiful heart, and rip the soul from it, then you'll leave and never step foot in it again. Never look back.'

Alexander tried to formulate a comeback. Failed. Sophie was telling the truth. There was no argument. That was exactly how the Fletcher Group went about business. Find a viable spot. Follow the format with complete disregard to what made a place special, then move on.

He focused on the lengths of wood in front of him, unable to face Sophie's antipathy for one second longer. Not because he couldn't handle it from *her* but because it was a reflection of how – if he were honest – he felt about the family business. Its impact on communities. Its impact on the people who lived there.

It was a feeling he'd tried to suppress for years. One that was his secret shame. If he ever voiced his concerns out loud to either of his parents he'd be letting them down. Not living up to their expectations of who he was meant to be.

Yet he'd heard whispers of what happened to communities once Fletcher money transformed their quiet, peaceful villages. And they weren't pretty.

Early issues were of infrastructure struggling to cope. Sewerage systems with burst pipes. Roading that crumbled under the increased volume of traffic. Road rage breaking out on bank holidays, putting pressure on the local police force.

He'd heard reports of increases in drunk and disorderly behaviour and petty theft. Not to mention the 'us' and 'them' mentality between those who were born and bred in the area and those who came to holiday in their flash cars, complete with sense of entitlement, rubbing up villagers in the wrong way, creating a friction that couldn't easily be smoothed over.

'The thing is, Alexander.' Sophie's voice cracked. She cleared her throat. 'The thing is, you're not the one who has to pick up the broken pieces. The broken people. You don't have to hold things together. And while I have no doubt that a Fletcher resort will bring money, opportunities and people to Herring Cove, it won't strengthen its soul. This place is not just where I live, not just where I work. It's as much a part of me as my heart is. It *is* my soul. And you're threatening to destroy it, which is why I'm going to have to ask you to put down that hammer and leave. You being here is just a reminder of everything you're planning to take away. And I've lost enough.'

The strength in Sophie's voice stopped Alexander from an attempt at rebuttal. There was no pity in her voice. No 'poor me'. Only a strong self-belief that she could handle whatever life threw at her, and his helping was only seen as interference.

He sucked in a breath and focused on the hammer, still in his hand. Pondered what his next move should be.

Quick footsteps on pavers followed by the click of the back door shutting told him he was alone.

Sophie didn't just have a point. She was right. But her being right couldn't change the future. The deal was going through. The resort was happening. He couldn't stop it, but he could say sorry in his own way.

He'd promised Sophie he'd help out. And he didn't break promises. Not to too-cute-for-her-own-good bookshop owners, not to his parents, not to anyone.

48

Especially not to himself.

His sense of self, his sense of worth, was riding on his doing the right thing by Sophie, because he was beginning to wonder if what they were doing in Herring Cove might very well be the wrong thing.

CHAPTER SIX

Sophie tried not to let the ripple of ever-growing irritation break through her customer-ready smile. Why was Alexander still out the back? What part of 'leave' did he not understand? And why was he still hammering away, physically and metaphorically?

'That noise has got to be driving you balmy.' Mr Johnson, a loyal customer who made a point of coming in every couple of weeks to buy a book, usually an autobiography or thriller, covered his ears with an empathetic grimace.

'I've got a guy helping me build some new shelving.' Sophie silently congratulated herself on not adding 'annoying' and 'pain-in-the-arse' before 'guy'.

'New shelving?' Mr Johnson's eyebrows rose. 'Does that mean business is picking up? Is Herring Cove seeing a turn of the tide? Is fortune finally favouring us? Is there a chance we can kick that horrid Fletcher resort out of the town before ground is broken?'

Sophie placed Mr Johnson's latest book of choice, an autobiography of some past-it politician, in a brown paper bag stamped with All Booked Up's logo, folded the top over and fastened it with a piece of sticky tape. 'I wish. People are falling like flies from what I can make out. Selling up and moving out. They've been trying to get me to sell, but I won't. Not that my saying no will stop them. Apparently I can be built around.'

'Disgusting. Ruining the special character of our village just to add more money to their coffers.' Mr Johnson shuddered dramatically. 'Good on you for not folding, Sophie. You're setting a good example. Perhaps once others know about your refusal they'll change their minds too. Until I see a bulldozer I believe we have a chance at battling this Goliath.'

'I don't think there's any chance of that, sadly. They seem determined.' So determined that one of the masterminds of the project was refusing to stop helping her. 'Either way I think it's high time this place was freshened up. She deserves to look her best, no matter what happens.'

'Indeed. Your parents would be proud of you, young lady. Keeping this place alive in the face of all sorts of adversity.' Mr Johnson waved his package in the air as he tipped his tweed cap, the lines around his eyes deepening along with his smile. 'I'm looking forward to seeing this place jazzed up, Sophie. I'll see you again once I'm finished with this.'

'Perhaps sooner? I'm planning a night market for this Friday. Will you come?'

'Of course. I'll pass the word around. Let's make it a night to remember before our beautiful village is tarnished by a tacky resort.'

With a wave goodbye he left, leaving Sophie alone with the tightness in her chest. She slumped down onto the counter and buried her head in her arms.

Would her parents be proud of her? The survival of All Booked Up was on a knife's edge, and the blame could be laid squarely at her own feet for trusting another to love and care for the place in the same way she did. To love and care for her.

Except he hadn't. Phillip had pretended to have a vested interest. To want to pour money into the place, to expand its offerings, to revamp the look, to go online. Instead he'd emptied thousands of hard-earned pounds from their joint bank account. Stealing not only money, but any chance of doing All Booked Up the justice Sophie believed it deserved.

Her parents had put their all into that shop. They'd died fighting for its survival. Arguing in the car over how best to keep it going. Their words causing her young self, who'd never heard them fight, to cry and plead for them to stop. Until they did stop. For good.

She knew the accident wasn't her fault, but she carried the guilt of surviving, of being part of what contributed to the accident. Because of that she'd long ago promised herself to never let their legacy go. To hold it tight, as she wished she could hold them tight once more.

The door chimes tinkled, followed by the pitter-patter of small feet racing off to the children's area Sophie's mother had created. Filled with picture books and toys, it was a great way to keep the little ones occupied while their parents browsed in peace.

Sophie lifted her head to see Natalie walking towards her, her forehead corrugated with concern.

'What's up, Soph? You look rotten.'

Sophie propped her elbows on the counter and placed her chin in her hands. 'Just what every girl wants to hear. I look a mess. Wonderful.' She winked to let Natalie know she wasn't insulted. 'Just a headache that won't budge.'

Natalie's head twisted towards the back where Alexander was still hammering away. 'With that going on I'm not surprised. What's that Fletcher guy doing out there, anyway? Not that I'm complaining. I may not be in the market for a man, but I still know how to appreciate a good-looking one when I see one.' Natalie fanned herself with a laugh.

'Ugh.' Sophie wrinkled her nose in disgust. 'He's too annoying to be good-looking. He's got it in his head that he wants to help me save my business by building shelves and helping me freshen the place up. I suspect there's a hidden agenda of some sort. Speaking of which…' Sophie caught Natalie's eye and held it. 'You've been hiding something from me.'

'Me?' Natalie shook her head. 'Don't think so. I know I didn't tell you about wanting to leave, but that was because I didn't think it would ever happen, so what was the point?'

'Not about leaving. About your website. You built it. Alexander told me. Ginny was here and it was as big a surprise to her as it was to me. Since when do you build websites? Since when are you really good at it?' Sophie skipped round the desk, hooked her arm through Natalie's, pulled her to the sofa and dragged her down to sit beside her. 'I thought a professional had done your website. It's that good.'

Natalie's cheeks flamed red. 'It's nothing, honestly. Just something I thought I'd try. I didn't have the money to hire anyone to do it for me and I've always been okay with computers...'

'Okay with computers? You were a right whizz at school. Able to fix things when we couldn't. We were always surprised you didn't take it further.'

'Taking it further would've meant leaving here. Leaving my ex. My life. It just seemed... easier... if I stayed here and took the hairdressing apprenticeship that was on offer. Get married. Have kids. Do the regular thing.' Natalie shrugged. 'I don't know, with business slowing up I had some time on my hands and I guess I wanted to see what else I could do. See if I could make web design a side business, or perhaps one day a full-time one.'

Sophie took Natalie's hand and gave it a squeeze. 'You can do anything you put your mind to, Nat, and I want to be your first client. You can make me a website. One where I can sell my books. Er...' Heat washed over Sophie's cheek as she realised she was going to have to talk money, or lack thereof. 'Erm, one thing though...'

'You know what?' Natalie tapped her finger on her chin. 'If it works for you, I'd like to do it gratis. As long as you don't mind me using it as an example on my business website and perhaps writing me a client recommendation?'

Sophie leaned over and planted a loud kiss on Natalie's cheek, grateful that her friend had helped her avoid a sticky topic, and for her generosity. 'You are amazing. Best friend ever. I'll write you the most glowing recommendation the internet's ever seen.'

Natalie clucked her tongue. 'You might not say that once you see it.'

Sophie went to reprimand Natalie for not having enough faith in herself but was interrupted by a coupling of pants and grunts.

The door to the backroom squeaked open, and a broad back – not that Sophie was looking, or found it attractive in any way, shape or form, even if she kind of did – greeted her, followed by a bookshelf that was so tall it had to be dragged in on an angle.

Sophie pushed herself up and rushed to help Alexander, her previous irritation with him disappearing as she saw him struggling under the weight of his glorious creation. She stopped a few feet away, unsure of what to do next. 'Do you want a hand with that? Or if I get in the way will that thing tip over and squash us both?'

Alexander waved her away. 'It's all good. I'm fine.' Then with one more grunt he pulled the bookshelf into the room, set it upright and gave it a loving slap. 'There you go. What do you think?'

She ran her hand over the timber and admired the bookshelf. It was simple but solid. In other words, it was perfect. The shelves looked to be evenly spaced, and she suspected if she were to get out a pencil and place it in the middle of a shelf it wouldn't roll to the left or right. As even as its creator was even-tempered. Because if she'd been Alexander, she'd have told her to pull her head in and stop being such a rude cow by now.

'You know you didn't have to do this. I mean, I told you to stop.'

'Is that your way of saying thank you?' Alexander tipped his head to one side, his eyebrows raising in amusement.

God, there she was being rude again. If he wasn't here to rip out the heart of the place she called home, she suspected she'd have found it easy to be polite to Alexander. They may have even been able to become friends. Sure, he'd come across as a bit of an arse when they'd first met in his slick suit and perfectly manicured everything, but standing here in his T-shirt and shorts, looking a little hot and sweaty, with a hint of a shadow peppering his jawline, a laughing smile that emphasised the sparkle in his green eyes, and his hair roughed up as if he'd just run his hands through it, he looked straight up sex—.

Nope. She closed her eyes, blocking the cause of her unexpected lusty thoughts. Out of sight, out of mind, and all that.

It didn't matter how good Alexander looked; at the end of the day he'd only come here to woo her into selling her home.

No. Wrong word.

Not 'woo'.

Persuade. Convince. Strongly suggest.

There would be no wooing.

'I must be a sight for sore eyes.'

'Ha?' She opened her eyes to find his smile had quirked to the side.

'Or maybe you're so overcome with the beauty of this shelf you can't stand to look at it for too long. Well, you'd better get used to it. There are more where that's coming from. You wanted to create a library ambience. I'm going to give you it.'

'Oh, sorry. The sun was reflecting off…' She glanced around looking for a reflective surface. Nothing jumped out to help her excuse viable. 'Off something. Or, you're right, just dazzled by the shelf. It really is perfect. Thank you.'

'Manners. She has them. Who knew?' Alexander threw his hands up in surprise.

Sophie went to defend herself, but stopped. He was teasing. And he'd just done something nice for her. That, and he had a point.

'Well when someone's not being all pushy in a suit that probably costs more than I make in a month, I can be quite pleasant.'

Alexander laughed. Deep and throaty, it filled the room. Open and warm. Pleasant. If Sophie didn't know better she'd have said it belonged to a man you could trust.

And what has he done to make you believe you can't trust him?

Nothing. Absolutely not a thing. Sophie hated to admit it, but Alexander had been straight up with her the whole time. In fact, it felt like he'd gone out of his way to be upfront, to be transparent.

Did that mean she should trust him? Logic suggested yes, the past screamed no.

'Wow. That's really impressive.'

Sophie spun round to see Natalie standing just behind her.

'Is there anything you can't do? Businessman by day, carpenter by… well, day.' Natalie flashed Alexander a dimpled grin.

Was it Sophie's imagination or was there a little flirt in Natalie's voice? And why did the idea that Natalie might find Alexander attractive niggle her?

Was she jealous? Nooooooo. She kicked the thought away. Not jealous, just irritated that her friend was appreciative of anything the man who was meant to be the enemy did.

'Thanks, Natalie. Kind of you to say. I'm looking forward to building more.' Alexander's attention moved from Natalie to Sophie. 'That's if seeing what I can do has changed your mind about me hanging around and helping you out?'

Hanging around and helping her out? He made it sound like she was doing him a favour by allowing him to build the shelves?

'It would be rude not to, Soph. It really does look fantastic.' Natalie raised her eyebrows, egging her on.

'And I'm happy to do it, honestly.' Alexander ran his hand up and down the length of the bookshelf. 'Were you planning to paint or stain it? Because I'd be happy to help with that too.'

Sophie crossed her arms. Physically and mentally reminding herself she had to keep her guard up. Alexander's openness, his honesty, was disarming and she didn't know what to make of it. How to handle it.

'I was planning to stain them dark brown. Keep with that old library feeling.'

'Love it.' Alexander nodded his approval. 'Now where can I put this?'

Sophie pointed to a blank bit of wall at the back of the shop. 'Pop it over there for the time being, please. Wouldn't want it falling onto a customer.'

Alexander hefted the shelf up and shuffled it over to the space she'd indicated. 'How many more of these do you want? I was thinking five more would really create that library look, and there's enough pallets for it. Then we could place them back-to-back for stability down the centre of the shop?'

'Five sounds good.' Natalie poked the small of her back. 'Don't you think, Soph?'

Sophie looked over her shoulder and glared at her friend. Her look was met with a slight shrug of shoulders and an unrepentant smile. She rolled her eyes at Natalie, then faced Alexander once again.

'It's kind of you to offer, Alexander, really, but it's not fair of me to waste your time building shelves when I'm sure you've better things to do.' Sophie waited for Alexander to accept her words, to back down, but his mouth didn't move. No backdown came.

What was going on? Why was he so determined to help her out when he didn't have to? He knew the score. Knew she wasn't selling. Knew she wasn't his greatest fan – the furthest thing from it – and yet he insisted on sticking round, which should have felt uncomfortable bordering on stalkerish, but for some reason Sophie couldn't put her finger on, felt anything but.

'Well, I'd love to hang around here all day and watch you two dance around each other…' Natalie nudged Sophie good-naturedly. 'But the kids and I have got to go. I told Ginny we'd meet her and Mike down at the pub for a drink. You should come.' Her gaze moved from Sophie to Alexander. 'Both of you.'

'Sounds great. I'm parched after all that work. What do you say, Sophie?'

Sophie drew her brows together and directed her fiercest glare at Alexander, who returned the look with a benign smile.

'My shout. It's the least I can do.'

The least he could do? Sophie's curiosity deepened. She was the one who was getting something out of this unorthodox, and unsettling, situation. Free shelves. Free workmanship. A fresh look for the shop. How was this benefitting Alexander?

Her annoyance dissipated as quickly as it had arisen. 'No, it has to be my shout. It's the least *I* can do, considering what you've made me today.'

'Great. That's that sorted.' Natalie's lips lifted in satisfaction. 'Joe, Bella, get a wriggle on. Time for lemonade and crisps.' The kids ran up and danced around her in excitement. 'See you two soon.'

With a waggle of fingers, she and the kids were off, leaving Sophie and Alexander staring at each other. Awkwardness sprung up from nowhere, like a boundary had been crossed in the past few moments. One that couldn't be uncrossed.

Alexander stuffed his hands into his short pockets. 'I probably shouldn't have answered for both of us like that... It's just a beer sounded really good and I thought you might like one, too.' He dropped his gaze and rocked a little on his heels.

Sophie went to agree with him, to tell him he was indeed wrong to answer for her, but something in his demeanour – a vulnerability – stopped her. This wasn't the confident Alexander who wore suits and expected the world to do his bidding. This Alexander appeared kind and thoughtful, capable of thinking about others' feelings and needs.

'It's fine, honestly. You're right, a beer does sound good. It's stinking hot and you've been out in it all day. And, before you get all gentlemanly on me, it really is my shout.'

A hint of a blush hit Alexander's cheeks. 'That's very kind, thank you. Is there somewhere I can wash up?' He showed her his palms, ingrained with dirt. 'I'd forgotten that building was dirty work.'

Forgotten? He said it like he'd once been an actual builder. Which explained how handy he was with tools. How well constructed the shelf was. How quickly he'd built it.

'There's a toilet just off to the side of the storeroom. It's got a basin, soap, you know... hand-washing stuff.'

He nodded his thanks and made his way towards the door. His forearm hair brushed against hers as he passed her. A tingle of... something... rippled over her skin at the touch. Spreading, infusing her with warmth.

She touched her cheeks. They were burning. And Sophie was willing to bet they were bright red, too. Thank God Alexander hadn't paused at the door to say anything to her or he'd have seen the effect a simple touch from a man had on her.

A man. Not Alexander. It could've been any man – *any man* – and she would've reacted the same way.

Sophie flapped her hands towards her face and hoped the hint of cool breeze would dissolve the flush of colour.

'Done.' Alexander filled the doorframe with little space to spare. All broad shoulders, toned arms and just the right amount of tall. He had the kind of body that would give a training-honed rugby player a run for his money.

Heat prickled her chest, threatened to rise once more.

'God, I need a drink.' She cringed when she realised she'd said it out loud. Could she be any more obvious?

Alexander took a step towards her. 'Lucky for us we're off to the pub.'

Sophie stepped back, then ducked down behind the counter under the pretence of grabbing her bag, and used the excuse to fan her face once more while attempting to breathe the heat out.

'You right down there?'

Sophie screwed her face up. Awesome. How was she going to

explain her self-ventilation? She tipped her head to see Alexander looking amused… and, if his angled brows were anything to go by, confused.

'Yeah. Fine. Just a bit flustered. I mean hot. Flustered because it's hot.' She mentally face-palmed her waffling self, then pushed herself up from her squatting position. 'You ready?'

'Absolutely.'

Alexander opened the door and Sophie walked through without even an attempt to tell him she didn't need men to open doors for her, because even though she was capable of opening her own doors, and never held back in saying so, for some reason she quite liked that this man did it for her.

Clearly the heat was getting to her.

CHAPTER SEVEN

Alexander kept pace with Sophie as she hot-footed it towards the pub. Her eyes forward-facing, her shoulders pushed back, her lips twisted to the side in a way that indicated she was deep in thought. Musing over something.

She'd been this way since they'd left the shop, and the silence was getting to him. In a matter of days he'd seen angry Sophie, happy Sophie, suspicious Sophie, but this silent Sophie flummoxed him.

Mainly because he had a feeling that he was somehow tied up in the reason for her silence. Though he couldn't put his finger on the reason why.

Either way, it wouldn't do. Not when he was about to enter a pub full of Sophie's friends and fellow villagers, who either saw him as the enemy or as the person who held their fate in their hands. He needed at least one person who, if not on his side, would actually talk to him like a proper human being.

But first he had to get said person to open her mouth and let words fall out.

'Do you ever get sick of that view, Sophie? Stupendous doesn't even begin to cover it.' He stopped in the middle of the road and took in the panoramic vista before him.

Thunderous clouds in bruised shades huddled close to the

water, turning it grey. Streaks of sun that had managed to break through the clouds sent glistening fingers dancing across the water. Ever present, yet ever changing.

Sophie stopped a few steps ahead of him and followed Alexander's gaze.

'I'd forgotten how beautiful it was. When you see it every day, I guess you forget it's there,' she shrugged.

Alexander jogged the few steps to catch up with her. 'I can't believe anyone would take something so beautiful for granted.' Alexander dropped his gaze from the view to face Sophie. 'I certainly wouldn't.'

Sophie's shoulders shuddered in a shiver. Strange, since it was still warm out.

'Cold?'

'Just a bit.' Sophie continued her march towards the pub. 'It may be summer, but the sea breeze still makes things a little chilly, especially with the sun ducking in and out of those clouds.' She rubbed her hands over her arms, grimacing as if to emphasise her point. 'Here we are.' Sophie stopped outside the pub, 'Reel Her Inn'.

Alexander took in the riot of colour spilling from the twin flower boxes sitting either side of the front door. Orange and yellow nasturtiums wandered their way over the edges, flanked by brilliant green foliage. A stunning contrast to the stark white walls of the pub. The windows were thrown open, and the sound of live piano floated into the street.

'After you.' Alexander indicated for her to go through with a small flourish of his hand.

'Not this time.' Sophie matched his hand flourish, then folded her arms over her chest and tapped one foot impatiently. 'After you.'

With a shake of his head, Alexander did as he was told and strolled into the pub. He paused and looked around, unsure of what he was seeing. More unsure of his place amongst the crowd that had gathered.

A rope had been affixed from one end of the pub to the other, creating an even divide. Two signs on either side of the rope hung from the roof. Written on one in bold black lettering was 'Pro', the other 'No'.

Knots formed in Alexander's stomach as he put it all together. This wasn't some village quirk, this was a village divided, literally. Because of the Fletcher Group's plans for Herring Cove.

He backed up, straight into Sophie.

'Careful.' She side-stepped around him and waved to the man on the piano, who was playing a jaunty jazz tune.

'Sophie, darling. Welcome! Pick a side!' he called, as his fingers danced over the keys. 'Before you do, though, are you in the mood for a little pop? I could switch. Although the muse of jazz seems to have filled my soul this good day.'

'Keep with the jazz, Rob.' Sophie silent-clapped his playing as she weaved her way round the tables dotted with local fishermen nursing pints of golden lager and families enjoying an early dinner of fish and chips with lemonades, lagers and crisp white wines to wash them down.

Alexander followed, unsure of what to do, what to make of the situation. Should he sit in the Pro area? That's where he belonged. Then again, if he was here as Sophie's guest it would be rude to sit there when he should be sitting with her in the No area.

'Hey Sherry, what's with the rope of separation?'

Alexander turned his attention to the conversation between Sophie and the woman standing behind the bar pulling their pints.

'A necessary evil, I'm afraid.' She placed one froth-topped glass down in front of Sophie and began to pour another. 'We hated putting it up, separating friends and family, but at least poor Rob's not having to break up fights every other minute. Honestly,' she shook her head, 'what idiot thought building a resort was a good idea in a place like this?'

Sophie muffled a snort with her hand and turned it into a cough. 'Sorry, breathed in wrong. No idea, Sherry. Hopefully they'll see sense and put a stop to it.'

'Wouldn't hold my breath. Money-hungry beggars like that don't think past their snotty noses.'

'Indeed.' Sophie's tone was solemn as she paid and picked up the pints.

All hints of solemnity disappeared as she handed Alexander his pint with a wink, an impish grin on her face.

His heart did a random flip-flop at the cuteness of Sophie's act.

And there was that word again. Cute. Yet she really was. Even when Sophie was telling him to bugger off, she was cute. From the tip of her cute button nose, to the bottoms of her cute petite sandalled feet, which he had seen on more than one occasion begin to lift up in what he guessed was a stamp before being slowly set down again. Even her self-control was cute.

She was so different to the women he socialised with in London. Women his parents deemed acceptable. All from good families, all driven by success, all understanding of what was expected of them as a potential partner of a future CEO of a multimillion-dollar company.

Yet none of them made his heart tumble and turn. Not like the woman whose grin had turned impatient as he stood staring at her like a gormless wonder.

'Oh, sorry. Was caught up in my own head. Business stuff. You know how it is. Always something to think about.' Alexander took a sip of beer to stop any more blather.

Sophie flicked her index finger in the direction of a spot behind him. He turned to see Natalie and the kids, Ginny and a man who, guessing by the proprietary fingers caressing the back of his neck, was Ginny's husband, Mike.

An unaccustomed swarm of nerves was making its presence felt in his stomach. It was one thing to sit with a group of people at a business meeting, or to catch up with old school friends at the pub, but to join a close-knit group of friends who shared history, a bond, and – based on their seating position – strong beliefs on the plans his family had for Herring Cove? Unsettling didn't even begin to cover it.

Although, at least with the pub divided in half it was easy to see where he stood with the villagers. More so at Sophie's friend's table as they'd dragged a table to sit square in the middle. The rope running across it emphasised the separation of thoughts and beliefs in the community.

Ginny was sitting on the 'No' side. Mike, beside her, had taken up residence on the Pro side. Natalie and the kids were also, unsurprisingly, 'Pro'. A seat was open beside Natalie's kids, presumably for Alexander. Another by Ginny was empty, clearly for Sophie.

'That rope wasn't here two days ago,' murmured Sophie as they excuse me'd their way around other customers to their table. 'Things must've really gone downhill.'

Alexander didn't reply. Didn't know what to say. He'd never seen anything like this. He knew there was always an element of discontent when a Fletcher resort was proposed in a community. Environmental groups, usually, who were worried about the effect population growth and potential pollution would have on wildlife and their way of life. But he'd never heard of friends and families having to be separated. Of a community literally divided.

Was Sophie right? Was Herring Cove the wrong place for the Fletcher Group to expand into? Would it do more damage than good?

Sophie sank into the chair left open for her, and indicated for Alexander to follow suit. He went to pull out his chair to sit in, but found himself pulling it to where the rope was. He lifted the chair and placed it squarely over the top of the rope, right in the centre. Half and half.

His parents would see his choosing neutral ground as a

betrayal, but his heart saw it as right. True to himself. To who he was. A man who wanted success, wanted growth, in a way that was fair to all. That lifted people up and brought communities together.

'Interesting place to sit.' Ginny raised her eyebrows. 'I hear you've been busy building shelves for Sophie?'

'Just the one. But I'm happy to do more, if she'll let me.'

'I'll make sure she lets you.' Ginny nodded, ignoring the sharp elbow that came from Sophie's direction. 'It's not every day a man offers to build shelves for free, no strings attached.'

'I wouldn't say there were no strings...' Sophie muttered into her beer. 'I suspect Alexander's still hoping he'll get me to change my mind about selling. Guilt me into doing it through good deeds.'

Ginny rolled her eyes. 'Always so suspicious, Soph.'

'And wrongfully so.' Alexander picked up the menu that was placed in the centre of the table and ran his eyes over it. 'I've accepted Sophie's decision. I've also been straight up in saying that her not selling won't stop the project going ahead and, as far as I'm concerned, that is that.'

'Well, I'm all for the project. I'm Mike by the way.' Mike offered Alexander his hand. 'One question though... Are you planning on using local suppliers, like myself, for your seafood? Assuming, of course, that the resort will have a restaurant.'

So much for a quiet drink. This had the potential to turn into a mini town meeting. Alexander silently thanked his father for teaching him how to be ready to field questions at any time. How to keep calm, to appear in control.

'To be honest, Mike, we do tend to use our trusted suppliers for our produce and meat. We prefer to use organic wherever possible and the quality has to be consistent, but in saying that, I think when it comes to seafood fresh is always best. Make sure you give me your number and I'll make sure it's passed on to the right person.'

66

Mike clinked his pint against Alexander's. 'Cheers for that. Appreciate it. She's been slow going the last few years. The boost will do us good.'

Ginny elbowed Mike and gave him a 'shut up' glare.

'What? I'm just saying what we're all thinking.'

'If we were all thinking it, there wouldn't be a daft rope in the middle of this pub. The last thing I want is to have to rope off sections of our house. I love you too much.' Ginny leaned over, cupped Mike's cheek and kissed him, softly, lingering, and just long enough that Alexander began to feel uncomfortable and found himself focusing on the bubbles trailing up from the bottom of his beer.

A gagging sound came from Sophie's direction.

'You two are incorrigible. Always with the public displays of affection. You'd think after all this time you'd be sick of each other. I'm just glad I haven't had anything to eat recently otherwise I'd be saying hello to it.' She picked up her beer and took a sip, a smile playing on her lips.

Ginny grabbed a crisp from an opened bag on the table and waved it at Sophie. 'I'd say you were jealous, my friend, but I know your feelings about relationships.'

'Indeed you do.' Sophie spun the bag of crisps round and took a handful. 'No man is better than a bad one.'

Alexander waited for Sophie to elaborate, but no explanation came. Unsurprising considering how locked down she kept her life, how private she was. Still, what had happened to give her that attitude? To see her shun relationships, when – considering how affectionate she was with her girlfriends – she seemed like the kind of person who had so much love to give.

'What about you, Alex?' Ginny turned her attention to him, her eyes gleaming. 'Can I call you Alex?'

No one called him Alex. Alexander had been his name for as long as he could remember. His nanny had once called him Alex in front of his parents and been admonished. His father believed

Alexander was a strong name, a winner's name, whereas 'Alex' sounded weak. The shortened name belonging to someone who'd give people a hand rather than rule with an iron fist.

But his father wasn't here to state his opinions, and Alexander quite liked the way Alex sounded. It sounded like a name that belonged to a guy who sat in a pub with friends, wearing shorts and a T-shirt, his hands raw after a solid day's physical work.

'Sure, you can call me Alex.' The word rolled off his tongue. It felt like the name he deserved. That belonged to him.

'Excellent. So, Alex…' Ginny rubbed her hands together. 'Tell me about you. What would you be doing if you were back home right now? Would you be at the gym? Working late? Out with a lady friend?'

Sophie groaned and buried her face in her hands. 'Really, Ginny?' Her hands slipped down. 'There's not enough beer in the world for this. I'm so sorry, Alexander. The moment I saw this one sitting here we should have hustled our behinds out of here. She's obsessed with love. Thinks because she's so in it that the rest of the world must be, or if they're not, then they should be.'

Ginny flapped her hand dismissively at Sophie. 'Oh shush. You love it, Sophie. Besides, I'm interested in what Alex has to say. It's not often we have a good-looking, successful man in these parts.'

'What am I? Road kill?' Mike took a swig of beer and put his glass down to reveal a frothy moustache.

'No.' Ginny wiped the foam away with the pad of her thumb. 'You're my everything. Best-looking man in the universe. But there are single ladies in the village and I feel it's my duty to play cupid since I was lucky enough to fall in love with you, my dear. Now, is our ego nice and solid?' She stuck her tongue out at Mike who mirrored the gesture. 'Good. So, Alex? Spill.'

'You don't have to say anything, Alexander.' Sophie shook her head, emphasising her point. 'It's none of our business.'

'No, it's okay. There's nothing much to tell. I live in London. Knightsbridge to be exact.'

68

'Fancy.' Natalie pulled her increasingly fractious daughter onto her knee and began to jiggle her up and down. 'You must feel like you're slumming it down here.'

'No, not at all. I'm enjoying it.' And, to his surprise, he wasn't being polite. He meant it. The chance to meander up and down quiet lanes rather than stride shoulder-to-shoulder down heaving streets. To breathe in the fresh, tangy air of the sea rather than exhaust fumes. A scent that had never bothered him until now. A scent he'd have to embrace once more, sooner rather than later. 'I've a mews house there. Nothing over the top, not compared to some of the other homes. Not that I'd be home at this time. I'd still be in the office.'

'So, it's a case of all work and no play? No girlfriend?' Ginny egged him on with an encouraging nod.

Alexander stifled a laugh as a groan of despair rose from Sophie. 'No. No girlfriend. I'm too busy with work to do a relationship justice. Besides, it takes a certain kind of woman to handle being with a person who has the kind of demands on them that I do.'

'Really?' Ginny's head tilted to the side. 'Do tell…'

Alexander's stomach squirmed with discomfort. He'd had it drummed into him by his father that revealing a soft underbelly was like pouring fish chum into the ocean… the sharks would soon swarm, then attack.

Had he revealed too much already? Was it right to reveal more? To trust a table of strangers in a pub where half the people hated what his family was planning on doing to their home?

'Give the guy a break.' Sophie's tone caught his attention. It was the voice of a person who sensed his discomfort and was handing him a lifeline. 'He's worked all day. He's come into a pub where if people knew who he was he'd spend the whole night being clapped on the back or having to explain himself. All he wants to do is relax, so we should let him.'

'Well you can't blame a girl for being curious.' Ginny shrugged, unperturbed by her friend's ruling. 'I was just interested to see what kind of girls rich, successful men go out with. I imagine they're beautiful, put together well with designer clothing, able to wear high heels for hours on end, and good at making small talk. Nothing too substantial though, because they wouldn't want to make their man look or feel less than.'

'Less than?' Sophie nearly spat out her mouthful of beer. She hastily swallowed and wipe her mouth of her hand. 'You make it sound like they're mannequins. Or one of those dolls where you pull the string at their back and they say something inane. I'd be bored stupid in seconds if I had to behave like that, let alone go out with someone like that.'

'Well it's not like you'll ever find out, given your stance on dating.' Ginny shot back with a laugh.

'Yeah, well.' Sophie shifted in her seat, her gaze dropping to her lap. She gnawed her lip, then released it and lifted her head. Her eyes were bright. Too bright. Her smile too wide. 'Better no man than a good-for-nothing one.' She followed the statement with a brittle laugh that cut out as quickly as it started.

Alexander sensed an unspoken conversation going on between Ginny and Sophie. Whatever Ginny had blurted appeared to be a sore point for Sophie and a point not to be made in front of an outsider, or even in public.

'Another round?' Mike scraped his chair back, ignoring the half-filled glasses on the table. 'Alex?'

Alexander nodded his head. He was in no hurry to leave. He wanted to hang around, find out more about the woman opposite him.

There was more to her than met the eye. She was astute in a way that was unexpected, not afraid of putting her foot down, or for sticking up for others even when the person she was sticking up for was in no way a friend.

For the first time in – well, ever – he wanted to dig deeper. To know more.

And not just about Sophie, either. He wanted to investigate this new side to himself. To find out who 'Alex' was. What he was capable of.

His phone vibrated in his pocket. Alexander fished it out, his spine stiffened when he saw who it was. His father. Ringing for an update. Expecting him to be heading back to the office.

He shoved the mobile back in his pocket, thankful that Mike was bringing back another beer, because the one in front of him was about to do a disappearing act.

How had a simple business trip become an existential crisis?

And would solving it mean disappointing his mother and father, the family name, or giving up who he believed he was, once and for all?

CHAPTER EIGHT

A wail of displeasure filled the car.

'Sophie, stop it.'

The window to Sophie's right cried with rain as she twisted and turned in her seat, hating hearing her parents argue.

'What are we going to do?'

'It'll be alright. Trust me. I have plans.'

'It's hard to trust you when our business is failing.'

Her parents' voices ratcheted up with every statement.

'Stop, Mummy. Stop, Daddy.' She raised her little voice as best she could to match theirs.

'Please, Soph—'

Her mother's plea cut off by the piercing squeal of tyres.

And all that was left was silence.

Then rhythmic banging.

Sophie fought to wake, strained to come to the surface, to rise from the nightmare, which no matter how many times she had it, never got any easier. Any less painful.

She forced her eyes to open and focused on the strip of sun coming through a crack in her curtains to light up one of the wooden floorboards.

The banging was still there. Not part of the dream. But happening below her window.

She rubbed her palm over her damp cheeks, swung her legs over the side of the bed and pushed herself up out of bed, determined to find out who was making that infernal noise so she could put a stop to it.

She padded to the window, pushed aside the curtains and glanced down to see Alexander's back hunched over a nearly finished bookshelf. 'Really? Are you kidding me?' Sophie reached for her bathrobe, shrugged it on and tied it securely. 'From one nightmare to another.'

She checked the time on her mobile phone. Just after seven-thirty. Barely sparrow's fart.

She thrust her feet into her slippers, then trudged down the stairs while trying to figure out the Alexander situation. It was kind of him to build the shelves for her, but it didn't feel right. To have a stranger helping her refresh her business in between planning to destroy the village she lived in? Something didn't add up.

Sophie paused at the little mirror she kept on the storeroom wall. Placed there so she could check her teeth or that her hair was in place before greeting a customer. She grimaced at her reflection. Her eyes were red and puffy from the nightmare. Her hair, still in a ponytail from the day before, had bunched to the side with random hairs sticking out. And a long pink line marked one cheek as a result of her face being squashed against a crease in the pillow.

If she wanted to frighten Alexander off, she just needed to head outside in her current state.

She rolled her eyes at herself as she pressed her fingertips around the contour of her eyes, hoping for a miracle de-puff, then released her ponytail, scraped her hair back and tied it up in a messy bun. As for the crease? There was no fixing that but Sophie patted her cheeks a little to colour-up her pallor.

It's like you care about what he thinks of you.

Ugh, whatever. She stuck her tongue out at her reflection. It wasn't what he thought about her that she cared about, it was how she felt about herself. Self-respect and all that. At least that's what she was going to tell herself, and that little voice whispering otherwise could bugger off.

The banging outside stopped.

Good, that meant she could greet him without scaring the wits out of him and causing him to knock a nail into his finger.

She opened the door and the 'Good morning' on the tip of her tongue disappeared. Along with any moisture in her mouth.

She ran her tongue around her mouth. Yep, dry as a bone. And she couldn't blame the two beers she'd had last night either. Not when Alexander was standing shirtless all of a metre away and the muscles she'd sensed existed the day before were now very much apparent. And – as much as she hated to admit it – glorious to boot.

His head turned to the side, as if sensing her presence.

Say something. Otherwise he'll think you're having a perve.

Which she most definitely was not. Not really. How was she to know he was about to become half-naked from the time it took her to leave her room and come downstairs? And her reaction to said half-naked body was… natural. Normal. Completely okay.

'Alexander.' His name came out a croak. She covered her mouth and coughed a little. 'Sorry, just woke up. Always takes a while for the mouth to warm up.'

She cringed. Did that sound dirty? Just a bit? And did he have to focus on her lips quite so intently?

'So, uh, what are you doing here?' She pushed aside her embarrassment, which was in no way tinged with lust. Alexander was lust-worthy, that was for sure, but he was also here on official business – the kind she wasn't on board with – and she had to keep that front and centre whenever dealing with him.

'Pass me that plank over there.' Alexander pointed to a piece of wood next to her.

She bent over, picked it up and passed it to him.

'Thanks.' His eyes flicked down towards her chest, widening for a split second, before meeting her gaze. 'And, er, you might need to rearrange your bathrobe.'

She glanced down to see her robe had gaped open revealing her nightie – all lace and silk and cleavage. 'God, sorry.' She spun round and rearranged the material.

'Nothing to be sorry for.'

His words were deep, raspy... and made her want to run upstairs, find her thick winter ankle-length coat and wear it until the day he finally left town. And not because his reply was creepy – the opposite. If she thought him attractive and he thought her attractive... well, that would take the situation from tense to potentially explosive.

No blurring the lines.

No engaging with the enemy.

Not that he seemed so enemy-like. Not after last night. The previous evening had been pleasant. Good conversation, a few drinks, followed by Alexander insisting on walking her home in that gentlemanly way of his.

'I know you can take care of yourself, but my mother would never forgive me if I let a girl walk home alone at night,' he'd said when she'd started to tell him she was capable of walking herself home.

That vulnerability she'd sensed earlier had returned, and she couldn't say no. Not when he was trying to be a good son. Not when she'd have given everything and anything to have a mother to do right by.

Sophie turned back round to see Alexander hunched over the frame of the bookshelf, nailing in what would eventually be the back of it. His concentration completely on the task at hand and not remotely on her. Good. That meant she'd misinterpreted his tone. There was no interest there. Just a man being polite to ease her embarrassment.

Typical gentlemanly Alexander behaviour. She hoped his mother was proud of him.

She picked up another plank and readied it to hand to him. The sawn edges were smooth, crisp almost. Like he'd taken great care with the work. Not just knocking them up in order to get the job done.

'How do you get it all looking so even? I took a closer look at the bookshelf you made yesterday and it's perfect.' She took in the immaculate workspace he'd created. Nails in a plastic jar. A small pile of off-cuts. Everything had its place. 'And I can't see any signs of a screw-up or wastage.'

'Measure twice. Cut once.' Alexander took the plank from her with a nod of thanks. 'That's what the construction manager at this site I worked on when I was younger told me to do. So I did exactly that. Except I measure three times.' His lips flattened out. 'Turns out you can double-check your work and still get things wrong.'

Sophie had the distinct feeling he was talking about their situation. So, he'd come to Herring Cove thinking he'd done his homework? Thinking he had all he needed to pull the whole deal together? And she'd put a spoke in his carefully laid out plans?

Or was Alexander talking about life in general?

'Yeah well, life doesn't always go the way we want. Can't prepare for everything. Can't expect everything to go to plan. And when it doesn't you just have to keep your chin up and figure out another way, right?' She picked up another piece of timber and ran her thumb pad over a small knot, enjoying its roughness against the soft flesh of her skin. 'You worked on a construction site? You hardly seem the type.' Sophie cursed herself. 'Sorry, that sounded kind of rude…'

'Don't worry, I'm getting used to it.' Alexander smirked, before banging in another nail.

'Smart-arse.' Sophie grinned. She liked how he wasn't afraid to pull her up. It was as if knowing she wasn't selling had loosened him up, and she was seeing the real Alexander. Not the smooth-talking besuited version he showed the world. 'It's just when you waltzed in here you didn't exactly look like the type of man who would know how to build a bookshelf, and I can't imagine the heir to the Fletcher Group needing "builder" on his CV.'

Alexander set the hammer down and sat on the ground, his legs stretched out before him, his elbows anchoring him to the ground. He rolled his neck round slowly, then reversed the stretch, a low moan escaping his lips. 'I forgot how hours of being hunched over can play havoc on your muscles. You're going to owe me a massage after this.'

An image of her hands running over Alexander's oiled-up back flashed through her mind. Her cheeks heated as an area low in her stomach tightened involuntarily. 'Once my revamp's complete and I've more customers, I'll send you a voucher to some fancy London masseuse.'

'You'll need to sell a lot of books... or you could just do it yourself...' Alexander's lips rose as he winked.

Sophie's pulse leapt to her throat as her heartbeat quickened. Was that flirtation? Was Alexander flirting with her? More importantly, why did she not hate the idea? She swallowed hard and forced her attention to the bookshelf. There was no way Alexander was flirting, at least not because he was interested. Flirting was probably second nature to him, something that couldn't be helped. Another way to turn a 'no' into a 'yes'.

"You haven't answered my question,' she pressed. 'Did you really learn those carpentry skills of yours working in construction?'

Two spots of pink flared high on his cheeks. He crossed one long, muscular leg over the other and tipped his head to the blue sky. 'I did. For a bit.'

Sophie waited for Alexander to elaborate, but instead he closed his eyes and lifted his shoulders high before dropping them.

'You must've enjoyed it then, since you were so quick to volunteer your services to me... Is building what you'd rather be doing?'

Alexander's eyes opened and met hers. Their expression was startled, like Alexander couldn't believe someone was seeing him, the *real* him. 'You're a surprising one, Sophie. I didn't expect you to be... you.'

Sophie didn't know what to say. How to react. The words warmed her. Made her feel... special somehow. Like to Alexander she wasn't just 'Sophie Jones whose parents passed away' or 'Sophie Jones whose boyfriend ran off with every penny she had'. She was 'Sophie Jones, the unexpected'.

'Well I'd hate to make your life too easy. Wouldn't want you thinking you've got me all figured out.' She grinned as she folded her arms and tapped her foot on the ground. 'And you still haven't answered my question. Spit it out.'

Alexander's smile returned as he let out a 'ha' of laughter. 'If you ever want a job you come see me. You're like a dog with a bone.'

'Don't think calling me a "dog" is going to distract me either.' She wagged her finger at him. 'Spill.'

'I'll spill for a cup of tea? I've been out here since the crack and I'm parched. Forgot to bring my water bottle.'

'Fine. I'll even make you Marmite on toast. Or there's honey if you'd prefer. Can't have my free labour keeling over from hunger.'

'Marmite's perfect, thank you.' Alexander pushed himself up and held out his hand to Sophie. 'Hand up?'

She paused. This time two days ago she'd have told him she didn't want his hand. Didn't want anything from him. But now?

Slowly he had begun to change her mind. Showing through hard work, and commitment to the promise he'd made to build the shelves and help revive the bookshop, that he was a man of his word. Someone who – if she lowered her barrier – she could learn to like. Maybe even learn to trust.

Sophie took his hand. His skin warm against hers, yet rough. It told her of time spent doing manual labour, not tucked behind a desk working on ways to take people's lives away from them in order to build the Fletcher empire.

He pulled her up like she was light as a feather, the momentum unbalancing her. She collapsed against his bare chest. And didn't move. A mix of embarrassment, shock and his scent – lemony, clean, yet fresh-sweat salty – rooted her to the spot.

Could a man smell any more manly?

'Sorry, Soph.' Alexander fingered a loose strand of her unbrushed morning hair and tucked it behind her ear. A small gesture, but too friendly. Too… intimate.

Pull yourself together, girl. 'It's all good. It happens. No harm no foul, and all that.' She took a step back, another, then turned her back to Alexander and made her way inside trying not to think how nice it had felt to be pressed against him.

How… right.

***

Alexander folded his arms across his chest. Now that he was out of the sun, away from his tools, he felt… naked. Which he technically was. Well, half was. Yet the way Sophie had looked at him, her eyes flaring wide, her pupils dilating. The way her perfectly shaped lips had parted, just a hint, then closed again as her heart thundered against his chest.

He released a long, quiet breath. Despite having dated a string of 'suitable' women, yet to meet the right one, he'd always believed he'd know a moment when he felt one. And he'd just felt one. Sophie had too if her refusal to stop buzzing about the storeroom, combined with the way she couldn't look him in the eye, was anything to go by.

'Here you go. Toast and tea.' A plate of two buttery bits of toast with a scraping of Marmite were thrust before him, along with a mug of perfectly beige tea. 'There's sugar in that bowl over there if you fancy it. Hope you don't mind my adding milk. Habit.

Usually only make it for Ginny or Nat and we all have it the same.'

'Looks perfect, thanks. Shall we sit out in the shop?' He'd spied the sun shining on the cosy reading area and it called to him. Seemed like a good place to tell her a little tale about a young man who'd found his passion, only to lose it to obligation and expectation.

'Sure, of course. After you.'

He didn't insist on Sophie going first. Didn't want to make the tension that had sprung up between them thicker, more complicated.

He placed his plate and mug on the coffee table, then relaxed into the armchair, running his hands over its wooden arms. 'I love this old-school Scandinavian style. I see some companies are replicating it, but there's nothing like the original.'

Sophie settled into the chair opposite. 'They belonged to my grandparents. They gave them to Mum and Dad when they were married.'

'That's an interesting choice of wedding present.'

Sophie's fingers played over the age-worn fabric. 'Not really. Mum and Dad had sunk all their money into the shop, and if my grandparents hadn't bought them the sofa and chairs they'd have had nothing to sit on.'

Alexander took in the bookshop with fresh eyes, a new respect. No wonder Sophie refused to sell. It was steeped in history. Part of her. Everything she'd ever known. Everything she wanted.

He picked up the pink and red rose-decorated mug. The heat from the liquid burned its way through the delicate china. The slight sting focused him. 'What you said out there? About me being a builder? You were right. If I'd had my choice I'd have 'builder' on my CV. I've always enjoyed working with my hands. Unfortunately, being a Fletcher meant I never stood a chance at being who I wanted to be.'

He glanced up from his tea to see Sophie's gaze had left her own lap to meet his.

'For someone not given the chance to be a builder, you sure have the knack.' Her eyes were hooded with suspicion, yet her tone held the quality of softness that told him she was treading carefully. That she wanted to know more.

And he wanted to give her more. Wanted to tell her everything. If only, for one moment, he could share what it was like to be a Fletcher. The pressure. The expectation. And something told him he could confide in Sophie. That it wasn't only her secrets, the details of her life that she held close. That she could be trusted to hold his secrets close too.

He thought back to when he was young, full of hopes and dreams, believing he could make a difference to the world. Believed he could make a difference to the Fletcher Group. Before reality was spelled out to him and his hopes and dreams had been tucked away, boxed up tight.

'When I was eighteen I spent a summer on a building site working for a charity that created homes for families who were homeless.' He paused, unsure whether to go on. How to go on.

'Is that some sort of thing you had to do? A way of keeping the Fletcher's name in good stead?' Sophie folded her arms across her chest and raised an eyebrow. 'So that if anyone were to say "you destroy homes" you could come back with "no, we help build them"?'

Alexander laughed. He couldn't help it. He didn't care that Sophie's eyebrow dropped, then drew together angrily with its mate. She couldn't have gotten the situation any more right.

'What's so funny about that? Companies do it all the time. Take part in charity in order to improve their appearance.' She folded her arms across her chest and held herself tight.

'What's funny is that you've hit the nail on the head. That's a very big part of why my father had me work there. His father had him work on a site as part of his training. The theory being you couldn't run a business built on building if you didn't understand what it was like to work on a site. My father took that

81

theory and decided to expand on it. He could have had me work on one of our sites, but it was more important that his son was seen to be doing good in the community, so he had me spend a summer building a home for a family who needed one. It was great PR. Except it backfired on him.'

'Backfired? How? Did you accidentally set fire to the site or something? Burn the house down?' Sophie's grip loosened, colour returning to her white knuckles.

'No, furthest thing from it. I did great on the site. The guy running it thought he would be dealing with some snotty-nosed kid who thought himself too good for manual labour. Except I didn't hate it. I loved it. Creating something that mattered. Something that would change someone's life. Being so hands-on. The camaraderie of working together with a group of people who had a common goal? It warmed me, fuelled me in here.' He tapped the area above his heart. 'It gave me all sorts of ideas for how the Fletcher Group could grow. Setting up our own charity for those who needed homes, with me at the coalface. Running the building sites. Working with people. Building communities.' Alexander laughed, a harsh sound that sounded more bitter than he would have liked, yet only emphasised how he felt. 'It's safe to say that my father was not a fan of my ideas.' Not a fan of? Total understatement. His father had told him it was idealistic. Too time-consuming for a business that was in the business of making money.

'"Your time is better spent building the business, son. If you care that much, if you want to make a difference, throw some money at a charity and let them do what they do best".' Alexander rolled his eyes, ignoring the stab of guilt that came with mimicking his father's stern voice.

A grin erased the last hints of Sophie's cynicism. 'Sounds exactly how I always thought fancy corporate companies worked.' Her hands came together in a steeple as she leaned forward in her chair, her elbows resting on her knees. 'What happened next? Did you just do as you were told and life went on as usual?'

'A bit. A little bit not.' Joy bubbled in Alexander's heart as he recalled his silent rebellion. 'I carried on being the son I was meant to be. Working in the family business, undertaking more responsibility as my knowledge of its ins and outs grew. But at the weekend I volunteered on building sites. Helped build more homes for those who needed them. I did it for years. My father never found out.'

Faint lines grew from the edge of Sophie's eyes as her grin widened. 'No? Really? And you were never caught?'

'I wore a hat. Kept to myself. It helped that the kind of people who volunteered had no idea who I was and the site manager was sworn to secrecy. I did it for years until my real job began to infiltrate my personal time and I had to give it up. Even then I set up a small workshop in the garage at my place and began to create furniture to go in the homes whenever I had an hour or so spare.'

Sophie's gaze turned thoughtful. 'Well, aren't you a dark knight. Your mother must be proud.'

'My mother?' Alexander set his cup on the coffee table. 'My mother would have been as horrified as my father if she knew.'

Sophie's head cocked to one side, her brows knitted together in confusion. 'But it sounds like she's a good person. She's taught you to be kind and gentlemanly and all that...'

'She's taught me to behave in a way that reflects well on the Fletcher name.' Alexander flinched at how hard, how cruel he'd made his mother sound. 'That's not to say she's a horrible person, she's not. But she comes from a good family. Was taught to keep up appearances. My father and her work so well as a team. They care about the same things. Building the business. Looking good to the outside world. Not being seen as weak. It's how they brought me up. For their son to be seen to care too much, to be seen as a soft touch, would leave the business open to attack. To under-hand dealings. And that is not how a future CEO ought to be seen.'

Alexander dropped his gaze to his feet. Panic threaded through his veins. He'd said too much. Trusted an almost-stranger with information that could be used against his family. Used against him.

'It must be tough to have that kind of pressure on you at all times.'

A pair of feet came into view, then two knees, as Sophie sank to Alexander's level.

'I can't imagine what it would be like to have that kind of expectation on my shoulders. I run this bookshop not out of guilt or obligation but because I love it. It has my heart.' A tentative hand fell upon his. 'You though? You've no choice. Even I can see that.'

Alexander met Sophie's gaze. Determination radiated from her narrowed eyes. 'So really, there's only one thing for it.' Sophie placed her hands on her hips and gave an affirmative nod, like she'd made a plan and it was already a done deal. 'You get out there and build those bookshelves. Build to your heart's content. I'm not going to stop you, or tell you to go. Hell, tell your father I'm being difficult if you need more time. Do what you love while you're here in Herring Cove, because it sounds like this might just be your last chance to do so.'

Alexander couldn't believe his ears. Sophie would back him? Just so he could be happy? He reached for her hand, tugged it away from her hip, gave it a gently squeeze.

'Thank you, Sophie. This all feels a bit bizarre. You've every reason to tell me to bugger off and yet you're helping me?'

Sophie's shoulders lifted and fell as her head angled to the side in a 'what are you going to do about it' way. 'Call it karma for the good you've done for others. Besides, I'll get furniture that won't fall apart and you'll get to be who you're meant to be.'

Who you're meant to be.

The words should have been a balm to his soul. Recognition that he was Alexander. Alex. A guy who liked to build things up, not tear them down.

Instead, they froze his soul.

He was meant to be a Fletcher.

Meant to be in the office giving the go-ahead for the demolition of the cottages surrounding Sophie, not avoiding his father's phone calls while knocking nails into pieces of wood.

He picked up the remaining half-eaten piece of toast. His throat thickened as reality set in, and he placed it back down on the plate.

He was trying to have his toast and eat it too. And by doing so he was playing a dangerous game. Not with Sophie. Not with his family. But with himself.

He couldn't fulfil his destiny with the Fletcher Group while playing make-believe out the back of Sophie's shop.

He had to be Alexander.

Even when who he really wanted to be was Alex.

CHAPTER NINE

'Aunsof! Aunsof!'

Sophie opened her arms wide and Bella ran straight into them, wrapping her little arms around Sophie's neck, the force of her affection nearly sending them crashing to the floor.

'Hey Bella.' Sophie sniffed Bella's hair and gagged. 'Oh Bella, have you been sick?'

'Yup.' She nodded enthusiastically and held up her hand. 'Five times.'

'And did your mum wash your hair?' She glanced up at Natalie and shot her a mock-glare.

'Yup.' Bella dropped her thumb down. 'Four times.'

Natalie shrugged. 'By the fifth time I wasn't sure what the point was. Typically, though, she hasn't spewed again, so I'll give her what will hopefully be the final hair wash tonight.'

'Tummy bug?'

'Looks like it. At least this one was over and done with quickly enough. She's back to eating everything in sight.' Natalie leaned down and planted a kiss on Bella's cheek, then straightened up and placed her hands on her hips. 'So, are you ready to see your new online store?'

'As I'll ever be. The laptop's all fired up.' Sophie jerked her head to the computer sitting on the counter.

'Joe, Bella, play nice. Don't destroy the store.'

Joe rolled his eyes as he took Bella by the hand and led her to the children's book section.

'He's sprouted up this summer.' Sophie ran her finger over the trackpad, bringing the black screen to life, then twisted it in Natalie's direction. 'She's all yours.'

'Sprouted up and grown an attitude to match.' Natalie's fingers flew over the keyboard. 'I wonder if it's because his dad's gone? Maybe he needs a male role model or something... Not that I have any intention of providing one anytime soon. Anyway,' Natalie tilted the laptop towards Sophie, 'here we go.'

Sophie's heart fluttered as she saw her store's name in elegant calligraphy appear on the screen. Behind it was an image of books arranged on shelves. Just like a library. Exactly how her store would look once Alexander had finished building the bookshelves and she'd stained them and filled them with stock.

'It's beautiful, Nat. I can't believe you've managed to do this in a couple of days.' She draped her arm over Natalie's shoulders and brought her in for a half-hug. 'It's amazing. You are amazing.'

'Oh shush.' Natalie flapped the compliment away. 'It's simple enough once you've done it once. It took me an age to figure out my salon's website – especially the online sales part – but now that I know all the tricks and stumbles, it's pretty much a breeze.'

'Take the compliment, Nat. I couldn't do this. Not in a million years. You're wonderful. So, what do I need to know so that I don't break it?' The familiar sound of the clomp-clomp of footsteps followed by timber being dragged across timber told her Alexander was bringing in his latest piece of work.

'Alexander, come, look. I have a website. All Booked Up's gone twenty-first century, thanks to Nat here.'

Alexander set the bookshelf down and strolled over. Sweat beaded his temples, and dark shadows under his eyes spoke of his early start, but made her wonder if he'd slept much the night before. He'd been distant all morning. Since their chat yesterday afternoon, in fact.

Sophie had put it down to his burning the candle at both ends, but she wondered if it was more than that. She suspected his family's demands placed a huge weight on his shoulders. Caused a huge division in him: who he wanted to be versus who he had to be, and the push-pull of his situation was wearing him down.

Despite all the warnings whispered to herself, all the reasons she regularly told herself as to why she couldn't trust him, shouldn't trust him, her heart went out to Alexander.

Their conversation the previous day had changed something. He was no longer the out-and-out enemy. Once stripped of his suit and his little squares of paper with numbers written on them, Alexander was a good guy. A really good guy. Someone who'd been pigeonholed. Forced to be someone he didn't want to be. And he'd done it for family, because how could he not?

That she understood. She'd do anything for family. Everything. And that meant saving the bookshop. Doing right by it.

Except… did she really have to? Was sticking to her guns going to see her stuck in a bad situation, like Alexander was? Was all this work going to end up with her losing that which meant the most to her? Leaving her with nothing? When taking the offer and moving across the road could give her a fresh start, while still doing that which she loved?

She blanked the thought. Their situations were totally different. Worlds apart. He came from a dynasty. He grew up knowing his fate. Alexander was forced to keep his family business thriving, whereas she *wanted* to keep her business alive. Wanted to breathe life into it.

'Soph? You okay? You've gone a bit… pale.' Natalie inspected her closely. 'God, maybe you've picked up Bella's bug? I've had so many of them I'm all but immune. Joe, too.'

'No, I'm fine. Sorry. Just… distracted for a second there. All this change, all this excitement, it's a bit much for this old girl.'

88

She faked a yawn, then smiled at Alexander as he came to stand beside them.

'Distracted.' Natalie's gaze went between the two. 'Because you're old. Riiiiiight.'

Sophie nudged Natalie's foot with her own and widened her eyes in a way she hoped conveyed the 'there's nothing going on here, he's just helping me out as a friend' message that she had been repeating to herself all day.

Stupid muscles. Dumb handsome face. Daft kindness. In any other world Alexander would be Mr Perfect. Just her type. But not in this world.

Not after what Phillip had done. Not when she could no more trust her heart, trust her instincts, than she could trust a man.

Alexander bent closer to the computer, his forearm brushing hers. Not moving. Like a magnet kept it there. Kept her arm there. Because as much as she knew she should move her arm away from his, she couldn't.

'That looks fantastic.' He looked over Sophie's head to Natalie. 'You really are very talented.'

Natalie shrugged the compliment off.

The second time today, Sophie noted. Had her friend's self-confidence taken more of a battering that she realised when her husband cheated on her, then left? Had she been that wrapped up in her own worry that she'd not noticed?

'It's paint by numbers stuff once you know how. It's only scratching the surface of what can be done, but it's a start.' Natalie moved the arrow to the top left corner and clicked. 'See here, Sophie. This takes you to the back end. It's where you can load up the inventory. You can create deals from here. Monitor who's visiting your website and from where. You can create campaigns and promote them on social media. I've added an email app so you can email clients about new books you've got coming in, and events. Which reminds me, how's the Midsummer's Night Market coming along? And have you managed to find a writer to speak at the shop?'

'I've not heard from Lucille Devine yet, but I've reached out to some other local authors to let them know we're available for book launches.' Sophie clicked around the website as she talked, amazed at how much her friend had achieved in such a small amount of time. 'And the market's coming along well. Lots of stalls confirmed.'

'And permission came through from the council this morning.' Alexander flashed her the thumbs up. 'All sorted.'

'You helped her?' A hint of a smile flitted about Natalie's lips.

'I figured I have the connections so I may as well use them.' Alexander shrugged like it was no big deal.

But it was a big deal. Huge. He could've left her floundering. Could've let her get herself in trouble by putting together a market that could have been shut down, making a fool of her in front of hundreds of people.

Except he hadn't. He'd given her a helping hand, above and beyond that which he had to, or felt obliged to. Like someone you could trust would.

'Alexander's being too modest.' Sophie smiled up a him. 'He's been such a help. Building bookcases. Fixing my display shelf.'

'You make it sound like I've done all the work.' Alexander shook his head. 'You've been at my side handing me wood, nails. Keeping me fed.' He patted his flat stomach. 'I'm going to miss that bread of yours once I'm gone.'

'Then maybe you shouldn't go.' Natalie winked at Alexander as her elbow dug into Sophie's side. 'You two make quite a team. Imagine what you could accomplish if you stayed.'

Sophie fought the urge to face-palm herself. This was why Natalie was acting strange the other day. She thought there was something between Sophie and Alexander. And here she was thinking Ginny was the matchmaker of the two. Although the way Ginny was digging for girlfriend information at the pub, it wouldn't have surprised Sophie if Natalie and Ginny were conspiring to bring the two of them together, even though they knew her stance on relationships.

She dared glance over at Alexander, who'd gone quiet. And a touch rosy in the cheeks. Poor bloke, he was just here trying to be helpful, not hooked into a relationship.

The shrill pitch of a mobile rang through the air. Not breaking the awkward moment, but distracting from it.

'That would be me.' Alexander pulled his mobile out from his short's pocket. 'I'll take it outside.' Alexander strode out of the room, leaving Sophie and Natalie alone.

'Well, that wasn't obvious at all.' Sophie forced her shoulders down, sucked in a huge lungful of air and tapped the laptop, bringing it to life once more.

'It was a bit on the nose, wasn't it? Here I was aiming for subtle.' Natalie screwed her nose and eyes up tight, then released them. Her eyes all apologies. 'I'm sorry, Soph. I've been so busy with the kids. The salon. I'm up half the night trying to improve my web design skills. I've totally forgotten how to be cool about things.' Natalie rubbed her eyes and Sophie noticed the bags under them. 'I do think you'd make a great couple though. You work so well together.'

Her friend wasn't just tired. She was exhausted. And delirious if she thought Sophie and Alexander were couple material.

'You haven't seen us bicker. We're good at it.' She waved the relationship talk away. 'You're right though, you've been crazy busy. And a lot of that has to do with helping me with the website. How about I take the kids out for the afternoon? I'll close up early and we can go have a swim at the beach. You stay home, have a nap. You deserve a break.'

'What about the shop? What if someone comes by?'

'No one comes by at this time of day in the middle of the week. Besides, I won't shirk my work completely. I can take this here…' She tapped the laptop. 'Link it to my phone's data and start loading up inventory. Now how about you show me what to do?'

Natalie wrapped her arms around Sophie and brought her in

91

for a hug. 'You're fab, Soph. What you're doing here is brilliant. And…' She lowered her voice. 'I wasn't joking about you and Alex. Maybe it's time you gave love another chance.'

'I'm not kidding when I say you need to get some sleep, Nat.' Sophie laughed off her suggestion. 'You clearly need it.'

She glimpsed Alexander out the window, his face a picture of seriousness as she spoke into his mobile.

Perhaps they did make a good team; perhaps she could trust him. Maybe Natalie was right. But there was no point starting something with someone who could never stay.

CHAPTER TEN

Sophie looked up from rummaging through her beach bag, checking to make sure she had sunscreen, to see Alexander standing in the doorway looking... dazed. 'You okay there? Important phone call? You looked the picture of a businessman being businessy just now. If you ignore that office inappropriate get-up you're wearing.' She whirled her index finger in the direction of his black T-shirt and olive cargo shorts.

Alexander ran his hand through his hair and blinked like he was trying to adjust from the bright sunshine outside to the relative gloom of the back of the shop. 'Yeah, something like that. Just my father firing a million and one instructions at me. Nothing I can't handle though.'

Sophie dropped her gaze down to her bag again, but glanced up from under her eyelashes at Alexander, inspecting him closer.

Something was off. He didn't seem himself. Alexander had a way of filling the room with his presence, but right now he seemed... shrivelled. And his skin was tinged with green, like he was coming down with something. Or maybe he'd been out working in the sun for too long and was suffering heatstroke.

'The kids and I were about to go down to the beach for a paddle. Do you want to come?' Sophie mentally slapped her forehead. Smart move. Inviting a guy you thought had endured too much sun to the beach, where it was blazing with no shade to be found unless you were willing to lug down a sun shelter or golf umbrella to sit under, which was impossible since the path was too treacherous to be doing that while minding two little ones.

Alexander rolled his shoulders back and tipped his neck from side to side. 'You know, that might be a good idea. I need some air, and what better air is there than sea air?'

'Indeed.' Sophie nodded, surprised he'd accepted. Part of her had pegged him as a man who didn't care much for children. But that was before she knew he was hands-on, that he loved creating. That he'd cared enough about people that he'd helped build a home for them. 'You did hear the bit where I said I was taking the kids down? That pretty much means you're going to be babysitting them with me.'

A slow smile lifted Alexander's lips, flushing away the unhealthy pallor, bringing a twinkle to his eyes. 'You don't think I'm any good with kids?'

Sophie shut her beach bag with a snap of the magnetic closure. 'I didn't say that.'

Alexander rose an eyebrow. 'You kind of did. At the very least it was inferred.'

'Well you can't blame me for thinking it... I mean, that first day you came in here full of bluster and bravado, confidence and cockiness, all sexy suit and fancy shoes. You hardly looked like the kid-loving type.' Heat flooded Sophie's face and raced down her chest, spilling through her body.

'Did you just say I was sexy?' Alexander took a step towards her. His chin dipped down as she tilted hers up in defiance. Their eyes met, locked. His lips kicked up in a knowing smirk.

Sophie crossed her arms over her chest, tried to create a barrier against the tension that had arisen between them. 'No, I did not say you were sexy. I said the suit was sexy.'

'But I was wearing said suit. Which means I made it look sexy.

Which means you thought I looked sexy in the suit.' Alexander's head angled lower with each sentence until his lips were inches from hers.

So close she could stand on tiptoe and kiss him should she want to.

Not that she wanted to. That was the last thing on her mind. First thing on her mind? Get out of this situation.

'It was the suit. Not you. We don't get a lot of suits in Herring Cove, so when we do we appreciate them.'

'Riiiiiiiight.'

Sophie narrowed her eyes at his disbelieving tone. 'Right indeed. I'm glad you've got the picture. Glad it's sorted.'

Alexander's lips quirked to the side. 'The thing is, Sophie, if it was just the suit, why have you gone such a charming shade of pink?'

'It's hot. And… and it's time to go.' Sophie skirted around the counter, putting a physical barrier between her and Alexander, scooped up her bag, shaped her hand into a cone and cupped it to her mouth. 'Joe, Bella, beach time!'

Quick steps told her the kids were heading her way, followed by the slower steps of Natalie who'd been reading to them in the kiddie corner.

'You're all ready?' Natalie scanned Sophie, then took in Alexander. Her dimples puckered in amusement.

Did she sense the standoff that had just happened? Sophie wondered. Had the flirtatious tension between her and Alexander left its mark? No, she was being silly.

'We are. Alexander's coming.'

Natalie's dimples deepened.

'If that's okay.' Sophie half wished Natalie would say it wasn't okay. That way she wouldn't have to look at Alexander with his ridiculously gorgeous green eyes that twinkled whenever he looked her way, and his lush lips that she'd been tempted to kiss in a moment of madness.

Natalie's hand went to her mouth as she let out a long yawn. The act releasing the grin. 'Yeah, it's fine. You're right, Soph. I need a rest. A break. Here…' She reached into her denim skirt's pocket and pulled out some money. 'Take this for an ice cream later on.'

'No, you don't have to—'

'I want to.' Natalie took Sophie's hand and pressed the money into it. 'Have a good time.' Natalie hugged and kissed the kids goodbye, then left, but not before shooting a meaningful wink in Sophie's direction.

Sophie replied with a glare. She'd have to pull her girlfriends aside for a chat. Their matchmaking, while coming from a kind place, was a waste of time. Her focus was on rebuilding her business, not on a well-built businessman.

'So, we have kids, we have me, we have you. Off to the beach then?' Alexander's lips by her ear startled her from her reverie.

'Sorry. Yes. Absolutely. Come on, kids, let's go.' She locked up the shop, then fished about in her bag for her bucket hat.

'Looking for this?' Alexander held it up. 'It fell out of your bag when you got the keys out.' He turned it round in his hands. 'Cute hat.'

'It keeps the sun off my face. That's the important thing.' She held out her hand. 'Pass it.'

Alexander shook his head and with one long stride was standing in front of her. 'Here.' He set it on her head and gave it a tug to ensure it was on properly, tucked his fingers under her chin and tipped her head back a touch. 'Cuter on you than not on you. You suit bright pink.'

Sophie swatted his fingers away. 'It was all they had at the shop,' she muttered while trying to ignore the bloom of pleasure the compliment gave her.

'Speaking of the shop. I haven't had anything to eat since breakfast, can we pop in there so I can grab a few things to nosh on while we're at the beach? The kids might want something other than ice cream, too. You know, something healthy.'

Sophie pressed her lips together to keep the smug smile that threatened at bay. Alexander may have made out he might actually be good with kids, but he can't have spent any time around them – not if he thought they'd want to eat anything other than sugar and cream. 'Hey Belles, Joe, quick question.' She squatted down to the kids' height. 'Do you want anything to eat that isn't ice cream?'

'Chocolate.' Bella said with a serious nod.

'And crisps.' Joe put his finger to his chin, his gaze drifted to the sky in thought. 'Maybe a fizzy drink.'

Sophie ruffled their hair. 'We'll see what we can do, hey?' She pushed herself up and placed her hands on her hips. 'Don't think they want anything healthy.' Alexander looked disapproving. 'They're kids, Alexander. And it's summer. And they've not had it easy lately. Let's get them what they want.'

Alexander's disapproval was replaced by a grin. 'I wish you'd been my nanny when I was growing up. She was all about the healthy life. I still can't bring myself to eat carrot sticks. And Brussels sprouts?' He mimed gagging, which set Bella and Joe off.

Sophie shook her head as the kids followed Alexander into the store chocking and fake-vomiting. What had she gotten herself into? And why was she so glad she'd gotten herself into it?

What was meant to be a two-minute trip ended up taking fifteen as Bella, Joe and Alexander weighed up the pros and cons of each and every item of junk food in the little shop that kept the villagers in milk, bread and essentials.

'Right? Do we have everything?' Sophie took one bag of groceries, while Alexander took the other two. 'Ooooph, this is heavy. Anyone would think we were going to the beach for a week.'

'If only we could abandon our jobs and do just that.' Alexander nodded to the bag in her hand. 'Give me those, I can handle them all.'

'Thank you.' Sophie transferred her bags to Alexander, then

shook her arms, which had begun to ache from the weight of the food. 'The path down to the beach can get a little steep and I'd like to have both hands free to help Joe and Bella.'

'Then I'm doubly glad to help. We can't have anything happening to these two little scallywags.' He turned his smile on Joe and Bella who grinned up at him. Affection shone in their eyes.

Two minutes with the man and they were already enamoured. Not that Sophie could blame them. When Alexander was being himself, being *Alex* – as Ginny had rechristened him – he was likeable. Very much so.

Perhaps too much so for her own liking.

She tore her eyes away from Alexander and took the kids' hands. 'Right then. To the beach.'

The trip down the zig-zagging cliff was uneventful. If you called shouting 'be careful', 'watch out' and 'wait for me' every five seconds uneventful. The kids, sugared up on sweets given to them by Alexander, had decided they were old enough to get down themselves, and Sophie had found herself having half a dozen minor heart attacks as they loped and tottered, tripped and skidded down the basic gravel path.

'Oh, thank God.' Sophie collapsed onto the golden sand, stretched her aching legs out and began to massage her calves. 'That path never gets any easier.' She watched the kids run down to the water's edge. 'Joe, you and Bella aren't to go into the water without us, okay? Be a good big brother and look after your sister while we catch our breath.'

Joe flashed her the thumbs up.

Safe in the knowledge the kids weren't going to get themselves in any trouble, Sophie sat back on her elbows and kicked off her sandals, digging her heels into the warm sand until she found the cool damp sand beneath.

Alexander set the bags on the ground and sat beside her. 'You're right. The path needs a lot of work. It's doable though.'

'And you'll be the one to do it, when Fletcher's builds its resort and transforms the town into the hottest new tourist mecca?' Sophie didn't even bother hiding her contempt – Alexander knew where she stood on the subject.

Alexander riffled through a bag and pulled out an apple. 'We'd have to. It's part of the agreement we have with the council. Besides, the last thing we want is for one of our guests to fall down and hurt themselves. It would be terrible press.' He pulled out another apple. 'Want one?'

Sophie looked at the shiny, red fruit. To take it was tempting. But she was beginning to wonder that if she took too much from Alexander she'd feel she'd owe him something in return. Something she wasn't willing to give. 'No, I'm good.'

He shrugged and took a bite, sending a fine spray of juice in her direction. Its sweet, fresh scent reminding her she'd not eaten and that she was, in fact, starving – more so after the traipse down to the beach.

'Must you make it look so good?' She leaned over and grabbed an apple from the bag.

'There you go complimenting me again.' Alexander tipped his head to the sun.

Sophie went to bite back, but decided saying nothing was the best retort and sunk her teeth into the apple. As good as it looked. Better.

They sat in silence, eating their apples and watching Bella and Joe draw pictures in the sand with long, thin pieces of driftwood.

The scene triggered a memory from long ago. A similar scene, but of only one child drawing pictures in the sand. An abandoned row of sandcastles behind her. A mother and father sitting on the sand, as she and Alexander were, but nestled beside each other. Her head on his shoulder, their hands tangled together. A happy family.

'Sophie? You okay?'

Sophie blinked and realised her lashes were damp. She swiped them away and hoped Alexander hadn't noticed them. 'Yeah, just… had a moment. Sorry.'

'Must've been quite a moment,' he murmured.

Of course he'd seen her tears. Alexander wasn't the kind of person to miss anything.

Sophie turned to him, expecting to see pity in his eyes, relieved to see simple curiosity. 'Do you ever wish you could change something?' The words were tentative, but she wanted to ask, wanted to know. Needed to know she wasn't alone. That she wasn't the only person who wished she could rewrite history.

Alexander transferred groceries from one bag to another and placed his apple core in the empty bag. 'Of course. All the time.'

Sophie waited for Alexander to ask her why she'd teared up, what all this talk of changing things was about. But no question came. No prying. No asking for elaboration. She should have been grateful, yet the longer they sat in silence the larger, the more pressing the tension in her chest grew. Hardening with every second until she felt like she might burst.

'My parents used to bring me here when I was a little girl.' The words came out in a rush; the pain in her chest lessened, but didn't disappear. 'I don't have many memories of them, of us, but our beach visits are something I hold onto, that I treasure. I was just remembering one of our trips. It's funny how a happy moment can make you tear up.'

'Tell me about it?' Alexander sucked in his bottom lip, released it. 'If you want. No pressure if you'd rather not.'

She paused to consider whether she could share the moment. Whether she should. Then remembered how much Alexander had opened up to her. How it hadn't made him appear weak. If anything, his honesty gave him a quiet strength.

A strength she would like to embrace. To experience.

She closed her eyes, drew the memory close, the rich, cloudless blue of the sky, the swish-swash of the water drawing in then slipping away from the sand, the echoes of gulls squawking above as they circled the small wharf further down the way, hoping for scraps from the few fishing boats that called Herring Cove home.

'It was a day like today but with not even a hint of a cloud, and the sea was still, calm. We'd packed a picnic. Not a junk food-fest like what you've bought, but old-school sandwiches wrapped in paper, a bit of fruit, biscuits for dessert. After we'd eaten, Mum insisted we wait thirty minutes before going in for a swim, and during that time we made sandcastles and I tried my best to bury my parents in sand. Failed abysmally.'

A warm laugh lit up the warm air. Sophie was surprised to realise it was hers. Usually her memories of her parents were bittersweet, even this memory. But today? Today the recollection brought her joy. Perhaps because she was sharing it with someone else. Spreading the happiness instead of clutching it tight.

'I managed to cover them from ankles to knees, but then I got bored. By then it was time to go swimming... well, paddling. It felt like we were out there for hours. Jumping over the tiddly waves. Lying in the shallows, letting the water wash over us. Standing and scrunching our feet into the wet sand until we felt like we were about to be sucked into it.'

'Sounds fun.'

There was a bereft quality to Alexander's voice. Like he'd never done such a thing, never felt the sand threatening to steal him away to the sea-side netherworld.

Sophie opened her eyes, let the memory go, and turned to him. 'You've never done that? Just... stood in the water and let the sand pull you down?'

'No. I've never done any of it.' His face was still. Not giving anything more away. 'My father is one for building seaside hotels and resorts, he's not one for the actual seaside.'

'And your mother? Did she not take you?'

'My mother was too busy supporting my father. When she paid attention to me it was to teach me a lesson in manners, etiquette, something that would benefit me as an adult once I began to work with my father. I asked my nanny if we could go once, but it was a kind but firm no from her. She was so fair that even stepping out in the watery winter sun for ten minutes would see her turn pink. Going to the beach was her idea of a nightmare.' Alexander shrugged, like it was no big deal.

Sophie suspected it was. Alexander may have had a family, but it sounded like it was in name only. That, like her, he'd missed the touches, the affection, the memories of joyful times spent together. Perhaps even more so than she had, because while her dreams of being part of a happy family could never happen due to her parents' accident, Alexander's family was right there, alive and well, but every bit as out of reach as her mother and father.

'Anyway, it all added up to me not going to the beach as a child, and I've not had the time to indulge such things in my adult years. My secret building projects were all I could manage to fit in.' Alexander's brows knitted together, his chest rose. Held. 'Tell me more about your day at the beach.' He managed a half-smile that did nothing to break the solemnness that surrounded him whenever he spoke of his family. Of his perfect-on-the-outside, but seemingly cloistered, life.

Sophie checked on Joe and Bella, who had abandoned their sticks in favour of collecting seashells, then closed her eyes once more, the memory playing like an old film. Fragmented, flickering, but clear enough to tell the story.

'Well, we played in the water. Then, eventually, once we were covered in goose pimples and our teeth were chattering, we dragged ourselves out, flopped on the sand and let the sun dry us off. Then Mum and Dad sat together and let me roam free for a while. When the sun began to set they called me to them and we huddled together – arms around each other, warding off the chill in the evening air – until it dropped beneath the horizon. Then we packed up and went home. Dad carrying me on his shoulders the whole way because I was too tired to walk. Mum made us hot chocolates and then we fell into bed. Me in the middle, snuggled up between them. It was perfect. I don't think I've ever felt so safe, so secure.'

Sophie turned to him, her eyes shy. A faint blush on her cheeks. 'I've never told anyone that story before.'

Her vulnerability, her courage, made Alexander want to wrap his arm around her slim shoulders. To pull her closer. To hold her tight. Protect her from the big, bad world. Protection he knew she didn't need. With all her independence, it would be an offer she'd reject, he felt sure.

'It sounds like the perfect day.' The words came out stilted as desire collided with common sense, leaving him out of sorts, unsure what to do next.

'It was.' Sophie's face edged into his field of vision. 'I don't think about it often. They passed when I was very young. When I was five. In a car accident.'

It was like sharing that one memory had turned on a tap; here she was revealing another. One that must have been painful to tell him.

One he knew all the details of.

If Sophie found out he'd looked into her past, would she be angry with him? Hate him? Would she run him out of town? Complete with pitchfork up his bum and a fiery torch thrown after him?

Was saying nothing, pretending he didn't know, worse? Was silence a lie? And was it right to lie by omission to someone who'd entrusted him with a huge piece of her past? Of her self?

'I need to tell you something and it might make you... upset. Upset being an understatement.' Alexander braced himself for a verbal beating. 'But I know about your parents' passing, and I could never forgive myself if I sat here pretending I was hearing about it for the first time.' He gritted his teeth and waited for Sophie's anger to hit him, full force.

Silence stretched, long and thoughtful. Followed by a soft exhale.

'I'm not surprised,' Sophie finally replied. There was no ire in her demeanour, just calm acceptance. 'I guess looking into a person's history when you're planning to work with them is part of the job, right? Know who you're dealing with before you talk to them? Something you'd have been taught to do by your father?'

'Something like that.' Alexander nodded. 'It's not my favourite part of the job, but it's a must if I'm doing a business deal with someone. Better the devil you know and all that.' He paused, not sure what else to say. He did what he did because he had to. Because it was expected.

'At least tell me I wasn't an easy mark.' Sophie nudged him with her shoulder. 'Admit it. I was a pain in the arse to research. I keep things tight.'

'I spent far more hours researching you than I should have.'

He turned to Sophie to see her face fall. He cringed, realising how harsh he sounded. Like she was a waste of his time. When she was anything but.

'That came out really wrong.' He reached across the sand and took her hand in his. Squeezed it. 'I'm sorry.'

Her gaze fell on their hands, but she didn't break the hold.

'How was it meant to come out?'

Alexander paused. Aware that what he was about to say could also be taken the wrong way. Afraid that if it was, their precious but tenuous connection would be broken.

'I'm glad that you were a mystery because … And before I say what I'm going to say, you have to know this is not a line or me being dodgy, it just is what it is.'

'Duly noted.' Sophie's eyes met his, and he saw humour in them. Curiosity. And a slight guardedness. Like she was bracing herself for the worst.

Alexander took a deep breath, exhaled. Forced the words, the thoughts, the feelings, from his mouth. 'I'm glad I wasn't able to find out much about you, Sophie, because it meant I had few preconceptions, and the ones I did have were completely wrong.

And because of that I've really enjoyed getting to know you. You're not like anyone I've ever met. You're different, your own person, and that makes me interested.' Alexander shut his eyes and groaned. 'Okay, that sounded way creepier than intended.'

'Actually, it sounded… perfect.' The flush on her cheeks deepened. Her hand twisted in his, so their fingers intertwined. Held.

Her mouth moved towards his. Her lashes fluttered shut. He breathed in. Ready to blur a line that shouldn't be blurred. Not caring that he was about to blur it.

'Aunsof? Uncle Alex? Can we please bury you?'

Sophie jerked away, her attention snapping to Joe, whose little hands were pressed together, his eyes pleading. 'Up to your heads?'

Bella jumped up and down, her hands mimicking her brother. 'Please? Please, please, please? Say yes, Unca Alex.'

Alexander glanced at Sophie to make sure she was okay, that she wasn't embarrassed by what nearly happened, but her focus was on the kids.

'First of all, Alexander isn't your uncle.' Sophie reached out and pulled Bella into her lap for a cuddle. 'Second, yes you can bury us. As long as Alexander has the time. We've probably taken up too much of it already, and I'm sure he has lots of work to do.'

Was it his imagination or did Sophie look relieved at the interruption? Like she'd been given a 'Get Out of Jail Free' card. Saved from making a mistake. Doing something she'd regret. As for all this talk of him being too busy? Business could wait. This was his first proper trip to the beach and being buried next to a woman who intrigued him more than any other had before was too good an opportunity to turn down…

Especially when a little girl and her brother had turned their big brown eyes on him and looked like they might cry if he said no.

'Work can wait. This is my first trip to the beach, remember? And what would a beach trip be without a good burying? Then

105

maybe afterwards we could go for a swim? What do you guys think?'

No confirmation was needed. Their little foot stamps and cheers of happiness said it all.

Alexander glanced at Sophie from the corner of his eye. Her lips were smiling but her eyes were cautious, like she didn't trust herself to be around him too long.

His father's stern face, his mother's constant expression of expectance, flashed before him, reminding him of his duties, that he was meant to preparing Herring Cove for their intrusion, not swanning about in the sun.

Intrusion.

Was that how he saw it now? And was seeing it that way a betrayal of his father? Of his family? For their hopes and plans for him? For the company's future?

Guilt threatened to rise, but he pushed it away. He had the rest of his life to do right by his family, but today he was going to make two kids whose father had taken off happy, and the warmth and fullness it created in his heart would carry him through the coming years of all-work and no-play. Of intruding on villages and towns that would rather be left alone.

'In that case…' He lay back in the sand, closed his eyes and crossed his hands over his chest mummy-style. 'Get digging. I'm not going to be buried that easily.'

CHAPTER ELEVEN

'Can we do that again tomorrow?' Joe plodded along next to Sophie, his hand in hers, the other nestled in Alexander's, Sophie noticed.

In the few hours they'd spent together these two had bonded, and Sophie could see that Joe already hero-worshipped Alexander. How could he not?

Alexander had been the perfect playmate. Letting the kids bury him up to his neck, then chasing them up and down the beach, before racing them into the water where they'd spent a good hour splashing and paddling.

'I'd love to, Joe, but I need to work. Your Aunty Sophie's got me building shelves, and after that a new sign and all sorts of things. Maybe another day?'

Joe nodded, his little face turning serious. 'Maybe another day. And maybe another day we could go camping? Daddy always said we'd go camping one day. But I don't know if he's going to any more and I still really want to go camping.'

Alexander's face as he looked down at Joe was wistful. 'I've always wanted to go camping too. It looks fun. So yeah, one day we should.'

One day? Sophie went to reprimand Alexander. To tell him it was wrong to make promises to children that you couldn't keep, but stopped herself. The way he'd said it, something in his tone... a clarity, an honesty, solidity. Alexander sounded like he meant it. Like he *would* take the kids camping. Like he wanted to come back to Herring Cove. Or to never leave.

She shook the thought off. She was being silly. Reading too much into it. Alexander would have to leave Herring Cove. For good. He was the heir to a huge company. He had no choice but to go, even if the unbelievable, the unthinkable, were to happen and he gave up everything to stay.

Could one kiss make him stay? She closed her mind to the possibility. What had happened – nearly – on the beach was a potential transgression she had no intention of being part of again. She'd been an idiot to allow things to get to that level. A few sweet words and a moment of openness and she'd all but swooned into his arms.

And where did swooning get a girl? Nowhere good.

Sophie breathed a sigh of relief as they reached their homes. She opened Natalie's door and herded the kids up the stairs, Alexander trailing in their wake.

'Nat? We're home. You decent?' Sophie peeked around the corner to see Natalie lying on the sofa, a magazine in one hand, a glass of wine in the other.

'Decent.' Natalie set the book and wine down and stood up. 'There are my babies. I missed you.' Natalie dropped down to her children's level and brought them in for a hug. 'Did you have fun?'

Joe and Bella nodded their heads, their sun and wind-reddened cheeks high with delight, their smiles so wide Sophie half wondered if their jaws were in danger of dislocating.

'Thanks so much, Sophie, Alex. It was nice to have the opportunity to miss them.' She brought the kids in for another hug. 'What do you say to fish and chips for dinner down at the pub?' She looked up at Sophie and Alexander. 'Would you two like to join us?'

A yawn overwhelmed Sophie. The combination of heat, sun and sea breeze along with weeks of worry and the excitement of turning the business round had drained her, more than she'd realised.

'I'd love to join you, really, but my plan to do work at the beach didn't quite pan out, so I've a night of loading up books to the online store ahead of me at home, and I want to solidify the last of the stalls for the Midsummer's Night Market.' Sophie turned to Alexander to tell him he could go without her, but he was already shaking his head.

'Could I take a raincheck? It's been a long day and I have to check my office email, then collapse into bed.'

'Right then. Looks like it's just us three.' Natalie ran her hands through Joe and Bella's hair, then waggled their heads a little, laughing as they ducked out of her reach. 'See you tomorrow?'

Sophie leaned over and gave her a quick hug. 'Of course. I'm not going anywhere.'

After Alexander waved goodbye to the kids, he and Sophie tromped down the stairs into the balmy evening air. Sophie breathed in the scent of the honeysuckle that weaved its way over the empty building across the road, which had once been a tea room and before that a bakery, and before that a butcher. Each venture had opened with enthusiasm, only for dreams to be destroyed as sales became scarce as the village shrank in size as people moved to bigger villages, towns and cities looking for greater opportunities, wanting more for their children or deciding the pace of a small fishing village wasn't so much laid-back as flat-out boring.

She'd sworn she'd never let All Booked Up go that way. And yet she had. One bad decision. One bad choice. Putting her trust in the wrong person had seen her shop's survival in peril.

She shivered, despite the night's warmth. One giant mistake and she'd become so afraid to take another wrong step that she'd made no steps at all. But no more.

She squared her shoulders as she unlocked the shop's door. Tonight she'd get a good chunk of the books loaded up, finalise the market, advertise her site through social media the way Ginny had shown her, and then she'd be up and running. She could reinvent All Booked Up without destroying its old school charm. She could, and she would.

A soft cough behind her made her jump. She twisted round to see Alexander rocking back and forth on his heels, his hands buried in the pockets of his shorts. 'Alexander, you gave me a fright. I totally forgot you were there.'

'Glad to know I'm that forgettable.' He tipped his gaze to the sky and shook his head. 'You spend a day with a girl, looking after two kids, and you become invisible. Who knew?'

'Oh shush. I'm just excited to get the online shop up and running, to start making proper progress.' She opened the door, then looked back at Alexander, who had restarted his rocking and was looking like a man who had nothing better to do, despite saying he had work to be getting on with.

A man who was waiting for an invitation to come in.

One she knew better than to extend.

'Alexander, would you like to come in for a quick cup of tea, or maybe even a beer?'

So, of course, she was going to extend it.

If she could start making leaps of faith in her business, perhaps it was time to make leaps of faith in others too – and herself. To learn to trust.

Alexander ceased his swaying, a slow smile spreading over his face, revealing a road map of creases that splayed from his eyes over his temples. 'I wouldn't say no to a beer.'

'But you would say no to dinner at the pub?' Sophie indicated for him to follow her as she made her way through the shop and into the backroom to the door that led upstairs. She paused at the threshold. Was letting Alexander up into her space crossing a boundary between kind-of colleagues to… friends?

Because spending a day at the beach having deep and meaningful conversations that lead to a nearly-kiss is such a kind-of colleague thing to do?

She pushed the door open and began to climb. The barriers between them had been breaking down all day, and would have fully eroded had they not been interrupted by Joe and Bella. Why stop chipping away at the wall between them now?

Sophie reached the small landing. 'This is me.' She stepped inside and waved Alexander in. Self-consciousness prickled her. What would someone like Alexander, who was born with a silver spoon in his mouth, think of her cosy, simple space?

'It's perfect. It feels like a home should.' He took another step in and ran his hand along the arm of her sofa, then perched on it. 'And I didn't want fish and chips because I've eaten enough junk today to last a lifetime.'

'Those two kids. Terrible influences.' Sophie laughed as she walked through to the kitchenette, opened the fridge and pulled out two bottles of icy lager, took the tops off, then walked them back into the lounge.

'Here you go.' She passed a bottle to Alexander, then took a seat on the sofa.

'So about today...' Alexander set the beer between his knees and fixed her with an intent stare. 'I just wanted to say thank you for thinking of me. Including me. It was an almost perfect day.'

'Almost?' Almost because they hadn't kissed and he wanted to finish what they started?

Sophie searched her mouth for a hint of moisture. Nope. None there. All gone. That'd make kissing him a desert-dry experience.

'Having sand biffed into my mouth by overenthusiastic people buriers wasn't my most favourite life moment ever.' He grinned and took a sip of his beer. 'But everything else was amazing. Everything I hoped a trip to the beach would be.'

'It's a pretty amazing spot to spend a day. Not that I've been to all that many other beaches.' Sophie allowed herself to relax into the sofa. Alexander hadn't misconstrued her invitation for a drink. Didn't expect to pick up where they'd left off. It was just two friends having a chat after a busy day. 'After my parents passed away my aunty came to look after me and run the shop. She wasn't much of a beach-goer, and the shop took up a lot of her time. If I did go, it was with Natalie or Ginny and their families.'

'It must be nice to have such close friendships.' Alexander's thumb circled the rim of the beer bottle.

'I'm lucky. They all but adopted me. They're more like sisters than friends. We can be brutally honest with each other one second, squabbling the next, teasing each other mercilessly minutes later.' Sophie grinned as she took a sip of her beer. 'I wouldn't be without them. They've made life bearable when it's been at its toughest.' Sophie bit her tongue so it would stop rambling on.

She'd shared enough with Alexander today. As much as she was comfortable with sharing. More than she'd intended, if she were honest. Talking about her family and friends was one thing, but to talk about the great mistake that was Phillip? She didn't want to look weak or stupid in front of Alexander. Didn't want to feel weak and stupid with a man ever again.

'I like Nat and Ginny, they seem like good sorts.' Alexander set his half-empty bottle on the ground. 'And the way you describe your relationship reminds me of how my school friends' siblings used to behave with each other. The ultimate love/hate relationships. One moment they'd be in a scrap, the next defending each other against the world.'

She felt Alexander's warm and strong hand encasing hers. Again.

He held it close, snug. And it felt so right. Like she had his support. His respect. That he saw her as an equal, despite the difference in their background, in their upbringings. She almost believed she could trust him. Which was daft. She barely knew him, and the last time she'd dared trust a man he'd nearly ruined her life.

But Alexander wasn't like Phillip. Phillip had hurricaned his way into her world. Whipping in, wooing her, moving in almost overnight. Promises of love and happily ever after. Everything her lonely heart yearned for.

Then just as quickly as he came, he was gone. No note. No sorry. Leaving her with not much more than the clothes in her dresser, the furniture in her home, and the books in the shop.

Alexander was the opposite of a hurricane. He'd been straight up with her from the start. As solid and dependable as the bookcases he'd built.

Her mind might caution her, might tell her to be careful, but her heart told her Alexander wasn't a liar. Or a cheat. He was a good man.

'Was it lonely? Growing up in your family?' She stared at the wall straight ahead. Embarrassed to have asked such a personal question, but desperate to know. To discover if Alexander understood loneliness in the same way she did.

'Unbelievably so. I didn't have cousins. Mum and Dad are both only children. Friendships were engineered based on social standing, so I never had a best friend. Never had a Ginny or a Natalie.'

Sophie inched closer to Alexander. Wanted to be there for him.

'God, I sound like a poor little rich boy. Woe is me with all the toys I could want, top-notch education, a guaranteed path in life, and not a worry in the world.'

'Liar.' Sophie whispered the word, not unkindly. 'You do worry. I see you worrying. See you upset. You were earlier after that phone call from your father. It can't be easy having so much expectation shoved upon you. Doubly so if you can't share those worries with anyone else.'

Sophie heard Puddles scratching at the door. The last of the sun's rays were hitting the wall opposite. Poor Puddles must have been starving.

She released Alexander's hand, stood and opened the door to

let Puddles in. He gave her a distinctly unimpressed 'hurry up' meow.

She followed him into the kitchenette, indicating for Alexander to follow her. 'As lucky as I was to have Natalie and Ginny there growing up, it wasn't always enough. I'd come home and feel… very alone. I didn't know how to talk about my feelings. That I was sad, that I felt guilty at surviving when my parents didn't. I blamed myself for the crash, you know? For a very long time. They'd been arguing before the crash and I'd gotten upset, begged them to stop. Believed my crying had somehow distracted them, caused the accident.' She opened a cupboard and pulled out Puddles' cat biscuits, grabbed a small bowl and shook them in. 'The more I kept everything in, the lonelier I felt.'

Sophie bent down and ran her hand along Puddles' sleek back. The action soothing her, centring her.

'I guess what I'm trying to say, Alexander, is that if you're lonely, I'm here.' Sophie squeezed her eyes shut and clapped her palm over them as a tsunami of heat raced through every cell in her body. Could she have sounded any more like she was hitting on him? 'Sorry, that sounded way less invitational in my head. I meant I'm here and you can talk to me. And whatever you say, I'll keep it to myself.'

Rich, rumbly laughter filled the kitchenette. 'I know what you mean. And thank you. I appreciate it.'

She peeled open one eye and split her fingers. Alexander had gone as red as she felt. Relief surged as she realised she wasn't alone in her embarrassment. Wasn't alone. Wasn't lonely. Which meant somehow, at some point over the week, Alexander had made a small home in her heart.

A home she'd have to evict him from because he wasn't going to stick around. He couldn't.

His life was in London, not in Herring Cove. And if she let that Alexander-shaped space in her heart grow, she'd only end up hurt. Left alone. Again.

114

Not going to happen.

She placed Puddles' food back in the cupboard and went to the door. Her footsteps as fast as the beat of her heart. She had to put a stop to whatever craziness was happening between them.

Sooner rather than later. Sooner being now.

'Right, well, now that I've offered myself up to you it's time for you to go. I really do have a lot of work to do. The books won't load themselves.' She opened the door and turned to see Alexander's eyes flashing with confusion.

'Are you sure? I mean, we didn't finish our beers and we were having a nice time...'

She met his gaze. Tried to ignore the hurt she saw in his eyes, and the hint of panic that quivered her core. 'I'm sure. Goodnight, Alexander.'

His mouth opened, then shut. And with a small shake of his head, like he didn't understand what was happening or why, he left.

Sophie shut the door behind him. Didn't watch him take the stairs. Pretended not to see his hunched back make its way down the street towards the cliffs as she stared out the window. Refused to let herself think about Alexander at all.

Her heart had to be in her business. In her home. She wasn't going to place it in his hands.

CHAPTER TWELVE

Bubbles frothed up the inside of the champagne glass as Ginny poured fizz into it.

'Woah, that'll do. There's still work to be done.' Sophie made to move the glass but not before Ginny managed to fill it to the top.

'Piffle. Life's short. We should celebrate everything, and you, my dear, are about to pull off Herring Cove's first market in years. Everyone's into it, even the people who are pro-Fletcher. I've seen buzz on neighbouring villages' social pages too. I think we're in for quite a crowd.'

Ginny half filled her own glass, then raised it in silent cheers. They clinked glasses and took a sip.

Tiny needles of nervousness prickled down Sophie's back. 'Do we have enough food stalls, do you think? The farmer's wife behind me has made huge pots of summer stews with couscous, and quiches and fruit pies. Sherry and Rob have ordered in extra. I've found a mobile pasty truck and they've said they'll come... And what if nobody comes and the stallholders sell nothing? They'll hate me.'

'Sophie. Breathe before you pass out from unnecessary worry.' Ginny placed her hands on her shoulders and frog-marched her to the front window. 'Look. What do you see?'

Trestle table after trestle table lined the street with vendors arranging their wares. Dotted around them were volunteers who were hanging bunting in all the colours of the rainbow from lamppost to lamppost. Unfamiliar faces wandered the streets, laughing, smiling and chatting.

'The market's hours away and already we're seeing people we've never seen before. The shop owner's worried he's going to run out of ice cream before the extra he ordered arrives. Sherry and Rob have had to ask locals to let them borrow their dining-room tables and chairs to fit all the people who're already here. The market's not even started and it's a success.'

Happiness soared in Sophie's heart. Ginny was right. The market was going to be fine. And she'd made her first online sale that day to a very grateful man who'd spent years looking for a book that had been sitting gathering dust on her shelves for years.

'It's going to be great,' she said as much to herself as to Ginny. 'Which reminds me, I need to set up my stall. Need to decorate it too if I'm going to turn any heads or compete with that stall over there.' She pointed out a glitter-encrusted table on which brightly coloured garden statues – gnomes and fairies, pixies and elves – were displayed.

An image of a box filled with sparkly party decorations that her mother had bought for her came to mind: pink and purple bunting, strings of faux silver and gold pearls. Glam enough to attract attention without being overly garish.

The doorbell jangled and, despite not being in direct sight of the door, Sophie knew immediately who it was.

Lemony-fresh scent and a vibrant energy that caressed her, despite its owner being a metre away.

'Bubbles, Alex?' Ginny rushed to the counter, grabbed an empty mug and began to pour without waiting for an answer. 'Sorry about the vessel, but it goes down the same.' She shoved it in his hands, then turned her attention back to Sophie.

'What are you waiting for, Soph? Go get yourself sorted. I can hang here and grab you if any customers come in.'

'What needs to be sorted?' Alexander took a sip and set the mug down.

'Nothing, really. I just have to get my stall ready, but first I need to get up in the loft and grab some decorations.' She picked up the bottle of champagne and offered it to Ginny.

'No more for me.' Ginny tapped her belly. 'Mike and I have made a bit of a big decision. We've decided to start trying. Two needs to become three. Our wee family is ready to become not-so-wee.'

Sophie's gut knotted up. More change. Natalie was going to move away with the kids. Ginny was going to become a mum. And what was she going to do? Sit in a falling-apart bookstore gathering dust like the books around her?

She sucked in a quiet breath, held it for three, then released. Blowing away the panic, the sadness. The loneliness that crept up, threatening to strangle the excitement of the event she'd created to bring the town together, the joy of making her first online sale; one of many, hopefully.

She wasn't being left behind. Her life was transforming every bit as much as Ginny's and Natalie's. But instead of moving on to a new village or creating a baby, she was experiencing a rebirth of her bookshop. Sure, it didn't hold her at night and whisper sweet words, or fly into her arms telling her every little thing that was running through their mind like Natalie's kids did, but her bookstore gave her the stability she needed. Gave her purpose. And, unlike a person, it wasn't going anywhere.

Not if she could help it.

She pulled Ginny in for a hug. 'I'm so happy for you, Gin. And excited. I can't wait to be Aunsof to a mini-you. You're going to be an amazing mum.'

Ginny squeezed her tight. 'And my future kiddiewinks are going to be lucky to call you Aunty. Love you, Soph.'

Sophie kissed Ginny on the cheek, released her and raised her glass. 'To the future sound of little feet pattering through All Booked Up.'

Ginny touched her glass to Sophie's. 'And to you for seeing opportunities in our darkest hour and running with them. For standing up to "the man".'

'Um, "the man" is standing right here, remember?' Alexander's brows raised in good humour. 'And I'd like to think "the man" has been a bit helpful. That I still might be.'

Ginny set her glass down and backed away. 'You know what would be helpful, Alex? Doing a one-eighty on this project of yours and just letting the town be. And with that said, I do believe that's my cue to leave.'

Sophie went to tell Alexander to ignore Ginny, but found the words halted on the tip of her tongue. Ginny said what she was thinking. What half the village were thinking. They didn't want their town changed, not in the way Alexander and his family were proposing.

'I don't suppose there's any chance what Ginny asked for could happen?'

Alexander shoved his hands in his pockets and shook his head. 'I don't see how, and that's the truth. Once my father decides something, it's as good as done.'

There was a dolefulness in Alexander's tone that Sophie had not heard before. Was he beginning to regret his part in the so-called reinvigoration of Herring Cove? Was there a chance it could be saved from corporate hands?

Hope bubbled in her blood, sent her heart into overdrive.

Maybe if the evening went really well, if enough money was made, if others saw what Herring Cove had to offer and invested in it, maybe that would change enough of the villager's minds that they could stage a full-on revolt. People lying in front of tractors and bulldozers. Marches down the lane. Articles in newspapers nationwide. Anything and everything to send the message loud and clear to the Fletcher Group that they were not welcome in Herring Cove.

Or maybe it was a case of the man standing in front of her

seeing what she saw in her home, and using his sway to convince the Fletcher Group to leave it be. Could Alexander take that stand though? Her hope settled to a dull simmer. Not likely. It would be even more unlikely that his father would pay attention to him if he did take a stand and say something.

'You were saying something about some decorations?' Alexander tucked one arm behind his back and half bowed. 'Because if it's help you need, I'm at your service, my lady.'

'In that case…' Sophie crooked her finger. 'Come. I'm going to need your muscles.'

'Ah, it's always the way. Women only want me for my brute strength.' Alexander's brows furrowed as his bottom lip protruded in a pout that was somehow cute and sexy at the same time.

'Well I can't speak for the others, but that's what this woman wants you for.' She reached over and patted his bicep. An innocent act, yet she couldn't help but notice the bulge in his arm was taut with muscle. Not a flabby bit to be felt.

'Are you going to give me back my arm anytime soon?' Alexander winked.

Sophie snatched her hand back like it had been burnt. 'Sorry. I guess it's been a long time since I felt anything that… hard.' *Hard? Really? Couldn't have chosen a less loaded word there, Sophie?* 'Er, that came out wrong. What I meant to say is that it's not often I touch anything hard. At all. Man-wise.'

She tore her gaze away from Alexander's bemused lips, which had twitched to the side and were trembling with silent laughter.

'Shall I find you a spade to dig a larger hole?'

A thigh-to-hip nudge followed, and Sophie became acutely aware that it wasn't just his bicep that was pure muscle. The length of thigh that teased her had no give whatsoever.

'Oh shush. You know what I mean. Now you can either continue teasing me or you can help me… Your choice.' She turned and made her way up the stairs, past her lounge to her bedroom door. 'Don't get any ideas.' She waggled her finger and opened the door to her bedroom.

He hovered at the threshold. 'I feel like I should close my eyes or ask for a blindfold or something.'

Sophie glanced around the room and mentally said thanks to her early-morning self for making her bed and tossing the previous day's clothing – including a pair of unsightly greying underwear – into the laundry basket. 'No blindfold needed, there's nothing to see here, but how do you feel about tight spaces?'

Sophie squeezed her eyes shut and mentally slapped her forehead as she jerked her thumb towards the loft hatch. Why were all her sentences sounding like some sort of invitation?

'For the record, just so you know, that's not some double entendre. I'm not trying to… I don't know… seduce you or anything mad like that.'

Slow, steady footsteps across the wooden floor followed, punctuated by that heady Alex-aroma.

Sophie turned around to see Alexander looking up at her, his head tilted to the side, amusement flickering across his face 'I know. Though I'm a touch disappointed. I feel like a Sophie seduction would be… interesting. Also, tight spaces are fine.'

'Great.' She forced the word out through gritted teeth. She had to ignore the heat that had made its way from her cheeks to somewhere far lower, and far more likely to get her in trouble. Her body may well be wanting to take a risk on Alexander, but her heart knew better. 'I'll just grab the step ladder.'

She rushed out to the kitchenette where she kept the step ladder tucked behind the door – grateful for the few seconds away from Alexander and all his… almost irresistible hotness.

Get it together, girl. He's just a man. Nothing special.

Even the voice of reason sounded doubtful. Still, it wasn't called "the voice of reason for nothing", so it was best to listen to it.

She squared her shoulders in an attempt to adopt a business-like posture, picked up the step ladder and carried it to the space

121

under the hatch. 'You go first, that way you can pull me up if need be.'

Alexander climbed the steps, moved the cover aside, poked his head through the hole, and made no further attempt to haul himself up.

'You right there? Not afraid of the dark, are you? Changed your mind about tight spaces?'

'Very funny.'

A dragging sound met her ears, followed by a plume of dust as Alexander ducked back down with a box in his hands. 'There's only a few boxes up there, all close enough for me to grab. So I thought it might be easier if we pull them down, check them out, then I can return whatever you don't need?'

She reached up for the box.

'Careful, it's heavy.' Alexander gently laid it in her hands.

She staggered under the wait. 'Ooph, you weren't kidding. What's in here?' She peered at a word written in black marker. 'Books'.

Not just any books. Her father's collection. His pride and joy. Something she'd not thought of, let alone touched, ever. Preferring to enjoy the comfort of simply knowing that something he loved was metres above where she slept.

'There's more where that came from.'

Two boxes later and Alexander had found the decorations. 'Closest to me, but on my left not my right.' He rolled his eyes. 'Typical. Could've saved myself an arm workout. Although, since you seem to quite like my arm muscles, maybe that bit of exercise wasn't a bad thing.'

He jumped off the step ladder, decorations in arms and strode through to the lounge. 'What's in the heavy boxes anyway?'

Sophie sank to the ground, grabbed a pen from the coffee table, used its nib to rip through the tape, then peeled back the flaps. The scent of aged paper wafted up as she gently took the first book out. She stroked the cover, navy with embellished gold script citing the title and author's name. 'Here's what's in them.'

'Books? Really? Shouldn't they be in the shop rather than stashed away?' His voice held surprise, and intrigue.

'Not just any books.' She opened the cover and checked the details. 'They're first-edition books.' She picked up another. The cover was a little tattered, but still in good condition. 'My father collected them. It was his hobby. They're not all rare, but I think for my dad it wasn't about the money he might earn from them one day, it was about treasuring something in its original state.' She opened the book up and breathed in. 'Musky and musty.' She set the book down next to the other. 'I'll never stop loving that smell. It's the scent of home. He used to let me sit on his lap as he read passages out loud to me from these books. It was our bedtime ritual for as long as I could remember.'

Alexander settled into a cross-legged position beside her, picked up the book she'd set down, pulled out his phone and began to swipe and type. 'Have you seen how much this one's worth?' He flipped his mobile around to face her.

'You are kidding me.' She choked the words out, barely hearing them through the blood roaring in her eyes and the now-jackhammering of her heart. 'That's. Ah…' Breath whooshed from her as she rubbed her heart.

'Now's not a good time to have a heart attack on me, Soph. Not when you're looking at something that could change your business. Your life, even.'

Sophie trailed her fingers over the embossed gold script. 'Do you think people would buy them?'

'I do. There's quite a market for them.' Alexander picked another book and began swiping and tapping at his phone. 'Your father must have had a real knack for it. This one's worth nearly as much as the last.'

Snippets of her parents' heated argument played through her mind. Guilt at what Alexander was suggesting, what she was contemplating, coiled tight in her heart. 'Dad didn't want to sell them though. Mum wanted him to. The business was struggling and she saw them as a lifesaver. Dad was against it. They were his hobby, his passion.'

'And what are they to you?' Alexander set his phone down and folded his arms across his broad chest. 'Are they your passion? Your hobby? Or could this be the lifesaver you need?'

'Maybe.' Indecision twisted and twirled within her. Would selling off her father's beloved books in order to secure the shop's future be a betrayal of his memory? Or would it honour all the hard work they'd put into starting All Booked Up? 'What would you do if you were me?'

Alexander took the book out of her hands and placed it back in the box, then bum-shuffled towards her until their knees were touching. Their faces inches apart. So close she noticed flecks of emerald in his forest-green eyes. Shards of colour she could stare into forever. Eyes that reflected the excitement, the triumph she should have felt at finding a way out of her financial troubles.

'If I were you, I would do what was right by the here and now. You can't change the past, but you can embrace the future. You love your shop, Sophie. Abundantly so. Can you tell me risking losing everything you've worked for is worth keeping a bunch of books stored away in a loft for memory's sake?'

Alexander reached for her hands, but Sophie pulled them away before he touched her, and tucked them under her thighs.

He was being so sweet, so nice, so… confusing. He should have been telling her to keep the books, hoping that her money problems would worsen and she'd have to sell or, worse, be forced to by the council.

'Why are you doing this? Being supportive, encouraging me to make my business a success, when it would be your interest to do otherwise. If I kept them, if the online shop failed, I'd be forced to sell. You wouldn't have to build round me. You'd get the resort you designed.' She hated how distrustful she sounded, but experience had taught her that if someone seemed too good to be true, they probably were.

Alexander tugged one of her hands out from its hidey hole and held it, his thumb drifting over her skin, sending a sprinkling of goose bumps up her arm.

'Because I care. Despite knowing I shouldn't. Knowing that it would be far better for me to keep my distance. Far safer.'

Sophie swallowed hard and tried to get her racing thoughts in check. This wasn't just any conversation. It was a precipice. One she should back away from. Yet some reckless part of her wanted to fall head first. To not back away as she'd done the previous day. To push forward, through her barrier, to risk embarrassment and uncertainty, just to know – one hundred per cent – that what she suspected was happening between her and Alexander wasn't just a figment of her imagination. To know that she could trust her instincts.

That this man could be trusted. That he would not hurt her.

She released her other hand from under her thigh and placed it around Alexander's. 'Safer? To keep your distance from me?'

'You heard me.'

His irises darkened as she brought his hands to her lips. Pressed a kiss on them. She waited for Alexander to push her away, to tell her she'd read things wrong. That the only thing between them was a business relationship that hinted at friendship. No more. No less.

'Remember when I offered to help you? It was partly because I'd hoped I could convince you to sell, an idea I quickly gave up on when I saw how determined you were to save your business, to reinvigorate your home.'

'You made a wise decision.' Sophie peppered kisses on each of his knuckles. 'You said partly. What was the other part?'

Alexander's chest lifted and his lips parted, like he was trying to figure out how to say what need to be said kindly, in a way that wouldn't hurt.

125

She braced herself for the gentle rejection.

'This was.'

One deft move saw Alexander's hand disentangle from hers. A cool hand cupped her hot cheek.

Friends didn't cup cheeks, not like this, not with desire in the eyes, and lips that moved closer with every passing second.

'Soph—'

Sophie shook her head in a small but definite no, silently shushing him. Words might ruin the magic, break the spell that had her head dizzy and her heart delighted.

The corners of Alexander's lips lifted, mirroring her own.

Was it possible to kiss through a smile? Through a light laugh?

Before she could ponder it further, his lips, soft and strong, met hers. Feather-light, touching, brushing… tempting.

Sophie curled her hand around the back of his neck and brought him closer. His lips parted, allowed her to taste him as he tasted her. Hints of coffee and the acid from the champagne combined with a slight saltiness that had her wanting more. Needing more.

Without breaking apart they uncrossed their legs and rose up on their knees, their bodies pressing together. Sophie ran her hand down Alexander's chest, feeling the muscles contract beneath his navy T-shirt. She slipped her hand under the soft material, her fingers dancing along the hard ridges of his stomach.

Alexander's hand tangled in her hair as he kissed his way down the length of her neck.

She melted against him. His arm circled her waist, holding her upright while he discovered her. Devoured her.

The tingle of door chimes broke the soft sighs and low moans that filled the lounge.

'Hello? Sophie? Ginny said you were up here?' The unmistake-able thud of footsteps on timber stairs followed.

Through half-closed eyes Sophie found Alexander's lips, kissed them once. Twice. Again, for good measure, then pushed herself up into a standing position and quickly ran her hand through her hair, smoothing it where Alexander's hands had mussed it up.

She fixed an innocent, open smile to her face and ran to the door just as Natalie was about to open it. 'Hey, Nat. How are you?'

'Good. Just checking in. Thought I'd make sure the website's going as it should. Ginny mentioned you'd had your first sale.' Natalie's brows drew together as she side-stepped around Sophie and made her way into the lounge.

Busted. Even if Natalie hadn't walked in on them kissing, Sophie was sure she'd sense the wired atmosphere. Her every nerve-ending crackled with energy. If a battery needed charging Sophie was sure she could power it up using the intensity that coursed through her.

She went to explain Alexander's presence, to try and distract Natalie from the event that – at least in her mind – was so clearly obvious, but Alexander had beaten her to it and was showing her the books they'd found in the loft.

'You never told me your father was a book collector, Sophie.' Natalie's tone was calm, but whenever she wasn't talking her lips would bunch up, like she was trying to stop herself from laughing, or squealing. Both.

She shut the door and went to sit beside Natalie, keeping her distance from Alexander, lest she lost herself in his scent, in his manliness, in his *there*ness and threw herself at him, embarrassing all of them.

'It wasn't something I'd thought about.' More like it was some-thing she'd kept to herself. Another memory of her family that she clutched tight.

Until Alexander came along.

She observed the books with new eyes. She'd kept them for so long because her father had been attached to them. Because, even though she'd not looked at them once, they held a place in her heart. A connection to a man she'd barely had the chance to get to know. Yet had his attachment been to his family and their livelihood, maybe he and her mother would be here today. Perhaps moving them on would be a way to move on from the past. To breathe life into her future.

Any residual guilt at the thought of selling them disappeared. These books would revitalise the business. Give it the fighting chance her mother had pleaded for.

'Er, Sophie?' Alexander got to his feet. 'I've got some work to do back at the B&B. So I'll be going.'

'Sure, I'll walk you out.' She turned to Natalie who was picking through the books. 'I'll be back in a minute, Nat.'

She followed Alexander down the stairs. Sparks of happiness zipped about her heart when he reached behind and took her hand in his, holding it all the way to the front door.

'Thank you for an unexpected, but wonderful, morning.' Alexander dropped a kiss on her nose, then her forehead, then on her lips. Less intense than the ones he'd showered upon her upstairs, but no less moreish. 'Those books are quite a find.'

'I know. Who'd have thought a martini-loving spy with an eye for the ladies could be worth so much?' She smiled up at him as she ran a finger down the length of his jaw, loving the way his stubble prickled.

Amusement deepened the lines around his eyes. 'Worth so much, hey? Is that your way of saying that because I pulled the books down and brought them to your attention that I might be worth a little something to you?'

Sophie paused as fear flared in her heart. Warned her against falling too hard. Against losing herself in a man who would one day soon leave, leaving her wanting more. She squeezed the fear away. She'd lived her life too carefully for too long. No longer. It was time to rebuild her shop, and her life.

'Yes, it is, and I mean it with all my heart.'

CHAPTER THIRTEEN

Alexander resisted the urge to literally skip down the street, or to flick his legs up in a high side-kick.

He settled for walking with a bounce in his step, only stopping when his mobile vibrated in his pocket. He pulled it out, afraid it would be his father pressing for his return to the office, as he had in every phone call and message the past two days. Each insistence heightening the burgeoning dread that had formed in Alexander's gut, in his heart, at the through of leaving Herring Cove. Of leaving Sophie.

See you at the market X

Alexander smiled, his lips stretching as wide as they could go.

Since that moment at the beach where he'd been seconds away from kissing Sophie, his imagination had been in over-drive. Her petite, yet perfectly shaped lips had floated through his mind more than once, and he'd wondered if her kisses would be as strong as she was. As determined. As soft and sweet.

His imagination had let him down.

Sophie's kisses were more passionate, more demanding, more than anything he could've hoped for. Or dreamed about. Her lips had seared, branded. As unforgettable as they'd been unexpected.

'Alex, what are you doing with that big grin on your face? You look like a bloke who's been up to something… and I'd like to know what that something is.'

Alexander followed the buoyant voice and saw the local publican, Rob, who he'd gotten to know a little over the course of his stay, waving him over from one of the pub's windows, open wide to embrace the beautiful day.

A reggae tune floated on the summer's air, along with waves of laughter and happy chatter from the customers inside the pub.

Before he had the chance to make a conscious decision, he found himself crossing the road towards Rob.

'Beautiful day for it.' Alexander propped his elbows up on the windowsill and breathed in the scent of hops and cooking oil, underpinned by cleaning products.

Nowhere near as heady as Sophie's violet and vanilla scent, but it held its own charm, especially on a day like today where the birds' chirps seemed filled with more joy than usual, the sun brighter, the breeze warmer.

'Beautiful day for *what* is what I'll like to know.' Rob winked. 'And what are you doing loitering about like that? Come in. I'll grab you your usual and we can have a natter.'

Emails that needed replying to, phone calls to return, the vow to head home to the office, all tugged at his conscience. Bugger it. Soon as he was back home his life would be restored to its all-work and no-play grind. What would one harmless lunchtime beer matter in the grand scheme of things?

'Why not? It's not like I've anything better to do.'

Rob ushered him in, then left him to take a seat at the window. The windowsills had been converted into built-in leaners, wide enough to hold a pint glass, a bowl of chips and a couple of pairs of elbows.

'There you go.'

A crisp, golden lager was set before him.

'Thanks.' He nodded his gratitude as he took a sip of the refreshing drink. 'Just what the doctor ordered.'

'She's a warm one.' Rob sat back onto his stool and took a long swig of his pint. 'Good day for the market. It's nice to see the place humming with people, like you'd think it ought to be at this time of year.' He set his glass down and stared out the window. 'Sometimes I wonder if Herring Cove is in some magical bubble that keeps most people out, but, every now and then that bubble will let someone in, and once here they find they don't want to leave.'

Alexander ran his thumb through the condensation on his glass. Rob's words were thick with meaning... but he couldn't quite catch what that meaning was. Couldn't. Or was afraid to admit he knew exactly what Rob was on about. 'Were you born here, Rob? Or did you make your way into the magical bubble of the village?'

Rob shifted in his seat, angled his body in Alexander's direction. His brow creased as his eyebrows knitted together. 'Made my way? That makes it sound like I wanted to come here. My arrival in Herring Cove was much more in the style of fate.'

Alexander found himself leaning in, not wanting to miss a word of the tale to come in Rob's deep and low lilt.

'I was a session musician once upon a time. Would tour around the country whenever required. Loved the lifestyle. Loved not sitting still. Rolling stones gather no moss and all that. I was never one for the idea of being bogged down by anything or anyone...' His shoulders shook with a shudder. 'I was so independent I wouldn't even travel with the band. Preferred to pack my stuff in my car and get there on my own. Then one day I took a wrong turn and ended up here. No big deal, or so I thought. I could just do a U-turn and find my way back to the main road. Except then I heard this thump-thump-thump.'

'Flat tyre.' Alexander's knuckles strained against his skin as he gripped his glass. Rob's wide eyes and lowered voice made it seem like a horror story. Yet he had his happy ending. Didn't he?

'Two flat tyres. And not a tyre shop in sight. So, I did the only thing I could.'

Alexander held his thumb and little finger out and put his hand up to the side of his head. 'Called for help?'

'No.' Rob let out a huff of disgust, his large nose wrinkling. 'I found the closest pub – or as it turned out, the only pub – ordered myself a beer and figured I'd sleep on the beach, then sort everything out the next day.'

'And how did that work out for you?' Alexander asked, even though he had an idea he knew exactly how things went.

'Well, I met this gorgeous woman who was working behind the bar. Turned out she owned the place. And, you know what? I think she must carry the magic of Herring Cove with her, because once I was in her bubble I didn't want to pop it. Or blow it.'

'Did you ever miss your old life? Feel trapped by your new one?' Alexander knew what Rob's answer would be, but wanted to hear it anyway. To see the emotion on his face.

A cheek-creasing grin appeared. The lines surrounding his eyes became crevasses. His eyes radiated love. 'Not once. I have a place to play my music. More friends – real connections – than I ever could have dreamed of. And the love of a very good woman. What more could I want?'

'You bleating on about the magic bubble of Herring Cove again, my love?' Sherry set down a bowl of chips and a ramekin of creamy aioli, wrapped her arm around Rob's neck and brought him in for a kiss. 'Don't believe him. There's no bubble. I just got very lucky that his car got nailed, literally, and that he liked beer.'

Rob shook his head. 'There's. A. Bubble.' The words were silent, but Sherry mussed his hair like she'd heard them anyway.

'Silly bugger. Now do you two need anything else?'

'Thanks, my heart, but I think we're good.' Rob kissed Sherry's cheek and sent her on her way with an affectionate tap on her bum. 'So, how's Herring Cove treating you? Have you got what you came for?'

Alexander's heart stilled. Was this friendly conversation going down the hard-word path? Was Rob going to give him grief for doing his job? A job he had little choice but to do.

'Breathe, lad.' Rob placed his hand on his arm and gave it a squeeze. 'You look like you're about to bring up your breakfast.'

Alexander did as he was told and filled his lungs with deep breath after breath until the beer in his stomach ceased swirling and the tension in his chest released.

'Sorry. Being here hasn't been the easiest. We've never been met with this kind of resistance. Tonight, at the market, I'm planning to make myself available to anyone who wants to have a chat. Hopefully I can ease some minds. Explain to them why a resort will be good for the village.'

Rob released his hold on Alexander and went back to nursing his beer. 'Maybe I'm reading things wrong, but you don't sound particularly convinced yourself that a resort's the best idea for the village.'

Was it too late to excuse himself, to leave this conversation? Or would doing that make it clear that Rob was right? That a Fletcher resort in Herring Cove was beginning to feel less and less like the right thing to do.

Alexander surveyed the hustle and bustle of people finishing off their display tables. Decorations fluttered in the breeze. Products were stacked high. The village buzzed. And there wasn't a five-storey resort anywhere in sight that could take credit for the vibrant ambience.

'Imagine all this,' he indicated to the scene before them, 'times twenty. That's what a resort would bring.'

'If that's what you have to keep telling yourself to help you sleep at night, son, then you keep the phrase on repeat.' Rob lifted his glass to his mouth, his eyes never leaving Alexander. 'Anyway, enough of the resort talk. I prefer it out of sight, out of mind. I'm more interested in your business with our Sophie.'

Alexander's gut constricted. From one difficult topic to another.

He barely understood what was happening with Sophie himself; to have to explain it to another person?

'I may not have kids but I can't help but feel a bit protective when it comes to Sophie and, from what I saw while tinkling the ivories the other night, I'd say that there was some interest, on both sides. The question I have is just how deep does that interest go?'

Alexander shifted in his padded seat. Seconds ago, it had been comfortable, now it could have been made from rock. And not because Rob was asking him a tough question. The easy answer was that he was very interested in Sophie. The hard thing to answer was, just how far could you take things with someone who inhabited a different world from you – in all senses. It wasn't fair to start something he couldn't finish. But something had already been started, and he didn't know that he had the power, or the will, to stop it.

'You see, Alex, Sophie may not have family of the DNA-derived type in this village, but she's got people who look out for her, love her, all through this tiny spot on the map. For all her independence, for all her outward show of positivity spiked with determination, she's got her fragile spots. That's why that wall of hers is as high as it is thick. She doesn't let anyone behind that wall easily, and if someone did manage to get through, then took a bulldozer to her heart?' Rob swung an imaginary mallet through the air. 'Well I don't know that Sophie would be able to rebuild that wall again. And even if she did, it wouldn't hold strong. And she sure as hell would never let anyone behind – or anywhere near it – again.'

Alexander gripped the back of his neck and tried not to think about how Sophie had not half an hour ago allowed him behind said wall. 'What you're saying is that if I hurt her you'll not so much see me out of town as throw me out?'

'That's if you choose to leave.' Rob finished his beer and set the glass down with a thump made Alexander jump in his seat. 'You've found your way into the bubble, remember?'

Alexander pushed his beer away. Any appetite for it gone. 'I would never hurt Sophie, not intentionally,' he said as much to himself as to Rob.

'That's the thing though, boy. All the best intentions in the world won't always stop you hurting someone you care about. Or love.' Rob reached out and slapped him on his back. 'But I do believe you when you say you're not out to hurt our girl. I just want you to know that if you do, you'd better leave and never come back. Small places have long memories.'

'Duly noted.' An uncomfortable mix of duty and desire sat heavy in Alexander's chest. He slid off the stool and nodded a silent goodbye to Rob, who returned the nod with solemn eyes.

Alexander pulled his sunglasses from his pocket and placed them over his eyes before heading out into the bright day. A smile rose unbidden as he saw Puddles attempting to catch a butterfly. Leaping up, his furry white paws missing as the butterfly ducked and weaved its way through the air. He squatted down and clicked his tongue, distracting Puddles from his mission. The cat trotted towards him and lay flat on the ground, belly up, waiting for some love.

Rob was right – Herring Cove had pulled him into its bubble.

He'd come expecting to expand the Fletcher empire. Instead he was on the verge of blowing his entire life up.

And a tiny, rebellious part of him didn't think that would be a bad thing.

CHAPTER FOURTEEN

'You keep touching your lips and getting this goofy grin on your face.' Natalie popped a piece of popcorn into her mouth and raised her eyebrows. 'How much longer am I going to have to wait before you finally admit that I walked in on you and Alexander having a moment of the kissing kind?'

Sophie focused on straightening up a pile of books. She refused to look Natalie in the eye, knowing that if she did the game would be well and truly up. Not that kissing Alexander was a game. In fact, it felt the opposite. Something not to be taken lightly.

She smiled at a woman who'd paused at her stall and was thumbing through a recipe book. 'Twenty per cent off all books this evening. Market special.'

The woman returned her smile, set the book down and wandered off down the lane towards the small stage where Rob had set up his piano and was playing songs on request, with the proviso that if he didn't know the song he'd donate money to the local community charity. Lucky for him he knew most of the songs or Sherry would have made good on the mutinous glare she'd shot him when he'd announced his plans to all and sundry.

The result had been a cheer from the community and added vibrancy to the event as he belted out hits from the past six decades.

'How long are we not going to have this conversation about you and Alex that I feel we really need to have?' Natalie picked up a book and swatted Sophie on the bum playfully. 'Because it's not going to work. I need the tongue-tangling nitty-gritty. I have to live vicariously through you these days because I've no intention of going down that path again.'

'Who's living vicariously?' Ginny strolled up, her cheeks red with exertion as she hauled about armfuls of bags, with flowers tucked under each armpit. 'Soph, can I leave these with you? I think I might have gone a bit overboard, and there's still more things I want. I saw the most adorable handmade wooden block set, and I have to get it for the nursery Mike and I are putting together.'

'Sure. Here, let me.' Sophie grabbed the flowers and placed them in the shade under the table, then relieved Ginny of the rest of her load.

'Thanks for that.' Ginny placed her hands on her hips and did a slow turn, letting out a long, low whistle. 'Would you look at this place? It's heaving. Are you going to make it a regular thing? Actually, don't make it a regular thing. My bank account couldn't afford it.' She tapped her chin. 'Or maybe it could. My wee stall sold out in an hour, I've made a killing.'

'I've done okay too.' Natalie tweaked a line of shampoo and conditioner. 'Moved some hair product, which will make life easier when I close the business and leave. And a few people have taken my website design business card, which is good.'

Grief twinged in Sophie's chest. She'd put Natalie leaving out of her mind. Refused to think about it. Promised herself she'd deal with it when the time came. But time was marching on, and the thought of saying goodbye to Natalie and the kids wasn't getting any less painful.

'I still can't believe you're going.' Ginny pouted. 'I'll miss you, but I can see how it's for the best. Nothing like a fresh start, a change of pace. Besides, you'll stay in Cornwall, yeah?'

'Of course. I don't want to be hours away from Mum and Dad, or you guys. Far enough away to erase the memories of that pillock ex of mine, but close enough that we can still catch up without it being in the too-hard basket. Although after what I walked in on this morning I suspect Sophie will be too busy heading up London way to visit little old me…' Natalie turned to Sophie, a smirk on her face.

'Are you suggesting what I think you're suggesting?' Ginny squeaked, her hands flying from her hips to her cheeks in delight. 'That's more than I could hope for. I had a feeling there was something between you and Alexander. A connection. You've every reason to keep away from each other, yet you've been circling each other with desire in your eyes since the moment you met.'

'You two are infuriating. And we have not.' Sophie rolled her eyes at Ginny, who was too busy jumping up and down in excitement to notice. 'There's no circling here. Just a man helping me out to ease the guilt of building a resort around me, and me taking advantage of free labour. Beggars can't be choosers and all that.' She pressed her chin to her chest, furrowed her brow in warning, and waited for Ginny and Natalie to back off from the topic of Alexander.

'Oh no, dear Sophie.' Natalie threaded her arm through hers. 'You're not getting off that easily. You two had passionate guilt written all over your faces. That and Alexander's T-shirt was rumpled like someone's hand had recently been scrunched up in it. Oh, and your hair was mussy in a way that wasn't "I did this on purpose" cute.'

'Oh, this is good. This is very, very good.' Ginny rubbed her hands together, glee lighting up her face. 'If Alexander meant nothing, Sophie wouldn't have hidden it, would you, Sophie?'

'Yeah, well…' Sophie fought not to look away, to confirm the truth through denial. Even if she was attracted to Alexander, and he to her, what was the 'truth' between them anyway? It wasn't like anything more could happen between them other than a

138

fling. He had a life in London. She had a life here. It couldn't be more. Even if she wanted it to be.

'"Yeah, well"? Is that as good as you've got?' Ginny tapped her chin with her finger. 'Methinks the lady is more smitten than she cares to admit.'

'Methinks you're right. Me thinks she's also freaking out about it. Big time.' Natalie draped her hand around Sophie's shoulders and brought her closer. 'Me also thinks it's nice to see you being vulnerable. Even if it means that my inner mummy wants to wrap you in cotton wool and bubble wrap to stop any chance of you getting hurt like last time.'

Sophie wriggled out from under Natalie's hold. 'And *I* think you both need to get into my shop, make your way to the language area – now situated to the back left of the shop, three bookshelves in – and relearn the English language.'

Ginny laughed. 'We've got her, Nat. She's taken to insulting us. I never thought I'd see the day.' Her features smoothed out as she shook her head, her eyes wide with wonder. 'Sophie Jones has fallen head over heels.'

'And you'll be pushed head over heels if you don't stop harassing me.' Sophie stuck her tongue out at her friend, then cracked up when her friend returned the gesture and upped it with a two-fingered salute.

'No can do.' Ginny turned around, stood on tiptoes and surveyed the crowds. 'Where is Alexander anyway? I want to see you two together.' Her body rippled in a shiver. 'How delicious. Love. Seeing people fall into it. Yum.'

'What's yum?'

Sophie jumped, along with Natalie and Ginny, at the sound of Alexander's voice behind them.

She clutched her heart and spun round. 'Are you trying to give us heart attacks sneaking up like that?'

Alexander grinned, sending a flurry of miniature lightning bolts zipping and zapping through her stomach.

'Wasn't sneaking. Just saw that it was easier to go behind the stalls in order to see you than in front of them, so that's what I did. This place is packed.'

'Oh. Right.' Sophie dropped her gaze as a warm flush hit her cheeks.

Big mistake. In avoiding Alexander's handsome face, she was faced with impeccable dress sense – olive-green cargo shorts paired with a navy polo – that only served to emphasise the muscles she'd noted during his shelf building sessions, muscles she'd touched far too briefly earlier that day. The man was perfection, through and through.

She glanced down at her red sundress flipping around her knees and was glad she'd dressed up for the market instead of wearing the faded khaki shorts and wrinkled grey marl T-shirt she'd had on earlier.

'You said you wanted to see Sophie, Alexander?'

The amusement, the 'knowing' in Ginny's voice was obvious, and Sophie wished she was standing beside her instead of across the table so she could dig a sharp elbow into her waist.

'I did. Actually, Ginny, I was hoping you might be so kind as to look after Sophie's stall so I can escort her around the event. Show her what she's managed to achieve? What do you say, Soph?'

'She'd love to go.' Ginny bustled round the table and flapped Sophie out of the way. 'Stay away for as long as you like.'

'Wonderful.' Alexander slipped his hand in Sophie's and pulled her in the crowd.

Sophie twisted around to see Ginny and Natalie waving her off, triumphant looks upon their faces.

She poked her tongue out at them and turned back round to see Alexander looking at her with amusement.

'Is that how you normally say goodbye to your friends?' Alexander nodded at acquaintances he'd made over the course of the week as they weaved their way through the crowds towards the back of the market.

He'd made progress with some of the locals today. The crowds and allure of money had seen those who'd been unconvinced that a resort would be beneficial to Herring Cove waver. New faces and money changing hands had that effect on people.

When stall holders had stopped him and asked if this was how busy other villages became once the Fletcher Group had moved in, he knew his job was about to get much easier.

He'd done as his father would expect and said yes it was. That it would, in fact, be busier. Not a lie. It would be. With the right marketing and implementation of facilities there was no reason why Herring Cove couldn't be as vibrant and alive as it was today all summer long.

His mouth had said all the right things, but his heart hadn't been in it. Not when the stories came out of how much Herring Cove meant to those living there, their histories long and rich, their love for the place – for its tranquillity and charm – so apparent.

One stall holder, a fisherman, spoke of going out on the boats with his father since he was knee-high, the way his father had before him, and his grandfather before that. He talked of days when local families would pick up bread and pastries from the bakery, ham sliced fresh from the butcher, and take it down to the beach along with fruit from the farm that would soon be a golf course. He reminisced about how those long, hot days became bonfire-filled nights where the kids would play, the adults would chat, and a community was forged, bonded.

A local dressmaker, who'd given up her shop on the small main street due to a reduction in her customer base, spoke of creating wedding dresses for women all around the area. How her business had then fallen over almost completely due to not having a store-front. How she hoped people seeing her dresses and skirts would re-spark interest. Perhaps enough that she could open a new store.

He didn't have the heart to tell her that once the resort was opened, lease prices would rise and she'd be priced out of the market. Along with so many people who'd turned up to sell their wares. Crafted straight from the heart, and deserving to be seen, to be loved.

'You've gone quiet.' Sophie shook his hand. 'Is everything okay?'

'Of course.' Alexander forced a smile. Now was not the time to get gloomy. Now was the time to show Sophie how successful her venture had been. How it had brought so much joy to both locals and people from the surrounding areas.

The small stage loomed. He caught Rob's eye and flashed him a subtle thumbs up. It was time for Sophie to shine, for people to see the brains behind the beauty of the market, and to hope-fully support her and her shop in the future.

'Don't get angry at me.' Alexander tugged Sophie to a stop.

Sophie's eyes narrowed as she turned to face him. 'I've yet to hear of a conversation that goes well when it starts with those words.'

'Well, there's a first for everything.'

Three taps on a microphone echoed over the crowd, followed by a slight cough.

'Hello. Good evening.' Rob's voice rumbled loud and clear, bringing the murmuring masses to a halt. 'Thank you for coming this evening to the first-ever Herring Cove Midsummer's Night Market.'

'First ever? He's making it sound like this is going to be a regular thing,' Sophie muttered, her brow furrowing more and more by the second.

'No reason it couldn't be,' Alexander murmured, tightening his grip on her hand in case she attempted to make a run for it.

'It's been fantastic to see our main street filled with people having a good time, and discovering what makes our place special. It's not just the beautiful beach and astounding panoramic views that make Herring Cove a wonderful place to visit, it's the people who live here who give it its heart, its soul. Speaking of which…'

Rob gave Alexander the nod, and Alexander pushed his way through the crowd, a reluctant Sophie in his wake.

'This event was the idea of one of Herring Cove's most beloved citizens and the owner of the most unique bookshop around, All Booked Up, which you can find up the way there and there is twenty per cent off all books for tonight only. May I introduce you to Sophie Jones. Get up here, Sophie. Say a few words and take a bow.'

Alexander reached the stage and gave Sophie the nudge she needed to step up.

'You are in so much trouble.'

He grinned at her growled threat. She could yell at him all she wanted, but this was for her own good. She needed to see how much support she had around her, how much love. To know that if she was ever in trouble again – whether it be of the personal or professional kind – she could ask for help and people would gladly step up. Not out of duty, but because they cared.

Sophie took the microphone from Rob and turned to the crowd. 'Er, this wasn't planned so I'm afraid I've not got anything witty or funny to say, but what I will say, I'll say from the heart.'

Sophie paused and, even from his distance some metres away, Alexander could see her eyes becoming glassy with emotion.

'Your coming to Herring Cove to support our wee village, to support us, means everything to me. You've given us reason to believe we have so much to offer. Things that those who don't live here want, and need. You've brought with you laughter, kindness and generosity. For that, I can't thank you enough. I have a feeling this is the first of many wonderful changes to happen to Herring Cove. With that in mind, please raise whatever you have that's raiseable and let's toast to new growth and new beginnings.' She raised the microphone, and the small crowd repeated the phrase, then cheered.

Sophie pressed the microphone back into Rob's hand and searched the crowd. Her eyes settled on Alexander as a huge smile lit up her face. One that told him he wasn't in big trouble, not even a little trouble; in fact, no trouble at all.

She stepped off the stage and made her way to him. The closer she came, the more pride surged through his body. Filling his heart.

Sophie Jones was an amazing woman. The best he'd met. She lived her life the way he wished he could live his. Free from expectation of others. Doing the best she could by those she loved, but not at the expense of what would make her happy.

Tonight, she'd built community camaraderie. All without destroying a single home or business. If anything, if the people of Herring Cove were left alone to their own devices, the village could flourish once more and become the bustling fishing village it once was.

Alexander eyed the rundown empty shop fronts. An idea sparked, ignited. With a little help, some investment, the revitalisation could be hastened, all while retaining the charming aspects of the village.

He pushed the plans that had begun to formulate aside as Sophie took his hands in hers and gave them a shake.

'You are a rotter.' The words were firm but warm. 'You're lucky I like you or you'd be fish food.' Her chocolate-brown eyes twinkled as the sharpness of her lips softened.

He was going to miss those eyes when he went back to the city. Going to miss *her*.

Sadness threatened to lower like clouds before a storm. He shrugged it off. Tonight was not for mourning the eventual. It was for celebrating the possible.

'Lucky you like me then.'

'Indeed.'

Silence stretched between them. Heavy with anticipation.

'I forgot to tell you how beautiful you look in that dress.' Alexander broke the silence. 'Am I allowed to say that these days? I know blatant wolf-whistling's out.' He winked to show he was joking.

Sophie laughed. 'I think I can take that compliment. And thank you. The local seamstress made it. She's very talented.'

Alexander angled his head so it was hovering just above Sophie's, kiss-close. 'Seems to be a lot of talent in Herring Cove.'

Sophie bobbed back a fraction. 'Alexander Fletcher, are you flirting with me?'

'I might be. Just a little. If that's okay with you.'

Sophie's hand left his, touched his hip tentatively, then brought him closer. 'It's okay with me. More than okay.' She stood on tiptoe and pressed a kiss to his lips.

He breathed in her sweet, heady scent. Committed it to memory. Their time together was limited, so he was going to make the most of it, and treasure every second.

The evening flew by in a blur of conversation, laughter, and – later on when the crowds had gone home, the stalls had been packed up and the locals had retired to the pub to celebrate – topped-up glasses.

Sophie and Alexander had parted ways during the evening but always found each other again. Their hands slipping into each other's so easily it felt like second nature. Like they were meant to be joined together.

It was of little surprise to Alexander that at the end of the evening after Natalie had yawned one too many times and taken the kids home to bed, after Mike had swooped Ginny into his arms and carried his heavy-lidded wife home, and Rob and Sherry had waved them off hand-in-hand, it was just he and Sophie left standing outside the shop.

'Tonight may well have been my most favourite night ever.' Alexander held his arms out for Sophie and she all but fell into them.

He wrapped his arms around her petite frame and pressed her against his chest. So close. Not close enough.

Alexander stroked the soft spot of skin between her thumb and index finger. A small gesture that felt hugely intimate. He was so comfortable with Sophie. So at home. It simultaneously comforted and scared him.

What if he fell for her? What if never wanted to leave? How hard would it be to tear himself away from her when he had to? And he would have to. Sooner rather than later. He'd told his father he'd stay for the market to press the flesh, but now that the market had been and gone he had no more excuses to stay.

'Alexander?'

The caution, the hope, in Sophie's voice brought him back to the here and now.

'I don't want to be too forward, but we could either stand here hugging each other all night… or we could perhaps go upstairs and hug horizontally?'

She cocked an eyebrow, her eyes sparkling under the light of the lamp post. Brighter than the stars above. More beautiful.

He resisted the urge to say yes immediately. The chemistry between them made his desire to do so easy, but they needed to know where they stood with each other. Had to know the outcome was never going to end in a happily ever after.

'I've had the best night, Sophie. Best ever. Being with you. Being with your friends. Not being seen as "that Fletcher fellow" but as me, as Alex? It's meant so much. And I want to hug horizontally with you. I do.'

Sophie's grip loosened. Her eyes lost in shadows as her gaze fell from his face.

His heart twisted, hating that his caution was causing her pain.

'I get what you're saying. I understand. It's no big deal.'

Sophie made to step back, but Alexander kept his arms around her.

'That's where you're wrong. It is a big deal, Sophie. You're not like anyone I've ever met before. You're raw. You're real. Determined. Independent. With a beautiful heart that's willing to give so much to those she loves. I'm afraid of how I'll feel when I have to leave. Because I will have to leave. I can't be here

146

forever. And I don't want you doing anything you'd regret. I don't want to hurt you. You mean too much to me.'

Sophie locked eyes with Alexander as her arms found their way around his waist once more. 'There's no way I could regret the time I've spent with you, Alex. Not ever. And you can't hurt me. I've experienced enough hurt that I'm immune to it.'

Her smile – one that was mean to make light of the situation – only deepened his thoughts and feelings around it. Sophie could say she was immune from hurt all she wanted, but he knew it wasn't true. Once she let someone in, once she cared, she could be hurt. All too easily.

'I promise not to get hurt.'

'You can't prom—'

Sophie cut the words off with a kiss. Slow, lingering.

The kind of kiss that would make the most rational man abandon all sensibilities.

Sophie broke the kiss, but kept her lips hovering millimetres away from his. 'One night. Just give us that.'

'Are you sure?'

Sophie turned away with a wink, unlocked the shop, tugged Alexander through the store and up the stairs, towards her bedroom.

Alexander had his answer. Sophie was sure.

At least one of them was.

CHAPTER FIFTEEN

Early morning rays of light struck Alexander's eyes, dazzling him despite his eyes being shut. He squeezed them tighter against the sun and patted his hands around the bed, looking for the person who'd kept him up so late that he was reluctant to wake up.

Not that he was complaining. The opposite.

Sophie had chased away the last of his reservations. Her lips soft against his. Teasing his concerns away until there was nothing but the pleasure of two people who wanted to be together enjoying each other. For hours, upon hours, upon more unforgettable hours.

'Soph.' The word came out a sleep-fogged mumble.

There was no reply, and the spot next to him was cold, like she'd been up and out of bed for hours.

He rolled onto his back, draped his forearm across his eyes and repressed a groan as his mobile phone's vibration mode buzzed on the wooden bedside table.

There was only one person who'd call so early on a Saturday morning.

And while, as his father, Frank had every right to, did he as his boss? Any other job, any other manager, and he'd have respect-fully asked that phone calls be made during office hours except for in the case of an emergency, but his father didn't believe in boundaries. Work was front and centre, twenty-four seven. And he expected his only son to believe the same.

And Alexander had, for more years than he cared to count.

Responsibility threatened to swamp his happiness and he was grateful to hear Sophie's light footsteps on the lounge's wooden floor. A reminder of what really mattered, of *who* really mattered.

He sat up in bed, gave his face a dry rub and quickly patted his hair in place in a cack-handed grooming attempt.

The bedroom door was nudged open by a bare foot, then Sophie appeared carrying her laptop. 'You're awake. Good.' She padded over to the bed and set the laptop on the bedside table. 'I was starting to think you were going to sleep forever.'

Alexander's heart sunk. She'd wanted him to be awake? So he could leave? So things could go back to the way they were? Business as usual?

So much for a romantic start to the day.

He'd imagined the two of them snuggled up in bed, drinking tea, catching up on the news on their phones… Instead he was getting kicked out like he was nothing more than a one-night stand…

Which he was. It was all he could be. The phone began vibrating again. A harsh reminder of the truth.

'Be back in a sec.' Sophie jogged out of the bedroom, her pink, cotton bathrobe patterned with white polka dots, flying behind her.

He reached over and turned off the phone. Bugger his father. If this was the only chance he was getting to spend with Sophie he was making the most of it. All attention on her.

'Here we go.' She stood in the doorway with a food-filled tray. 'I figured you'd be starving because I'm beyond famished.'

So much for being kicked out. Sophie had made enough breakfast to keep them bed-bound for a week. Something he would not object to.

She placed the tray in the middle of the bed, leaned over and kissed him full on the lips. 'I hope you like toast, yoghurt and fruit.' She kissed him again, before straightening up, arranging her pillows against the lemon-yellow washed headboard and settling onto the bed.

Alexander's stomach rumbled as he took in the pile of toast, smothered in melting butter and coated in golden honey, which was plated next to a mountain of juicy red strawberries and plump blueberries.

'I heard that.' Sophie reached over and patted his grumbling tummy, then sat her laptop in front of her and started typing. 'Ignore me. You get stuck in. I'll eat soon as I check my emails. See if any orders have come in overnight.'

Alexander picked up a piece of toast, cupped his other hand under it to stop butter or honey dropping onto the mint-green bedsheets, then bit into it, relishing the crunch, the salt, the sweet. 'Yum,' he let out a low moan of satisfaction. 'That's so good. Just what I needed.'

Sophie smirked. 'Working up an appetite will have that effect. You'll be in raptures when you try the strawberries. Fresh from the farm round the road.'

'More raptures?' He finished off the toast and licked each finger before reaching for another piece. 'I thought last night was as rapturous as things could get.'

Sophie reached for a blueberry and popped it in her mouth. 'Yeah, it was pretty good.'

He reached over and tickled her waist, laughing as she squeaked and bum-shuffled away from him. 'Pretty good? Is that the rating you're giving it? After I—'

Sophie picked up a strawberry and pressed it against his mouth. 'Kidding, Alex. I'm amazed I didn't hear a choir of angels singing, or the sky splitting open to reveal marshmallow pink clouds and golden light spilling over us.'

Alexander bit into the strawberry, then went to wipe the juice that dribbled down his chin.

Sophie took his hand. 'Uh-uh. That's mine.' She leaned over and kissed the juice off his chin, then lingered on his lips. 'Mmm, delicious.'

She made to move away, but Alexander wrapped his arm around her waist and pulled her closer. 'Oh no, Miss Jones, you're not going anywhere after that. You've given me a taste of dessert, and now I'm ravenous for more.'

'Is that so?' Her leg slid over his as Sophie came to hover inches over him. 'In that case...' She took another strawberry, placed it in her mouth and brought her lips down to his.

Desire surged hot and heavy through Alexander as he ate the strawberry in one bite, anything to get to the sweetness that lay beyond. 'Delicious, but that wasn't the dessert I was talking about.'

Alexander tangled his hands through Sophie's hair and brought her down for another kiss, loving how her body collapsed onto his, inch by inch. All resistance gone.

He could get used to this. Could live like this.

Forever.

And the thought didn't frighten him. Not one bit.

***

'No more distracting me.' Sophie wagged her finger at Alexander as she grabbed her laptop and set it down in front of her, laughing as he placed his hand on his bare chest with an innocent 'who, me?' widening of his eyes. 'I wasn't kidding about checking orders, and I have research to do. I don't want to sell my dad's books too cheaply, but I don't want to put people off buying them either.'

'Is this your way of telling me I need to leave?' Alexander rearranged the tangle of sheets, tucking them up around their bodies. Covering them. 'There we go, all decent.'

'Got a sudden case of shyness, Alex?' She stuck the tip of her tongue out between her teeth and wrinkled her nose at him.

151

'Pretty sure after last night and this morning there's not a lot left to hide between us.'

'I'm just preserving my modesty. Wouldn't want you to lose interest too soon.'

Sophie grinned at his proper tone, complete with a prim tilt of his nose.

Alexander had the most amazing ability to combine cute and sexy. It was moreish.

Except more was not an option and she'd had to remind herself of that more than once already that morning. She'd sprung out of bed before dawn in an attempt to create some distance between the night they'd shared and the reality of their situation. However, contented snores and the lift of his lips as he smiled ever so slightly in his sleep scuppered any boundaries she'd wanted to build, and she found herself pulling on yesterday's clothes and a pair of trainers on a mad-woman run to the fruit and veg stall to gather breakfast supplies so he could eat. So they could spend a little more time together before reality set in and they had to part ways.

'Soph? You okay? You've gone all quiet.' Alexander's eyebrows drew together. 'You mentioned you were hungry, but you've not really eaten. A couple of blueberries is hardly breakfast. Shall I get up and make you toast? Return the favour?'

Alexander was already half out of bed before Sophie had a chance to say no.

She caught his hand and drew him back into bed. Into their bubble.

'I'm fine. Honestly. Blissed out.' She pasted a bright smile on her face and hoped it hid the small, but no less, brilliant pain that flared in her chest.

Sophie loaded up her email, and hoped working would distract her enough that she could put Alexander's inevitable return to London out of her mind.

Her heart seized as a name she'd not expected to see flashed up.

'Are you kidding me?' She clicked on the email, peered at the screen. Her heart kicked back into action, this time in double speed, as she scanned the contents of the email. 'This cannot be happening.'

Alexander touched her forearm. 'Is something wrong? Are you okay? Can I help?'

Sophie dragged her eyes away from the email. 'I am more than okay. I'm going to be fine. Better than fine. Lucille Devine has agreed to give an author talk.'

'Lucille who?' Alexander peered over her shoulder.

'Only one of the UK's most celebrated romance authors. I sent her an email asking if she'd consider an author talk here since I'd read she was touring the area. I never thought she'd say yes, but she has.'

A slow smile curved Alexander's lips. 'This is a great thing, right? If she leaves happy, then she'll recommend you to other authors for talks and signings and people will come from all over?'

'Ten points to the hot, mostly naked man.' Sophie rubbed her hands together. 'There's only one catch. She wants to come tomorrow. It's her day off from the tour, but she heard about Herring Cove from a friend who came to the market yesterday and raved about it, and when she heard I'd set the market up, she remembered my name from the email I'd sent and was intrigued by the story: a bookshop owner determined to save the village she lives in from economic ruin. She reckons there's a book in it.' Sophie giggled as she reached over and ran her hand through Alexander's hair, then cupped his neck, stroking the soft skin of his nape. 'I'm starting to think you're my lucky charm. Only good things have happened to me since you arrived in Herring Cove. I'm going to have to tie you up so you can never leave. Tell your father I'm holding you hostage but there'll never be a ransom note because I refuse to let you go.'

Alexander looked away. His jaw tightened. His Adam's apple bobbed up and down.

Sophie bit her tongue. Idiot. She knew the score. Knew Alexander had to leave. Knew it was going to be painful when it happened – for both of them. Making light of it only emphasised that point.

There was no getting out of the situation or of finding a way to change what had to happen. She couldn't sell the shop and move to London. Not for a man she'd just met. Not for anyone. Herring Cove was home and leaving it was non-negotiable. And because she understood how important home was, she would never ask Alexander to leave London. Not that she'd expected he would. He had his family there, his mother and father. Not to mention a job that he was committed to. He had to be in London. She had to be in Herring Cove.

Was long distance an option?

She shoved the idea away as quickly as she'd entertained it.

If the ache she felt deep inside existed already when she thought about Alexander leaving, she wouldn't survive a long-distance relationship.

'This' could only be the here and now. No more.

'Well, I guess I'd better shower. Get ready for the day. Get my thinking cap on if I'm going to impress Miss Devine.' She swept her legs out of bed and pushed herself up. *Keep it light, keep it easy, keep it simple.* 'I've never missed a day opening, and as much as you're worth it – and I'd love to continue the day as we started – I'd hate to disappoint a customer.'

Alexander's shoulders bunched towards his ears as his spine stiffened. She didn't have to see his face to know her excuse had fallen flat.

His shoulders inched down as he turned to her, his expression unreadable. No delicious lines of happiness radiated from his eyes. The corners of his lips were neither tugged up in amusement, nor curved downwards in disapproval.

Sophie told herself she was doing what had to be done. While Alexander may have brought immeasurable pleasure, she knew the more she grew to like him, the more attached she became, the greater the pain would be when he left.

She had to protect herself. Keep the loneliness at bay before it further entrenched itself in her life. In her heart.

'Well, in that case, I'll be off then.' He swung his legs out of bed, bent down, picked his T-shirt off the floor and tugged it on. Covering the beautiful swathe of skin she'd stroked, licked and adored for the better part of the night into the early morning hours. He pulled on his shorts, shoved his feet into his shoes and made his way over to her side of the bed.

She went to duck backwards, forced herself to stop. She wasn't going to run from Alexander. What was between them would reach a natural conclusion sooner rather than later, and she refused to hurt him by rejecting him.

He cupped her cheek, tenderness softening his eyes. 'It's probably a weird thing to say, but... thank you.' His fingers tucked under her chin. She allowed him to tilt her chin up so his lips could meet hers. A brush of skin that created a ripple of heat inside that made her want to toss all her good sense aside and take things further.

Alexander broke the kiss, his hand slipped from her cheek, and just like that he was gone.

Sophie wrapped her arms around herself. Held herself tight. And told herself she'd done the right thing. For both of them. Besides, it wasn't over. Not yet. Alexander would have told her if he was heading straight back to the city. Surely.

Yet two questions circled in her mind.

Why had Alexander's 'thank you' seemed like a goodbye?

And how come she wasn't running out the door to stop him?

CHAPTER SIXTEEN

Alexander turned on his phone. Determination pulsed through his veins. It was time to sort things out with his father once and for all. Time he took his life into his own hands and changed it for the better. Time he did what he'd been put on earth to do – to create things that brought happiness, brought hope to people's lives.

He pulled up his father's mobile number and hit the call button. The ring tone barely starting before it stopped.

'Alexander. I've been trying to get hold of you all morning. What's the situation down there? Did the market go as planned?'

Alexander drew a big breath in. His future, his happiness, counted on him getting this conversation right.

'Dad, I'm going to be straight up. I don't think the resort is the best option. Not for the village or its people.'

His declaration was met with ominous silence. He took a deep breath and carried on. If his father wasn't yelling, he was listening.

'The villagers want their home to revert to how it used to be. To keep the rustic vibe, to have people visit it because of what they have to offer, not what we force on them. In the week I've spent here I've come to think that they might well be right. That we could help them achieve their goals.'

'Really? And how do you propose to do this, Alexander? Wave

a wand? Have each villager rub a lamp and grant them three wishes?'

Alexander stiffened at the sarcasm. Refused to let it put him in his place. If he was going to run the Fletcher Group one day, he needed to be heard. To be understood. To be trusted.

'I have ideas to revive the village, Frank. Ones I believe will work. It won't be an instant cash cow like the resorts. But over time I believe we could reap the benefits from investing in Herring Cove by rebuilding the village while keeping its charms. It's a model I think would work in many places throughout the area.'

'Where is this coming from, Alexander? You know that's not how we do things. That's not the Fletcher business model. What's gotten into you?'

Auburn hair paired with brown eyes, the cutest nose and most invigorating, inspiring personality he'd ever met came to mind.

'Nothing's gotten into me. I just don't believe that a resort is the only way forward. I think it would be a mistake.'

Stone, cold silence met him. His father wasn't buying it.

'I'm coming down, Alexander. I'll hold a town meeting. Talk some sense into them. You too. I expect you to head back to London today, be back in the office on Monday, and I'll see you at the family dinner on Tuesday.'

Having issued his instructions his father ended the call.

So that was that? Fait accompli?

Alexander shoved his mobile in his pocket as a wave of defiance surged through him.

Herring Cove was too quaint, too special, to be allowed to be turned into just another holiday destination. He wouldn't see the town swamped with people who took its natural beauty for granted, people who'd expect the locals to bend over backwards to accommodate them, not thinking once about their impact on the small village. But that didn't mean Herring Cove couldn't and shouldn't be given the opportunity to thrive.

He could see the main street lined with boutique shops: an

artisan bakery, café, florist, cheesemonger and gift shop. The empty houses dotted along the cliffs could be bought and turned into tourist accommodation, its booking run through websites, with the day-to-day operations managed by a local. A surf school could be started up. Fishing charters could operate. There was no reason the farm land behind Sophie's couldn't still become a golf course, or pool and spa. Or an entrepreneur could keep the farm land and create rustic accommodation alongside a five-star all-organic restaurant that showcased the area's seafood, meat, vegetables and fruit. The sky was the limit – and there wouldn't be a towering monstrosity of a hotel blighting the skyline.

He picked his way down the cliffs, wanting to breathe in the tangy sea air, to let the sand run through his fingers one more time before heading back to the city.

Alexander collapsed onto the sand, closed his eyes and began putting his ideas in order in a way that his father might under-stand, which meant showing how the money would be made, and how money could be saved.

'You're a hard man to find, Alexander Fletcher.'

The words were puffed out, the tone teasing. Joy chased away worry as Alexander turned to see Sophie traipsing through the sand, her hands on her hips, her chest heaving.

'Also, do you know how much I hate running? Lots. More than just about anything else in the world. Almost as much as I hate climbing up and down that evil cliff path.' She plopped down beside him with a grin, then bumped her shoulder against his. 'But I couldn't let you leave the way I did. Couldn't let you think this was just some one-night thing where we'd carry on with our lives as if nothing had happened.'

'I didn't think you—'

Sophie held her hand up. 'You did. I could see it in your shoulders, they went all hunched, then they went all droopy. And I don't blame you. I was so casual, so cool. The way I always am when I'm afraid I'm going to get hurt.' Sophie clucked her tongue in disapproval. 'That made me sound like I've got a steady stream of men coming and going from my bedroom. Which, for the record, I don't. I've steered clear of men since…' She paused, her gaze drifting to the horizon.

Sophie wrapped her arms around herself, then plopped down onto the sand in one graceful, leg-folding movement. Alexander sank down beside her, giving her space, but making sure he was close enough that she could reach him, should she want to.

'The reason the bookshop has been in such trouble was because I made the mistake of putting my trust in the wrong person. The wrong man, to be exact.' She blew out a breath. 'I was an idiot. Phillip came to Herring Cove to work on a fishing boat not long after my aunty moved away. Despite Ginny and Nat being with me whenever they could, I was lonely. Desperate for connection. Ripe picking for someone like Phillip, who swept me off my feet the first night he came to town, moved in with me after that first night, and never left. Until he did. With all the money I'd saved for a rainy day. And when that rainy day came, it was more of a downpour and I didn't have any savings to stop it.' Her shoulders shuddered. 'I feel ridiculous blurting it out like that. Truth be told, I've not talked about it in years. Blocked it from my mind as best I could. Keep calm and carry on, and all that.' Sophie lifted her chin in that proud manner she had.

Alexander placed his hand, palm up, on the sand. Sophie took it without hesitation. Her fingers interlaced through his, curled around him, strengthened him. Strengthened each other.

'After Phillip's betrayal I found myself afraid to take risks. To put a foot wrong. I became stilted. Stuck. In all parts of my life. Terrified to change anything at All Booked Up, scared to let anyone in. I even had to think really hard about taking care of Puddles when I found him. Because what if I was no good as a cat mum? What if something happened to him on my watch? What if by caring for something or someone I opened myself up to hurt again?' Sophie huffed out a frustrated breath. 'I guess I became convinced that the best way to live life was to stick to a routine and never deviate. Never give anyone a chance to show me any other path. Emotional safety first.' She rolled her eyes at herself and shook her head.

Tightness clutched at Alexander's heart as the last piece of the Sophie puzzle fell into place. No wonder she'd been so suspicious, so resistant to offers of help. Her whole life had been an exercise in letting people in only for them to go. Each time with heart-breaking consequences.

Not this time. He wasn't going to be that guy. He may have to return home, but he wasn't going to go before giving Sophie fair warning of what was to come. Wasn't going to leave her without her knowing just how much she meant to him. How much of an impact she'd had on him.

'I get where you're coming from, Soph. I understand what it's like to follow rules, to be afraid to go off page. I've followed my father's rule book all my life. Done as I was told. Never once have I risked disappointing him, or my mother. Until now.'

Sophie's cheek met her knees as the little frown line between her brows appeared. 'What do you mean "until now"?'

'I just told my father that I didn't think we should build a resort in Herring Cove. That we should invest in the village more organically.'

A smile chased away the sadness in Sophie's eyes. 'Really? Do you think you could do that? Do you think it could work?'

'I think it could.' Alexander pressed his lips together, hating that he was about to rob Sophie of her hope. 'But my father doesn't think so. He thinks the idea's bonkers, and to that end he's coming down here to hold a town meeting, which – in his mind – will put an end to any dissent from the villagers.' Alexander sucked in a breath, knowing it wasn't the only thing his father would do. 'And don't be surprised if he tries one last time to get you to sell.'

'But I won't.' Sophie straightened up. 'Between the author talks, the online sales, my father's first editions, and the market potentially becoming a regular event, I can dig myself out of this hole. I know I can.'

'I know you can, too. The thing is, my father is used to getting his own way. His methods are… tough. To say the least. I just want you to be prepared. To be ready. He'll throw anything and everything at you to weaken you. To force you to change your mind.'

Sophie's eyes widened. 'He sounds like a monster.'

Alexander nodded. 'I can see how you'd think that, but he's a businessman of a successful company, and he didn't get to where he is by playing nice.'

Sophie shuffled closer to him until they were shoulder to shoulder. Leaning against each other in mutual support. 'They say the apple doesn't far from the tree, but I think your father's tree was built on a cliff and you fell right to the bottom.'

Warmth rushed through Alexander's heart, flooded his body. Sophie didn't see him as an extension of his father, of the Fletcher Group. She saw him for who he was.

No woman before ever had. They'd seen his late model car, his designer suits, his black credit card, and saw a Fletcher. They didn't see an 'Alex'.

'That might be the kindest thing anyone has ever said to me.' He dropped a kiss on Sophie's shoulder. 'Thank you.'

'I said it because it's true. I didn't trust you one bit when you walked into my shop. In fact, I thought you were a right knob. A hot knob. But still, a knob.' Sophie laughed, light and easy, before turning her serious eyes back on him. 'But you've shown me over this past week who you are. You've always been straight up and honest. Your words have been followed by your actions. You're one of the good guys, Alex, and I'm so glad I let you into my life.' Sophie buried her face in her knees. 'God, that sounds lame when it's said out loud.' The muffled words were dense with embarrassment. 'I sound like a right loser.'

Alexander tucked the tips of his fingers underneath Sophie's chin and tilted her head back his way. 'It makes you sound amazing. No one has ever understood me like you do. Ever given me a chance to just be me. I'm the one who's lucky.'

Comfortable silence filled the air around them.

Alexander spotted a piece of glass, tumbled smooth by the elements, half buried in the sand. He picked it up and turned it over in his fingers. 'Being here has reminded me of who I want to be. *How* I want to be. I've worked so hard to be someone else – to be the future CEO I'm expected to be – that I'd lost myself.' He passed the piece of glass to Sophie, who took it with a smile and tucked it away in her short's pocket. 'It's nice to be reminded of who I am, what I'm capable of. It's as if being around you, experiencing your strength, your determination, has given me some of my own back.'

Sophie shook her head. 'Yeah, I'm so strong and determined that I nearly let my fear of change, of making a misstep, run my business into the ground.'

'You can't be blamed for that. You can't blame yourself. That's all on that Phillip guy. Not on you. You reacted how thousands of others would have. But you mobilised when you needed to. When it mattered.'

'With your help.'

'Just a little. It was mostly you.'

'I guess I can't be expecting to have your help forever. Not if you can't convince your father to change his ways, his beliefs.' Sophie met Alexander's eyes. Clear and sincere, sad but strong.

They both knew the score. He couldn't stick around.

'We could keep in touch…' Alexander started, then shook his head. 'But we wouldn't.'

'We wouldn't. We couldn't. It would be too hard. I'm sorry.' Sophie rubbed her heart, like the thought of him leaving gave her physical pain.

'We still have today. Tomorrow. Tomorrow night, even.'

Alexander wasn't letting her go. Not that easily. And if that meant disobeying his father's orders to return immediately, so be it. 'I could help you organise the Lucille Devine author talk. Put up messages on local social media pages. Get the word out. Go door-to-door if I have to. Then I can leave first thing Monday. I have to be back in the office that day, but being a few hours late isn't going to matter. Who's going to tell off the future boss?' He pushed himself up and reached his hand out to Sophie.

'You're such a rebel.' She rolled her eyes and laughed as he pulled her up, wrapped his arms around her, kissed her long and slow.

And promised himself he'd find his way back to Herring Cove.

CHAPTER SEVENTEEN

Alexander appeared in the storeroom doorway and gave Sophie the thumbs up to get the evening started.

She nodded and blew him a kiss. He'd been a godsend the last thirty-six hours. She'd given him access to All Booked Up's social pages and he'd put the word out that Lucille Devine was speaking, then gone down to the pub and worked the crowd, telling them about the event. He'd bought, at his own expense, a ridiculously expensive bottle of champagne for the guest of honour. Tracked down the baker who'd had a stall at the market and persuaded him to put together delicious platters of finger food. RSVPs has come flying in and if she was busy with a customer, Alexander was quick to pick up the phone or type out a reply.

And in between all that he'd found moments to make her feel special, feel alive. Small touches as he passed her. Kisses dropped on the back of her neck. Shoulder rubs while she loaded up her father's books ready for sale. Never asking anything in return, just happy to be there for her.

The only thing he'd refused to do was to MC the event, telling her it was her place to shine.

Nerves prickled over her skin as stage fright sent bile rising. She swallowed it down. Now was not the time to let fear get in the way.

People had poured through the doors, then proceeded to buy every Lucille Devine book she had in stock and ordered in books she didn't have on hand, and now their excited chatter had reached fever pitch. The perfect time to introduce the woman they'd come to see.

Sophie made her way to the front, clapped her hands and waited for the audience to settle down.

'Thank you all for coming this evening.' She gripped her hands, pressed her knees together and hoped the audience couldn't see how much she was shaking. 'No one was more surprised than I when Lucille Devine replied to my email enquiring about giving an author talk. The Queen of Romance here in Herring Cove? It seemed too good to be true.' She sought out Alexander and found him leaning against the counter. One leg crossed in front of the other, arms loosely folded, totally at ease.

He met her eyes. 'You're amazing,' he mouthed.

His belief in her eased her case of the wobbles. 'Though if there's one thing life has taught me, it's that it's full of surprises. And sometimes when something seems too good to be true, that's because it's as simple as that. It's good. And it is true. There's no ulterior motive, just a desire to see others happy. Much like the romances our guest tonight writes. Honest, beautiful, heartfelt books that make you believe in love.'

Her words were directed at Lucille's fans, but meant for Alexander. He was good. He was true. And nothing would ever or could ever make Sophie regret falling for him.

'Now, put down your glasses and put your hands together in a warm welcome for the one, the only, Lucille Devine.'

Applause bounced off the walls as Lucille made her way from out of the storeroom where she'd been stashed away with a bottle of champagne and a stack of sausage rolls and club sandwiches. Both of which she'd been enjoying if the brightness in her eyes and the crumbs on either side of her cheeks were anything to go by.

Sophie caught her eye and surreptitiously wiped at her uncrumbed mouth. Lucille nodded and mid-wave swiped away the pastry with a nod of thanks.

'Thank you, thank you so much. It's so lovely to receive such a kind welcome from such a wonderful crowd.' She settled herself on the couch and rubbed her hands together. 'So, do tell, who has read one of my books?'

Most of the crowd raised their hands.

'Who has read two?'

No hands dropped.

'Three or more?'

A few hands fell down, but the majority remained.

'Brilliant.' The gold bracelets on Lucille's arm jangled as she clapped her hands in joy. 'That's what I like to see. It means I'm surrounded by people who believe in hope. Because that's what a romance is at its core. A story about hope. And I do love hope.' She took a sip from the glass of champagne they'd placed on a side table for her. 'Almost as much as I love champagne.' She downed half the glass. 'Joking. Although I hope there's more champagne on the way. This is moreish. Almost as moreish as that moment in a romance when people figure out what it is that they really want and then put aside their fears to go get it.'

Sophie sidled her way around the edge of the audience until she was at Alexander's side, then stood on tiptoe so her lips were millimetres away from his ear. 'It feels like she's talking to me. I didn't know what I wanted until I met you.'

No sooner were the words out did she realise what she'd said. How it sounded. Like she had fallen in love with him and couldn't imagine her life without him.

'I mean, I wanted the store to survive more than anything. I just didn't realise how much.' She ducked her head as heat raced over her face and flowed down her neck.

'Sure that's what you meant.' The words tickled her ears, teasing and light.

166

Sophie glanced up to see Alexander grinning down at her, a knowing smirk on his face.

'Shush,' she mouthed and pointed at Lucille for emphasis, before turning her attention back to the makeshift stage.

'Another reason I love writing romance is that it shows something I dearly believe – that there's someone out there for every person. Someone who shares our interests. Who has our best interests at heart. Who'll be there when the tough gets going, and will – when required – challenge us and practice a little tough love. I believe everyone deserves to find love. To experience it. People dismiss romance books as being a pile of fluff to help you while away a few hours. I'd bet my next book's royalties that those who say this have never read one, because if they had, they'd know – as you wonderful, smart, gorgeous people do – the magic a romance holds. The hope that no matter what our past holds, it won't impact on our chances of experiencing our own happy ever after in the future.'

The crowd broke out into spontaneous applause, and Lucille took a deep bow.

'You're all too kind. Too kind. Now, are there questions from the floor? And can I get my glass refilled?'

Sophie raced to the backroom for a fresh bottle, grateful to get away from Alexander for a chance to think.

Her heart pounded in her chest, her mind dizzy with thoughts, feelings and an awakening self-awareness that could only be called agonising.

Was she letting go of Alexander too easily? Was some part of her past holding her back from her future? Could she convince Alexander to stay? Or would she have to make the ultimate sacrifice to be with him? To sell up and move to London. To start afresh in a city where she knew no one and would no doubt spend most of her time alone because her future-CEO boyfriend would be busy working day in, day out?

Sophie pulled the bottle of champagne out of the mini-fridge, unscrewed the label, popped the cork with a gentle hiss, then made her way back into the shop and discreetly topped up Lucille's glass as she waxed on about her writing process, which seemed to involve copious amounts of tea and people-watching at her local café.

Alexander caught her eye, his eyebrows rose in a questioning manner. 'Are you okay?' he mouthed.

Sophie nodded. She must look as sick and confused as she felt. 'Fine,' she mouthed back. 'Tired.' She brought her hands to her face, angled her head and closed her eyes, to emphasise the point.

If she was serious about her feelings about Alexander, if she didn't want to let the best thing to ever happen to her slip away, something had to change. Or someone. And she suspected that someone had to be her.

***

'Thank you for coming. I hope to see you soon.' Sophie ushered out the last of her guests and turned to face Lucille, who was draped on the couch finishing off the last of the champagne straight from the bottle.

Sophie sunk into the seat to the side of Lucille. 'Miss Devine?'

'Call me Lucille.'

'Okay, Lucille. I just wanted to thank you so much for coming tonight. I hope you had a good time…'

'Marvellous time, my dear. Brilliant. A massive congratulations to you. You've been the best host. Far better than the bookshop a few towns over. They didn't supply the good stuff.' She waggled the bottle in the air. 'And their sausage rolls were nowhere near as good. If you ever want me back, I'm yours. I'll be sure to have my assistant plug your store on my pages. There's a few hundred thousand people who need to know about this little gem.'

Sophie flushed at the kind words and tried not to think that they were fuelled solely by the bubbles.

'Well, it's time for me to bid you adieu. One needs her beauty sleep.' Lucille pushed herself up off the couch and ambled towards the front door.

Sophie quickened her pace so she could open the door for her guest. 'Thank you again for coming, Ms Devine – er, I mean, Lucille. You being kind enough to be here tonight has really changed things round for me. In many ways.'

Lucille placed her hand on Sophie's shoulder and gave it a rub. 'I'm glad, my dear. And I mean it when I say I'd love to come back. All you have to do is ask.' A quick waggle of fingers and she was off into the night, ever so slightly weaving her way down the street towards the village B&B.

Sophie shut the door and pressed her forehead onto the cool pane of glass.

Three quick footsteps met her ears, followed by strong arms that encircled her waist and pulled her back towards the couch. 'Finally. I was getting impatient.'

Hot lips nuzzled her neck as she nestled onto Alexander's lap. 'You should've stayed out here. I could've introduced you. You helped make tonight happen. You deserve an equal amount of congratulations.'

A lazy smile spread on Alexander's face. 'Oh, I intend on getting my congratulations.' He raised his lips to meet hers. Brushed them against her sensitive skin.

A trail of delicious need burned its way down her spine, rippling out over and through her body.

She wasn't going to let this go. Couldn't let Alexander go. She wasn't sure how, but she was going to find a way to make this work.

The door chimes tinkled as the shop door opened. Beneath Sophie Alexander's body stiffened, and before she knew what was happening, she found herself seated at the other end of the couch, with a tall, besuited man looking at her like she was something smelly you'd found on the bottom of your shoe.

169

'Busy smoothing things over with the locals? Busy doing *something* with the locals. Really, Alexander? Is this why you've not bothered returning to the office?'

Sophie abandoned her plan to find a weapon with which to defend herself. This was no maniac, this was someone who knew Alexander.

Who even looked a little like him.

Navy suit. On a Sunday. Perfectly pressed. Tie knotted round his neck so tight she was surprised his eyes weren't bulging out of their sockets. Black shoes, leather, shiny enough she'd bet you could see your face in them. A square jawline. Straight nose. Lips that were full, but harsh-edged, just like...

'Dad.' Colour drained from Alexander's face, emphasising the guilt that filled it. 'What are you doing here? You were meant to be coming down tomorrow.'

'I wanted to get a head start. The sooner I get this sorted, the sooner I leave.' He brushed an invisible speck of dirt from his sleeve, his nose wrinkling in distaste as he turned his attention to Sophie. 'Alexander has explained you'd rather not sell. I'm here to tell you that would be a grave mistake.'

Sophie drew herself up as tall as she could. 'Well then, I'm going to make a grave mistake, because I'm not selling.'

'You'd be a fool not to.' Frank raised one groomed eyebrow. 'I have it on good authority, Miss Jones, that you've financial issues. Overdue power bills. Late on your water charges. And there's a little matter of the council rates...'

The churning in Sophie's stomach intensified with each statement. There was only one person who knew how bad things were. He'd seen the email. Knew her situation. But she'd never thought he'd use that information against her.

She spun around to face Alexander, her hands balled into fists. 'You. You did this? You knew I was in trouble. Saw exactly how much I was in trouble. And what? You set up a plan with your father? Decided to lure me in with affection because you could see just how sad and lonely poor little Orphan Sophie was? Then what? You had your father swoop in right when I began to think we could be more? That I could sell this place in order to be with you?' She blinked as the pain in her heart threatened to mute her.

This couldn't be happening. Not again. Falling for a person, trusting someone, who only wanted to take what she had? Would she ever learn?

'Sophie, I didn't do this. I didn't say anything.' Alexander's gaze darted between Sophie and his father, unable, or incapable, of settling on one of them. 'I mean, I did. When we first met. Before I got to know you. Before we became...'

'Intimate.' Frank's tone was flat. Unimpressed. He reached into his jacket pocket and pulled out a card. 'I can see now's not a good time, Miss Jones, so I'll leave my card on the counter and you can call me to discuss the sale.'

'I'm. Not. Selling.' Sophie gritted each word out, astounded at Alexander's father's thick skin.

A no is the beginning of the negotiation. It's the first step towards getting a yes.

The words Alexander had said on the day they met came to mind. Of course Frank wasn't taking no for answer. He didn't believe in no's. It's where his son had got that belief from.

She retightened her balled fists. Well, both the Fletcher men were about to learn what a firm, unshakeable no sounded like.

'Leave your card, but don't hold your breath for a phone call.'

Frank smiled mildly, then turned and left without a word of goodbye to either herself or his son.

'As for you.' She took a step away from Alexander. 'You can get out. I never want to see you again. Perhaps you didn't think twice about telling your father the miserable state of my finances because we didn't know each other, but they weren't your finances to discuss. They were on my private laptop. They were for my eyes only. My problem. Not yours. Especially not yours to use

171

against me just to get your own way. Just to get a yes out of a no.'

Alexander made to step towards her. Stopped as she took another step back, holding up her hand to ward him off.

'I've really stuffed this up. I'm so sorry, Sophie. I want to make this up to you. Tell me how I can make this up to you. I can't leave you like this. Leave *us* like this.'

Us? He thought they were an us? So much for the apple falling far, far away from the tree. Alexander was every bit as thick-skinned as his father.

'There is no us. There never could be. Even before I discovered how untrustworthy you are, we knew that. You live in London. Your life is there. My life is here. In my bookshop. In Herring Cove.' Her throat constricted as a maelstrom of anger, heartache and hopelessness threatened to overwhelm her.

'Just go, Alexander.' She spun on her heel, marched to the door, held it as he shuffled from the shop, shoulders hunched, head hanging.

The moment he'd disappeared into the darkness she shut it firmly, then slid down until she was huddled in a ball. Her knees became damp with frustrated tears.

She was an idiot. Falling for a pretty face and a charming demeanour. Thinking Alexander was different from Phillip. That he could be trusted. That, despite his agenda in Herring Cove, he had her best interests at heart.

She was a fool to have hoped, to have trusted.

Never again.

Soft fur brushed against her shins. She lifted her head to see Puddles looking up at her. His eyes shining with affection.

'Puddles, I guess the only man I can trust is you.' She scooped the cat up, cuddled him to her chest and dropped a kiss on his furry head. 'Time for bed, hey? Maybe if I go to sleep I'll wake up tomorrow to find this was all just a really bad dream.'

Puddles nuzzled into Sophie's chest as they climbed the stairs.

His rumbling purrs did nothing to soothe the nausea churning in her stomach. The self-recriminations that marched through her mind.

The realisation that she was, once more, alone. Again.

As always.

CHAPTER EIGHTEEN

Alexander stood outside his parents' home, the place in which he'd grown up, and tried to ignore the knot in his gut that tightened with every passing minute. He took in the imposing white, stucco house and wondered when it had begun to feel alien to him. All manicured gardens on the outside and an elegant mix of modernisation that blended seamlessly with the home's Regency features on the inside. A property designed to impress, while understatedly displaying their family's status.

There was no personality within those walls. No splashes of colour or age-bobbled throws draped over sofas. No musky scent of books. No random wads of moulting cat fur to be picked off rugs. Or hints of violet perfume.

There was no Sophie.

Two days he'd been home. Two nights. And during that time he'd been unable to think of little else but her. Was she okay? How much did she hate him? Had his father bulldozed her into selling by playing on her past, on her financial troubles, on any and every little piece of weakness he could find?

Sophie had survived so much. Her parents' passing. The betrayal of a lover. Nearly losing her shop. Despite all that she held an inner strength, a positivity, an attitude that nothing could get her down for long – but could that attitude withstand Frank Fletcher?

He drew in a deep breath. He'd soon find out. His mother had informed him their father would be joining them for dinner. She gave no hint as to his father's mood. Neither had she let on that she knew what had happened in Herring Cove.

His mother, as always, was loyal to the Fletcher name. Loyal to her husband.

Rather than go through the front door, he made his way around to the back garden where he knew his mother, Veronika, would be sitting on the patio enjoying a pre-dinner Pimms.

'Alexander darling, it's so good to see you. I missed you at dinner last week.'

He bent over and kissed her cheek as was their customary greeting, then took a seat opposite her, relieved that her welcome was warm. That, unlike his father, she was not going to drag him across the coals for straying from the Fletcher way.

'I missed you too, Mum. It's good to be home.'

Veronika raised her eyebrows in disbelief.

She knew. Everything. Of course she did. Veronika and Frank were a team. Always had been. And their game plan was to raise a son who would take over the business and carry it on in the same way his grandfather had started it and his father had expanded it.

'You know what happened down there.' No point in niceties; he knew what was to come. Gentle disapproval from his mother, followed by a firm talking to by his father.

Veronika waved a bejewelled hand. 'Your father filled me in. I was surprised to hear you'd taken up with a local girl. If you're lonely, Alexander, I can set you up with any number of appropriate women. Mary's daughter's doing very well for herself. Works in marketing. She understands business, is very well presented, has what it takes to charm people into doing what she wants.'

Alexander didn't bother hiding his shudder. She sounded awful. 'I don't want a manipulative woman at my side, Mother.'

'You make it sound so tawdry, Alexander. Charm is just a

different way of getting what you want. I use charm, your father uses information. You, my dear, use a mix of both. Would you call yourself manipulative?'

Alexander pulled a glass towards him, reached for the mint and fruit-stuffed jug and poured the tawny liquid into a glass. 'I'd like to think that I offer people the best option – that's why they respond to me. I don't believe I could force a person into doing something they didn't want to if I knew it was a bad idea.'

'And you thought that girl signing away her bookshop was a bad idea? That's why you didn't pressure her?'

To the outside world, Veronika Fletcher was an attractive wife, a wonderful hostess, a polished conversationalist. What many didn't see was her intelligence, her ability to get to the heart of any matter in a way that didn't feel confrontational.

'Sophie. That's her name. And you're right. I couldn't pressure her. There was no point. She was never going to sell.' An image of a folded square of paper that would never be opened came to mind, and a smile found its way to his lips. The first one since leaving Herring Cove. 'We went in there thinking she'd sell because she was stuck with a bookshop she felt she couldn't sell because her dead parents had opened it. We assumed that guilt and duty had kept her there. We were wrong.

'She genuinely wanted to be there.' Veronika nodded in understanding. 'It wasn't her place of work, it was her home.

'It's her heart. She's been through so much, Mum. It's the one constant she's had in her life, and even though business had been declining, and it was so close to being taken from her, she refused to give up. She started a market to bring business into the area, an online shop, was prepared to sell her father's first editions – something I don't know that I could have done had I been in her shoes. She's not just "the girl" or "a girl"; she's an amazing, intelligent, determined woman…'

'And you're in love with her.' Veronika summed it up with a raise of her eyebrows.

The breath whooshed from Alexander at the bluntness of his mother's words. At the truth of them.

Had he really fallen in love with Sophie over the course of the week? Could love hit that hard? Maybe it was just infatuation…

'You've dated plenty of women I would deem "intelligent", "amazing" and "determined", Alexander, but you've never put your career on the line for them. Never risked disappointing your father for them.'

'And have I? Disappointed him?' Anxiety swirled in his stomach. The answer was clear. Obvious in the pause his mother took before answering. In the way she couldn't meet his eyes.

'You have. You've never let him down before. Never not got the job done.' Veronika freshened up her glass. 'It's not just the business side that's upset him. It's the manner in which you conducted yourself. He's since spoken to some of the villagers and heard about your day at the beach, your pub dinners with the locals, your helping this Sophie of yours to rebuild her business when you were meant to be securing ours.'

The ever-present guilt that lurked beneath the surface since he'd returned home rose, squeezing his chest, reminding him of his duty to his family. Professionalism over pleasure. Family over friends. Work first, life last.

How could he say he was sorry though? How could he promise to never let it happen again? He couldn't. Not when he wasn't sorry. When if he could see Sophie again, if he could make things right, he would. In a heartbeat.

'Your father is struggling to understand why you've done what you've done. I think I understand though, Alexander. Love doesn't always make sense. Doesn't always make us see sense. It can make us do things that make no sense.'

Alexander sat back in his chair, surprised by his mother's words. 'You sound like you know something of the nonsensical. Did you love someone before Dad? Before you were put together by your families because it made sense?'

Veronika placed her manicured hand on her chest and laughed, long and loud. 'Oh, sweet boy. Your father is the only man I've ever loved. Yes, our families had a hand in bringing us together. They thought we'd be a good match and, initially, I was not happy. I had plans, you see. I didn't want to be a wife of a man of industry. I wanted to go overseas for a bit, find myself. Maybe be a waitress. Work in a zoo. Go skinny-dipping on an exotic beach...'

Alexander held his hand up. 'Whoa, too much information.'

'I'm not sorry. You've only ever seen me as the woman I am now. Not the woman I was then. I met with your father under duress, and in seconds his straight-talking nature had me charmed. I tossed away what I thought I wanted and embraced the life I was meant to lead. And I've never regretted it. Not once.'

A new potential jolted the guilt stirring in his belly, as excitement began to pulse through him. Was his mother suggesting what he thought she was suggesting? That if he'd found love, it was his duty to do right by it?

Hope filled his heart, wove a silver lining around the grey cloud that had befuddled his mind since returning to London.

'I know you and Dad only want the best for me. That you think my following in both Dad and Grandfather's footsteps is the path I need to take if I'm to continue the Fletcher Group's successful trajectory, but what if there's another road I can take? One that will mean diversifying, but in a business-positive way?'

Veronika cocked her head. 'I'm listening...' She gave him an encouraging nod.

Buoyed by her interest, Alexander continued on, telling her his vision for Herring Cove.

'It's a beautiful place, Mum. Picturesque, quaint, untouched. With rugged cliffs that drop down to a golden beach. I want to transform it without destroying it. I want to create a boutique village that capitalises on its charm in order to encourage people to holiday there.'

Veronika shifted in her seat, lines ran horizontally across her forehead as she stared into the middle-distance. 'I see what you're getting at, but how would we make money? From what I can make of it, your vision would attract fewer people than a resort would, simply because there wouldn't be the accommodation available.'

Cottages, empty but for the spiders that had set up home in the eaves and corners of the windows, came to mind. 'There are plenty of homes that are unlived in. Abandoned, really. We could buy them, upgrade where necessary, rent them out at a premium price. They have unobstructed views of the water, and the sunsets are unlike anything I've seen before. I'd pay above and beyond for those alone.'

Veronika further furrowed her brow.

Think man, think. He hadn't won her over. Not yet. The Fletcher Group cared about money. Making it. Saving it. And they cared about having the upper hand over their competitors. Surely there was an angle there...

He sprang out of his seat and began to pace the patio, hoping movement would get the ideas flowing. 'We wouldn't have to massively upgrade infrastructure, so we'd save money there. The farm we were planning to put the golf course on could be transformed into a five-star B&B, with private cottages complete with outdoor baths dotted around the property. It could house a restaurant specialising in local, organic produce, as well as fresh fish caught locally. Free-range meat from local farms. I know a chef who could be interested. He's always up for a challenge, and he's into the slow-food movement. Not unamenable to some show-ponying in food magazines either. From a PR perspective, it's gold. A company known for throwing up resorts taking a different approach, one that's in keeping with the local way of life? One that will revive a dying village? It's got the feel-good factor written all over it.'

Alexander paused and took a sip of his drink. His mother hadn't cut him off. Hadn't clucked her tongue. Hadn't given any

179

indication that she hated the idea. She was a master at hiding her true thoughts, but he was sure he saw a sparkle in her eye, one that grew as he'd outlined his plans. 'I know it seems so far from what we do, but I have a good feeling about it. And my good feelings are never wrong.'

Veronika tapped her chin. 'Your father will think it a terrible idea. He prefers wealth creation to be fast and furious.'

'Don't I just.'

Alexander twisted round to see Frank in the doorway.

'Don't tell me you're still going on about Herring Cove.' Frank poured himself a drink and took a seat, indicating for Alexander to sit opposite.

Alexander didn't budge, instead drew himself up tall as he could. 'Dad, I mean this with all respect, but if I'm going to be the future CEO of the Fletcher Group, you are going to have to trust me. Trust my instincts. Trust that I am capable of doing a good job of keeping what you and Grandfather built, on my own terms.'

Frank hooked a leg over his knee and leaned back in his chair.

Alexander had seen that move more times than he could count. It was a power play. It said 'I'm willing to hear you out', but what it really meant was 'I'll listen, but I'm never going to agree.'

Alexander relaxed his demeanour and took his seat, kept his hands loose. His smile easy.

His father wanted to play? He'd play.

To win.

180

CHAPTER NINETEEN

'Has she said anything to you, Nat?' Ginny's hushed voice was blatant with worry.

'Not a thing. Keeps acting like there's nothing wrong.'

'It's like when her parents died, remember? She'd always smile and say she was fine.'

'And no one who says they're fine ever means it.'

'Exactly.'

Sophie poked her head over her laptop screen where she'd been emailing a potential buyer of one of the first editions. One that would see her council tax bill cleared, and any chance of Frank Fletcher hassling her again well and truly gone.

'I can hear you. And I am fine. I promise.' She flashed a thumbs up at Ginny and Natalie, who were huddled on the couch together, mugs of tea in hand, their brows furrowed in matching looks of concern.

Ginny set her mug down and glared at her. 'Fine is not the same as being good, Soph. You know that. Can you tell me you're good? That you're happy?'

Sophie shut the laptop and indicated for the girls to get up. 'I've got to straighten up these shelves. They're still higgledy-piggledy after Lucille's talk. How about instead of worrying needlessly about me, you help?'

Natalie folded her arms, unconvinced. 'If we help, will you be straight up with us? Tell us how you really feel?'

'There's *nothing* to tell.' Sophie held her arms up, palms flat to the ceiling and widened her eyes for extra honest-to-goodness-I-really-am-fine effect. 'Promise. But if my telling you I feel nothing means tidying up this place will take one-third of the time, then I'll tell you I feel nothing.'

'There we go. She feels nothing.' Ginny grunted as she pushed herself up off the sofa. 'She's numb. Broken. No wonder she says she's fine. If you're not feeling anything of course you're fine.'

Sophie rolled her eyes as she reordered a line of books alphabetically. 'Look, I just don't see the point in thinking too hard about what happened. I can't change it. He has a life to live in the city and that's all there is to it.' *He.* And that's how much it hurt: she couldn't even say his name. Let alone think it. But she wasn't telling her friends that. She wasn't telling them anything. It was too embarrassing to admit she'd fallen for the same tricks again. Instead she'd let Ginny and Natalie believe he'd had to go back to London for work.

Ginny came to stand beside her and slung an arm around her shoulders. 'Maybe he'll come back for you. Wouldn't that be romantic.' She sighed deeply and faked a swoon.

'It would be inconvenient. I'm busy with the bookshop. The online business is picking up. I've had some big thriller author get in touch about a book signing after a recommendation from Lucille Devine, so I need to organise that. If he came back I'd be too busy for him.'

Tiring of the topic, Sophie left Ginny and Natalie to finish off straightening up the books and made her way back to the laptop. She pulled up the courier's website to check the tracking on a batch of fresh books due to arrive.

Sale by sale, the bookshop's finances were rising from the doldrums, but even that hint of success did not distract from the pain that pulsed through her heart every time Al—... *he* entered her thoughts or was mentioned by Ginny or Natalie, who hadn't stopped asking after her well-being or if she'd heard from him since he'd left nearly three weeks ago.

Nineteen days ago, to be exact. Not that she was counting.

Sophie ran her hand through her hair and tried to concentrate on the courier's tracking page. Failed. It was all too hard.

She should be happy right now. Thrilled. Instead her heart was hollow, and that feeling weaved its way through every aspect of her life. Her beloved bookshop tainted with sadness. Her home no longer her sanctuary, but a place she wanted to hide from. The beach was out of bounds, the memories forged there in recent times flooded in whenever she caught sight of the blue waters, heard them whisper as they washed over the sand. Every part of her home, of Herring Cove, pushed *him* to the front of her mind, when what she wanted – what she needed – was for him to be well gone from it.

Was this how Natalie felt? Was that why she was so happy to sell up? To leave?

'Have you found a new place to buy, Nat?'

Natalie poked her head around the bookshelf. 'Not yet. The money's not come through. There's been a hold-up. They said not to worry though, that it would be sorted soon.'

Sophie knew what the 'hold-up' was. More to the point, who it was. She was to blame. She'd dug her heels in when Frank Fletcher had returned to the shop, trying again to get her to sell. She'd even gone so far as to press her hands over her ears and sing 'la la la' so she couldn't hear his emotive arguments. Eventually he'd given up with an ominous 'you're making the biggest mistake of your life'.

It took all her self-control not to reply with a 'the biggest mistake of my life was falling for your son'.

The screen blurred before her as reality hit, hard.

She repeated the same mistakes with men.

She stuck stubbornly to her own safe ways, even when it was detrimental to her life.

Even now she refused to sell the bookshop, even though she couldn't muster any joy being here. Even though it had begun to feel like an albatross round her neck, rather than her happy place.

What had been her safety net was now a daily reminder of every misstep she'd ever made.

She slumped onto the counter and buried her head in her arms.

Seconds later she was smothered in a hug by Natalie and Ginny as they shushed kind nothings into her ear.

For the first time since that fateful night, Sophie allowed the tears to flow freely. To ease the tension coiled in every muscle. To wash away her anger at putting her trust in the wrong person, the fear that she could so easily be hurt, the heartbreak at feeling so deeply for another, only to have it all be a lie.

Long minutes passed. Her shoulders shuddered one last time. Ginny and Natalie's grip on her loosened, but they didn't let go.

'I'm glad you let it out,' Natalie whispered. 'You couldn't hold it in forever.'

'If you had you'd have exploded.' Ginny kissed her cheek. 'And I'm not game to clean human innards off books and furniture.'

Sophie blinked away the last of her tears, then wiped damp streaks from her cheeks with the back of her hand. 'I'm so lucky to have you both.'

'The feeling is entirely mutual.' Ginny wiped away a tear. 'Stupid hormones making me leak all the time. I swear they've gotten worse since I decided it was time to make a baby.'

'Just you wait until you've actually made one.' Natalie leaned against the counter and shook her head. 'You'll be begging for the regular hormones to make a return. Speaking of returns…' Natalie turned her attention to Sophie. 'I take it Alexander didn't go back to London just for work?'

Sophie breathed deeply, then exhaled, long and slow. 'He didn't.' She paused, unsure how to go on. Perhaps the first step to healing… to letting him go… was opening up. 'He went because I told him to go. He wasn't who I thought he was.'

Ginny's eyes narrowed. 'He seemed so nice. Like a proper good guy. Man, I wish he was still here so I could stuff fish bait into his car's muffler. Or just dump a bucket of it over his head.'

Despite herself, Sophie laughed. 'I wish you could too. It's my own fault though; I trusted him. He knew about my financial problems and he told his father.'

'That arse.' Ginny folded her arms and glared. 'I can't believe he'd do that. When? How?'

'He saw an email by accident on his first day here, an overdue bill. I guess he must've told him that day. His father used that information to come here after Lucille's talk, all guns blazing, and tried to use it against me. Told me I was silly not to sell. That I'd regret it.' Sophie hugged herself. Part of her was beginning to think Frank was right.

'Soph, don't take this the wrong way, but did you tell him *not* to say anything?' Natalie's words were hesitant, like she knew she was treading on shaky ground.

Sophie squeezed her eyes shut. She knew what Natalie was trying to say – that if she'd not explicitly asked him to keep that knowledge to himself, then she could hardly blame him for doing what any other businessman trying to secure a deal would do – but part of her didn't want to hear it.

Acknowledging that would mean she acted wrongly, tossing Alexander out the way she had. That the only person she could blame for her situation was herself. That had she stopped, breathed and heard him out, she wouldn't be walking around the shop wishing she could be anywhere but. Contemplating doing the one thing she'd sworn she wouldn't do.

Natalie rubbed Sophie's arm. 'You can't be blamed for jumping to conclusions and thinking the worst of Alex. Not after the Phillip situation, combined with the pressure of the last week and his father turning up like that and bothering you. It would be enough to make anyone do something rash.'

'Like considering selling up and leaving? Because that's what I'm thinking I might have to do.'

The silence was so complete you could have heard a loose leaf from a book fall to the ground.

Sophie wished she could take the words back. Not because she didn't mean them. She did. It had been playing on her mind since Frank Fletcher, on the day he'd left the village, had slipped another folded piece of paper, with an even larger number written on it, underneath the shop's door. But by saying the words out loud she was giving her friends the chance to talk her out of it.

Ginny's mouth opened. Her chest inflated.

Sophie shook her head, held her hand up. Stopped Ginny just as she went to talk. 'Don't try to talk me out of it. My everything has always been tangled up in the place. The good and the bad. And until recently the good managed to outweigh the bad – even after Phillip did what he did. But now? After Al—' She bit her tongue. Stopped herself from saying his name out loud.

What good was it doing holding it in, though? Perhaps if she could use it freely, she could move on faster.

'After this thing with Alexander, well, I don't know that the scales are weighted on the good side any more.'

'I understand.' Natalie threaded her arm through Sophie's. 'That's why I want to move on. Sometimes you need a fresh start. But just make sure you're doing it for the right reasons, okay? You don't want to look back a year from now and wished you'd chosen another path.'

A chirpy meow came from the storeroom, and Puddles sauntered in seconds later, before plopping down in the middle of the floor for a spot of grooming.

Memories of Alexander flared in Sophie's mind. Alexander stroking Puddles absentmindedly as they sat on the couch watching a movie. His pleading to be allowed to break Sophie's one cat rule that meant Puddles wasn't to sleep in her bed. His bemusement when she refused to budge, saying if she let Puddles do it once he'd want to do it forever. That he shouldn't be encouraged. The way that he'd then picked up Puddles, held him nose-to-nose and apologised for failing to change her mind.

There was no way she could find her way back to that path. Even if she wanted to. Alexander had his place in the world. His future all mapped out. She had begun to suspect that she was still finding hers. And maybe a fresh start was the only way she'd get the clarity she needed to illuminate the path ahead.

She broke away from the girls. 'I've got some thinking to do. I've made enough mistakes trusting others. If I'm going to sell this place I need to know that my instincts are right. That I can trust myself to make the right decision.'

Natalie and Ginny gave her one last hug and wished her good luck, before waving goodbye and heading into the late afternoon sun, which was becoming more watered down with every passing day as autumn's chilly fingers took hold of Herring Cove.

Sophie hugged herself tight. She may not have the happily ever after she'd dared hope for, but she had her friends and she had her bookshop – for now.

Soft fur brushed her ankles. She glanced down to see Puddles weaving his way through her legs. And she had Puddles. Which meant Sophie had all she needed.

And with all of that she could distract herself to the ends of eternity pretending it was enough.

CHAPTER TWENTY

Bang. Bang. Bang. Bang. Bang.

'Noooooo.' Sophie rolled over, grabbed the spare pillow and curled it round over her head.

Bang. Bang. Bang.

The repetitive noise, now muffled, was no less annoying.

'Are you kidding me...' She felt around her bedside table for her phone, dragged it under the pillow and peeled open one sleep-deprived eye. 'It's not even eight.' She groaned and pulled the duvet up over her pillowed head.

Maybe if she smothered herself she'd get the rest she was in desperate need of.

Rest? She needed more than rest. She needed the deal she'd made with Frank Fletcher to be over and done with so she could move on with her life. But, of course, even that hadn't been easy. Story of her life.

She'd have thought Frank would have lauded her decision to backtrack and been a patronising arse. Instead he'd paused for long enough that Sophie had been struck with fear that he was going to tell her the offer was off the table, and that she'd just have to live with a resort surrounding her for the rest of her life.

Instead he'd told her he'd send someone down that following week to walk her through the contract, and that was that.

Sophie huddled into a foetal position and prayed – as she'd done every day since – that the person he was sending down would be anyone other than Alexander. Not that she thought it would be. She was sure he had better things to do than tie up a loose end such as herself.

Bang. Bang. Crash!

An expletive filled the air, matching the one in Sophie's head. *Enough.* She threw back the covers, sprung out of bed, all vestiges of tiredness erased by boiling grumpiness. She shoved her feet into her red wool-lined slippers, grabbed her fluffy heart-covered bathrobe and tied it at the waist as she ran down the stairs and charged into the street to find out where the noise was coming from so she could give the creator of the racket a dressing down for not starting work at a more polite time.

The shop windows around her were in darkness. No surprise since most were abandoned anyway. That left Natalie's place and Mr Murphy's. But he'd left a week ago. Decided to move out early. Turned out he'd saved enough over the years to retire to Tuscany, and the money he'd been offered from the Fletcher deal was just the icing on the cake.

Sophie turned her attention to Natalie's. Had she had an attack of the DIYs? Or decided to take up a new, loud, bang-making hobby? That would explain the noise. But the cursing had been distinctly masculine.

Maybe something more nefarious was going on and Natalie and the kids were in trouble? Trapped by the world's loudest criminal?

Sophie knew she was being ridiculous, but tried the door to Natalie's anyway. If it was locked she'd know she was safe and she'd find out what the banging was all about later. If it were open…

The door creaked open.

Sophie's pulse picked up. There was no going back now. She couldn't just shut the door and pretend everything was okay.

Because what if it wasn't? What if her ridiculous imaginary scenario was actually real?

She sucked in a breath and summoned the courage to creep up the steps, cringing every time one creaked as her weight bore down on it.

Once she reached the landing she pressed her back to the wall and opened the door that lead to the lounge inch by inch. When no axe murderer came rushing out, she poked her head through.

'Finally. I was wondering how long it'd take for you to get up here to tell me off.'

Sophie froze. Blinked. Rubbed her eyes just to make double-sure she was seeing what she was seeing. *Who* she thought she was seeing.

'I know how much you love a good hammering in the morning.' Alexander winked, slung the claw end of the hammer through the wall and yanked it out, scattering plaster over the floor.

'What are you doing? Nat's going to kill you.' She stepped into the room and reached for the hammer. 'Give me that. Before you do any more damage.'

'But I'm not doing damage. I'm working on it.'

'Working on it? As in you're tearing this place apart piece by piece before building the resort?' Sophie took in the toolkit, the pails of paint, the paintbrushes and rollers. It made no sense. Why would he need paint when he was wrecking the place? 'Are you going to somehow incorporate this place into the resort? Turn it into some quaint extension? Because I can tell you right now that it'll just look ugly. And why aren't you in London? Why are you here? What part of leave and never come back did you not understand?'

Alexander's head tipped back and laughter filled the room. 'Did I ever tell you how cute you are when you're outraged? Because you really are, you know. So cute. The first day I met you I thought you were cute. At the time I thought it was strange that I would have that kind of feeling about you. It's not unusual to think someone's hot the second you see them – and you are that too, don't get me wrong – but to think of someone as cute you have to know them a little. And I felt like I knew you. Right from the moment we met.'

Sophie took a step backwards. She needed space. To think. To breathe. To figure out whether she needed to talk sense into Alexander or to swoon at his feet.

No. No swooning. Don't let his charm fool you. You've been down that road already.

'Don't think you can get away with doing whatever it is you're doing by sweet-talking me. I'm not that kind of girl.' There, he knew where he stood with her. Nowhere. Well, nowhere if his plan was to make himself comfortable in Herring Cove for the foreseeable future. She didn't need a constant reminder of how stupid she was to trust another man. How daft she was to fall for the wrong guy, again.

'I know you're not that kind of girl. It's one of the many reasons I feel the way I do about you. You are independent. You are strong. You are kind. You have the biggest heart of anyone I've ever met, even if you do your best to shield it.'

Alexander moved towards her, and this time she stayed rooted to the spot. She breathed in his clean, lemon scent. Damn it. She'd missed it. Missed him.

But that didn't mean she was going to throw herself at him. Good looks did not equate to a good soul. Even if he was saying all the right things.

Even if a rather large part of her knew she'd been too harsh, too quick to judge that night she'd found out he'd told his father about her financial crisis.

'So, the plan is…' Alexander came to her side, then turned around and faced the empty space. 'I'm going to knock down the wall between the lounge and the kitchen. Convert it into open-plan living. Bring some more light into the room. And then I'm going to hire someone to fix the roof. Then I'll re-sand and revarnish the floors. Then I'm thinking a fresh coat of paint, an AGA in the kitchen and lots of rugs and a cosy couch will make it a place that I can call home.'

If seeing Alexander's handsome face smiling at her when she'd entered the room hadn't been enough to give her a heart attack, this piece of news was.

'You what?' Sophie crossed her arms and pinched the soft underside of her flesh. This must be a dream. It was all too weird. 'You're not going to build the resort?'

'Of course not. What we're planning to do is a million times better than that has-been of an idea.' He slung an arm over her shoulder. Light. Non-committal. Giving her the option to move away should she want to.

Sophie didn't want to.

'What's going to happen is I'm going to move in. I've bought the place off Natalie. Not for what we were originally offering, but she seemed to be more than okay with the money I presented. It meant she could buy the place off Mr Murphy next door and still have some money spare.'

Sophie glanced around the room. In her shock at seeing Alexander she'd yet to realise there was so sign of Natalie and the kids. No laundry. No toys. No empty mugs. Just a bunch of furniture pushed up against one wall opposite from where Alexander was working.

'Where is Natalie? And the kids? Have they already moved into Mr Murphy's?'

Alexander shook his head. 'Not yet. They're staying with her parents until it's all sorted. And before you get angry at her for not telling you about all this. She wanted to, but I wanted to make sure everything was in order before I returned. I didn't want to let you down again. Didn't want to hurt you.'

'I have got to stop eating cheese before bed and figure out a way to stop Puddles sleeping in my bed and waking me up at all hours for a patting session. No more. This is crazy.' Sophie hooked a step ladder that was sitting in the middle of the room with her foot and dragged it towards her, ducked out from under Alexander's arm and crouched down to sit on it. Sticking to the lowest rung in case she had a case of the dizzies and fell off. 'You're meant to be in London. Working for that horrible father of yours. Selling your soul to the devil. Not moving in next door and making it so my best friend doesn't have to move away.'

Alexander sunk to his haunches and placed the hammer in Sophie's hands. 'See it's real. That hammer is as real as I am.'

Sophie ran her thumb over the smooth grain of the wood. 'This is madness.'

'Well, love is. Isn't it? No one's ever written about how sensible love is.'

'Love?' The hammer slipped out of her hand and fell to the ground without, strangely, making a sound.

Alexander's smile morphed into pain as he leapt up and hopped around the room. 'Ow, ow, ow, ow, ow, ooooooooow.' He collapsed on the ground and held his booted foot in his hand. 'This. Is. Meant. To be. Romantic.' The words were forced out between deep breaths. 'Grand gestures. All the things that happen in romances.' He pulled his shoe off and inspected his toe.

'Is it okay?' Sophie made to touch his toe, but it was pulled out of reach before she got to it. 'Sorry. Dumb idea. Who'd want their sore toe touched when they were in agony? Is it broken? Did I break it?'

'No, I think it's fine.' He flexed his toe and grimaced. 'Mostly, sort-of fine. And what's this about Puddles waking you up at night? You never let him sleep with you, even when I begged.'

Sophie tried for a nonchalant shrug but couldn't stop the smirk appearing on her face. 'Well, it turns out once you let someone into your bed it can quickly become a habit.'

Alexander's cheeks flushed a curious pink.

'That's for the "hammering" comment.' She scrambled onto

her knees and shuffled over to sit by Alexander. 'So, what's the deal? Why are you back? And be honest.'

'Because I want to be back. I want to be with you.' His eyes darkened with sincerity. 'And I believe that Herring Cove is lovely as it is, but has potential to be even better. Here, this will explain it better than I can.' He reached into his back pocket, pulled out a sheet of paper and unfolded it.

Sophie scanned its contents. 'You've got businesses here, but there aren't even buildings in that spot.' She jabbed at the roughly drawn map where a bakery and gift shop sat beside each other on a lot that was currently barren.

'If it all goes to plan, there will be.'

Alexander was so confident, so sure of himself. How could he be when Sophie's stomach was churning with excitement and fear and the sheer possibilities of his project.

'Initially I want to fix these places up. I've also bought the farm out the back because I didn't think it was right to go back on the agreement we had.'

'But what about your father? Have you left the company? Have you abandoned your family to do your own thing?'

'No. Well, not quite. The thing is building the resort wasn't making me feel good in here.' He touched his chest, where his heart lay beneath, and patted it twice. 'Leaving my family didn't make me feel that way either, but I couldn't keep doing what I was doing if I wanted to feel right within myself. Which meant I had to stand up to my father and make him see that there were other ways we could make money. That reinvigoration didn't necessarily require destruction.'

Sophie tried to piece together what she was hearing. It sounded right, but it also sounded too good to be true. 'And what? He just went with your idea? Folded? He doesn't strike me as a man who bends.'

'You're a good judge of character, Sophie. He didn't just bend. We struck a deal. If I can raise half the capital to do this, he will provide the other half. If my vision works, we'll integrate it into the Fletcher model.'

'And how much money do you need to raise?'

Alexander mentioned a figure that sent Sophie's gut into freefall. 'That's ridiculous. An insane amount of money. How would you make it work? And why would you? You could lose everything.'

'Or I could gain everything.' Alexander shrugged, his face the picture of sincerity. 'I've spoken to the bank. I've put my savings into this. My home in London is on the market, and the money from that will be invested into the project. I'm all in. If I can pull this off, and I'm confident I can, I'll be able to do work that matters to me, while leading the Fletcher Group in an exciting new direction.'

Sophie massaged her temples. Tried to get her brain around the scope of Alexander's project. 'This is all well and good, but there's not enough people here to support something of this scale. You've seen what it's like. A handful of locals. Empty houses dotted along the clifftops.'

'Exactly. Empty houses. That could provide income by becoming rental accommodation to tourists. They'd pay a pretty penny for those views. Once we've bought them, all we'd need to do is tidy them up, take photos, upload them to accommodation sites and employ someone local to run the day-to-day operations. Other locals might take the opportunity to lease a shop at a reasonable price and start a business. Or fresh faces could be attracted to the area to do the same. The main thing is we can retain the charm of Herring Cove while making it a place where tourists will come and stay, have fun, relax, spend money… all without destroying the heart and soul of the place.' Alexander tugged the paper out from her fingers and set it to the side, then took hold of Sophie's hand. 'I've thought it all through. Run the numbers. There's no reason why we can't make this a success.'

'We'. Why did she feel like Alexander was including her in that word? And how could he so easily throw himself into a project

195

so risky? How, when he was putting literally everything he had on the line, did he not fear failure? Fear the repercussions?

'It's all so big, Alex. So *much*. Your vision is beyond anything I could ever imagine for the place, and if anyone could make it happen, it's you. But there are plenty of other places where you could test out this reinvigoration of yours. Ones that aren't so rundown. That wouldn't need as much work. I simply can't understand why you'd uproot your life, everything you've worked for, in order to move to a tiny seaside village and risk... well, everything.'

'Like you were about to do? Offering up your bookshop to my father? Preparing to sell and move on like you weren't going to lose your heart in doing so?'

I lost my heart when you left. Sophie held the words tight. Couldn't say them. Didn't want to risk the rejection. Alexander may be making out like everything was fine between them... but it wasn't.

Not when she had one thing left to say.

'I'm sorry, Alex. I shouldn't have attacked you the way I did that night. Shouldn't have doubted your openness, your honesty. I should have given you a chance to explain.' Sophie shook her head and let out a huff, releasing the tension she'd held in every fibre of her being since that night. 'I'm trying to take more risks, trying to be more open, trying to be like *you*. It's not easy for me. This kernel of loneliness that sits so deeply inside has caused me to make such mistakes. It's hard for me to trust.'

'Well then, there's only one thing for it.' Alexander took her hand and held it to his heart. 'You need to stop being lonely. Then the kernel will disappear.'

'Easier said than done.' Sophie became aware of Alexander's thumb stroking her hand, back and forth. It wasn't horrible.

'It's easily done, Sophie. If you trust yourself. I understand what it is to feel lonely. I'm yet to meet a person who made me feel whole inside... who got me. Then I met you. And everything

I'm doing here is because of you. You've made me see that my life had no real purpose. Yes, I was good at my job. Yes, I could get yesses out of no's. Yes, I was on track to be the perfect CEO of our business that my mother and father wanted me to be. But my heart was never in it. Demolishing beautiful buildings – part of our heritage, our history – in order to modernise with paint-by-numbers edifices, and making money off quaint spots while destroying what made them special, is not what I want to do. I wanted to be like you. To revel in my job. To turn up to work each day glad to be there. Not wanting to be anywhere else.'

Sophie turned her attention to the tired, vine-covered building across the road. Imagined it freshly painted white with sea-blue trim. A flower box out the front alongside a sign that boasted fresh, handmade pasties or organic meat, or a florist with fresh blooms in buckets bursting from its front door. The possibilities were there, but could one person take on a whole town and turn it around?

Sophie shook her head. 'I can't let you do this. You could end up with nothing.'

Alexander lifted her hand from his chest to his lips and pressed a kiss against her palm. 'Sophie, you can't stop me. Besides, if it doesn't work?' He shrugged. 'With love on my side, I'll have everything I need.'

Sophie's heart squeezed and grew all at once. Did Alex just talk about love, talk about it being at his side? Was he talking about... 'Er, this love you're talking about. Um, just so we're clear...'

He dropped a kiss on her nose. 'I'm talking about you, Sophie Jones. Only you. I love you. And I know it's soon. I know it's quick. But I know what my heart tells me. Also, if that "arse" of a father of mine has taught me anything, it's that you should strike while the iron's hot. That is if the iron is still hot. Or luke-warm?' His eyes widened as his lips kicked up in a hopeful half-smile. 'I can work with lukewarm.'

She'd thought she'd lost Alexander. Believed she'd driven him away. Had been too afraid to apologise. To consider a second chance.

But here he was, sitting in front of her, telling her he loved her. Putting his heart, his trust, his hope on the line.

Two could play at that game. And for the first time ever, she wasn't afraid to try. Wasn't afraid to fail. Because with Alexander by her side she didn't think she could.

Sophie leaped to her feet. 'Can you stand?'

Alexander wriggled his toe experimentally. 'I think I can hobble about on this thing.'

'Good.'

She reached her hand out and he took it, and together they pulled him into a standing position.

'I can't believe you nearly broke my toe.' Alexander ran his hand through her hair, then cupped her cheek.

She closed her eyes and leaned into his touch. 'I can't believe you just confessed your undying love for me.'

'The way you wield a hammer, it might well be short-lived. You drop that thing on my head…'

Sophie opened her eyes and playfully pushed Alexander. 'Cheeky. Keep giving me grief like that and…'

'And you'll what?' He snaked his arm around her waist and pulled her close.

Sophie went to greet his question with a sharp retort but found nothing on her tongue. She was too happy. Too… complete. 'I'll keep hanging around. That's what I'll do. Pinch me?'

Alexander tweaked her nose. 'That's as good as you're going to get.'

She ran her thumb over his lips. 'I did dream about you after you left. Dreamed of us together. Not "in the past" kind of dreams, either. Like future dreams. Us walking down the beach as a sunset I've yet to see sank below the horizon. Drinking beer in the pub as Rob played a punk-pop mish-mash of all things. Beautiful dreams. Dreams I never thought would come true...'

'Well, I can't guarantee Rob's going to punk-pop it up anytime soon.' Alexander grinned, his tongue peeking out between his teeth. 'But I think beer in the pub and long walks on the beach at sunset could well happen.' His smile disappeared and his eyes grew serious as his hand circled the back of her neck. 'Did you dream about us... you know...'

'Oh, every night. Dreamed you put on quite the performance. You've got a lot to live up to.' Sophie's giggle disappeared into a kiss. Long, slow, deliberate. Filled with promises for the future.

Sophie broke the kiss off. If she was going to do this, if she was going to commit to Alexander, she was going to do it properly. She was trusting her instincts. She was going all in.

She took hold of his hand and dropped down onto one knee.

'Sophie? You okay? Did you lose something?' Alexander peered down at her, his brows knitted in concern.

'I'm fine. Just have something important to do. So, shush.' She placed a finger upon her lips. 'Alexander Fletcher, when you came into my life I nearly made the second-biggest mistake I've ever made. And that was push you out of it. Thankfully – well, thanks to Ginny – I was forced to let you stick around.'

'I've always liked that woman.'

Sophie shot Alexander a warning look and he zipped his lips.

'Had you left that day, I'd never have met anyone who got under my skin the way you did, who forced me to tear down my boundaries, to let you inside. I kind of feel like you Trojan-horsed me, and I'm not mad about it. In fact...' Sophie took a deep breath. It was now or never. 'In fact, I love that you did. Because I love you. I never thought I could let anyone that close again, could risk my heart like that, but you're worth it. If you can move your life from London to Herring Cove, then I would like you, Alexander Fletcher, to move in with me.'

Alexander clutched his heart. 'Bloody hell. For a moment I thought you were going to ask me to marry you.'

'And what would you have said?' Sophie pushed herself up to full height and wrapped her arms around Alexander's waist.

'No.'

'Really?' She opened her mouth in mock-outrage. 'If I had said "Alexander Fletcher, will you marry me?" you'd have said no?'

'Maybe.' Alexander dropped a kiss on her lips, then pulled back.

Sophie tapped her chin. 'Hmm, you know, a wise man once told me a no was the first step in a negotiation to getting a yes.'

'Is that right?' Alexander tipped his head to the side. 'Well, how about this… I quite like the sound of this marriage idea, so I'll move in with you if one day you promise to walk down the aisle with me.'

'Can I wear a poofy meringue dress, massive tiara, have a thousand bridesmaids, and a twenty-tier fruit cake with two icing lovebirds on top?'

Alexander's eyes widened in mock-horror. 'Is it too late to take this conversation back?'

Sophie shook her head. 'Definitely too late. Besides, you started it by thinking I was proposing to you. So, do we have a deal?'

Alexander held his hand out. 'In that case, yes. We have a deal. I will move in with you. But we're going to have to further negotiate the wedding terms. Two bridesmaids, two-tier chocolate cake, and you can wear the poofiest dress and the grandest tiara in the entire world.'

'I'm going to regret the dress and tiara comment, aren't I?' Sophie met Alexander's hand and revelled in its strength, in how sure it was. Like he knew they could survive anything life would throw at them, like he knew that together they would succeed.

Even more amazing, she believed him.

In Alexander Fletcher, Sophie Jones had met her match. And she knew, without a doubt, she could trust him. With all her heart, and all her soul.

EPILOGUE

Sophie smoothed a wrinkle that wasn't there from the creamy swath of flowing silk fabric that fell to the ground, straightened up and faced the mirror as Ginny buttoned the tiny pearls that had been hand-sewn on the back by the local dressmaker.

'Just breathe. Put one foot in front of the other. And try not to arse over whilst walking down the world's longest aisle.'

It had seemed like such a good idea at the time. A wedding held on the beach where she and Alexander had first truly begun to bond. To understand each other. The place where they'd spent countless hours since walking and talking, paddling and splashing. Not to mention kissing. All the kissing. So much kissing. With some hand-holding too.

It was where he'd officially proposed. Where she'd said yes.

And today she was going to upgrade that 'yes' into an 'I do'.

'Can't blame you for staring at yourself.' Ginny came up behind her and tweaked the flower-embroidered caplet sleeves. 'You look beautiful.' She touched her burgeoning stomach. 'And I look like a whale in lavender chiffon.'

Sophie rolled her eyes at Ginny's wrinkled-nosed reflection in the mirror. 'You look stunning. Here.' She reached behind her and picked up a velvet navy-blue drawstring bag. 'This is for you, to say thank you.'

'It's your wedding and I get the presents.' Ginny took the bag and opened it, pulling out a silver chain bracelet with three charms attached. 'A book. An angel. And a heart.' She passed the chain to Sophie and held her wrist out.

'The book for me. The angel for Nat, since she's always kept an eye on me. The heart for you, since you've loved me unconditionally, at my best and at my worst.' She fastened the bracelet and pulled Ginny in for a hug. 'You've got the biggest, fiercest heart I've ever met, Ginny. Love you.'

'Love you too.' Ginny squeezed her tight. 'Love you even though you're making me traipse down that shocking track to the beach when I could drop at any moment.'

'You make it sound like the track is treacherous. It's anything but since Alexander's business had it all fixed up.' Sophie smiled to herself. *Alexander's business.* He'd come so far in the last year. His plans for Herring Cove had been more successful than either of them could have dreamed, and his father had promoted him to Co-CEO, with Alexander in charge of taking the growth model he'd created in Herring Cove and working with other small Cornish villages that were in need of a hand to elevate them to boutique tourist destinations in keeping with each village's individual charms.

'Time to go, Soph.' Ginny picked up their bouquets, brimming with sunflowers, gypsophila, roses and delphinium and passed one to Sophie. 'You ready?'

'More than ready.' Sophie checked her reflection one more time and loved what she saw in it. Her cheeks were flushed, her eyes sparkling. A smile that wouldn't quit her lips. More than that, she saw peace and contentment. A happy soul. Not a single kernel of loneliness to be found or felt.

They made their way down the stairs and into the bookshop. Her fingertips trailed the spines of the books in the closest shelf as she floated to the front door. She breathed in the crisp, clean scent of new books mixed with the aromatic muskiness of the first editions she and Alexander went hunting for on their one day off.

It was the smell of home. Of happiness. Of security, trust and love.

Ginny opened the door and gasped. 'They outdid themselves.'

Sophie stepped into the bright sunshine and followed Ginny's delighted gaze up the street.

Silver and gold bunting hung from lamppost to lamppost. The flower boxes were freshly made up with blooms that matched the colour scheme of her bouquet. Solar-powered fairy lights circled the lampposts, ready to illuminate the lane, their love, when the sun sank beneath the horizon.

She laughed as she saw a miniature bride and groom had been placed on the shop sign Alexander had carved by hand. A stack of books, perfectly chiselled, so much so they almost looked real, with the spine of the top book reading 'All Booked Up' in gold script.

She didn't think her smile could grow any larger, yet it had. 'It's beautiful.'

'It's all Alexander.' Ginny clapped her hands with glee. 'He rounded up anyone and everyone he could to help. Not that he had to try all that hard. He's got the villagers wrapped around his little finger.'

'He's always had that ability, that son of mine.'

Sophie twisted round to see Frank standing a few steps away, looking dapper in a three-piece dove-grey suit, complete with top hat and cravat.

'Would you look at you, Mr Fletcher. Don't you scrub up well,' she teased, laughing as Frank's cheeks bloomed pink.

'Well it's not every day you get to welcome a new member to your family. One we're thrilled to have. Thrilled being an under-statement.' He stepped forward and crooked his arm.

Sophie slipped her arm through. 'You're too kind. Keep it up. I like it.' She squeezed Frank's forearm, and marvelled at how far their relationship had come.

Frank had not been the easiest nut to crack, but little by little he'd come out of his shell. Seeing how Alexander and Sophie worked as a team, supporting each other and thriving on it – personally and professionally – had eased his initial concerns that Sophie and Alexander weren't suited, were too different in background, to survive.

'Right.' Ginny clapped her hands to get their attention. 'I'm going to waddle off, fast as my pregnant elephant cankles can carry me. You two wander down. I'll have the band start the music in seven minutes, okay?'

Sophie lifted her flowers to her forehead. 'Yes, sir.'

Ginny rolled her eyes, blew a kiss, then hurried down to the cliff's beach entrance.

'Waddling elephant cankles, my arse,' Sophie muttered, which earned her a hearty laugh from Frank.

'You set, my dear?' He tightened his grip. 'And tell me I'm not the only nervous one.'

'You're the only nervous one.' Sophie grinned. 'I'm too happy to be nervous. I get to marry the love of my life. It's not something that happens every day.'

'No. No, it's not.'

Frank and Sophie set off at a leisurely pace, taking the time to accept the good wishes that came flowing from the bustling shops on either side of them. It may have been a Sunday, but Herring Cove was filled with out-of-towners enjoying pastries from the local artisan bakery, cheeses from the newly opened cheesemonger, and discovering local arts and crafts at the gift shop.

Alexander's dream for their village had come true, and he was beloved for making it happen, by no one more than Sophie.

They reached the cliff's pathway entrance just as the string quartet began 'Here Comes the Bride'.

'Right on time.' There was no hiding the admiration in Frank's voice. 'If that Ginny ever wants a job she can have one. She'd have my contractors going at double speed.'

Sophie hitched her skirt up a little as they made their descent, the faces below tipping towards them. 'I think she's about to have her hands full. Doubly so now that the online store Natalie created for her has seen her skincare business take off.'

'Well, I'll slip her my card along with the offer in case she ever wants a change of pace.'

'You Fletchers and your inability to take no for an answer.' Sophie grinned as she saw two small figures standing beside Ginny jumping up and down with excitement. Bella stopped to twirl around, sending her pink dress skirt out in a circle. Joe tugged at the tie Natalie had insisted he wear, telling him a ring bearer had to look extra dashing.

Ginny flashed her the thumbs up, took Joe and Bella in hand, then walked them up the aisle to where Natalie was standing, looking gorgeous in the lavender bridesmaid dress, even more so because of the smile on her face. One that had grown in the past few months as her website business had flourished, along with her self-confidence.

Frank and Sophie took the last few steps down to the beach and were greeted by Veronika, looking regal in an emerald green boat-necked, form-fitting dress.

'You look stunning, Sophie. An absolute vision.' She threaded her arm through Sophie's as the three of them began to walk down the aisle towards Alexander, his back turned to her.

She smiled as she saw his foot tapping impatiently. Stopping when Mike, who had struck up a solid friendship with Alexander and had happily stepped up to be his groomsman, nudged him to let him know his bride was near.

He turned, his mouth falling as his eyes widened – and misted up. 'You look beautiful,' he mouthed.

'You look hot,' she mouthed back, fanning herself with her bouquet for extra effect.

Hot was an understatement. In his black, tailored suit, paired with a crisp white shirt, left open in keeping with the casual environment, Alexander had never looked so handsome.

'Thank you for allowing us to walk you up the aisle.' Frank raised her hand and kissed it as he stepped back.

'I'm so glad to have a daughter in the family.' Veronika pressed a kiss to her cheek. Completely at odds from the cool air-kiss Sophie had received on their first meeting.

Sophie returned the kiss. Her heart full for the woman who'd taken the time to get to know her. Never pressed. Never fussed. Sophie had taken Veronika's initial distance to mean she was not fond of her, but over family dinners, which became weekends spent together searching out first editions when Alexander was too busy to come along, she realised she'd mistaken dislike for a natural reserve. One that hid a warm, generous woman, who hadn't just accepted Sophie into her family, but ensured she felt very much a part of it.

Sophie passed her flowers to Natalie, blew her a kiss, then with a deep breath turned to her soon-to-be husband.

Their hands found each other and the ceremony began.

Rob, who'd attained his celebrant certificate specially for the occasion, officiated with his usual charm. Weaving a tale of how the two met, having their guests in fits of laughter one moment, dabbing their eyes the next.

'And now for the important bit.' Rob gave them an encouraging nod. 'The vows.'

Sophie swallowed hard, terrified she'd forget the words she and Alexander had spent hours crafting, then more hours trying to remember.

They were simple words. And few of them. But they meant everything. Embodied their love exactly.

Alexander held her gaze, sent her strength. She returned his support with a squeeze of hands, then took a deep breath…

'I, Sophie, promise to never let fear see us fall. To risk everything to ensure we grow. To trust in us, always.'

'I, Alex, promise to stand up for us. To catch us should we fall. To keep us steady no matter what life throws our way.'

'I promise to love you with my heart.'

'I promise to love you with my soul.'

'For you are mine.'

'As I am yours.'

'Forever.' The last word said together, in perfect unison, as they slipped a gold band onto each other's ring finger.

'And with those beautiful words, I now pronounce you husband and wife. You know what to do next....'

Their guests laughed as Alexander pulled her closer, and they sealed the deal the best way they knew how.

With a kiss.

One that spoke of unshakeable foundations. Good bones. A solid roof.

And a lifetime of love.

ACKNOWLEDGEMENTS

Where would I be without you, wonderful reader? Thank you for taking the time to read my book. For taking a chance on my writing. For all your support.

My eternal gratitude to my husband and daughter. Thank you for putting up with a messy house, thrown together meals, and the odd moment of 'are there any clean undies?', while I write, edit... and have the odd existential crisis.

To those who help Englishify things for me when my Kiwiness gets in the way, Natalie Gillespie, my copy-editor Clare, and the fabulous HQ Digital writer crew - your knowledge-sharing is truly appreciated. Thank you.

Ah, the editor. Where would a writer be without one? This book would be an entirely different kettle of fish if it were not for the fabulous Charlotte Mursell. Charlotte, I've loved working on Herring Cove with you. Your ability to see what I'm trying to say, point it out, and make it better, blows. My. Mind. It's like you know my brain better than I do. You're one in a million. A goodie. A keeper. Never leave me!

Dear Reader,

Thank you so much for taking the time to read this book – we hope you enjoyed it! If you did, we'd be so appreciative if you left a review.

Here at HQ Digital we are dedicated to publishing fiction that will keep you turning the pages into the early hours. We publish a variety of genres, from heartwarming romance, to thrilling crime and sweeping historical fiction.

To find out more about our books, enter competitions and discover exclusive content, please join our community of readers by following us at:

🐦 *@HQDigitalUK*

🅕 *facebook.com/HQDigitalUK*

Are you a budding writer? We're also looking for authors to join the HQ Digital family! Please submit your manuscript to:

HQDigital@harpercollins.co.uk.

Hope to hear from you soon!

If you loved *The Little Bookshop at Herring Cove* then turn the page for an exclusive extract from *The Cosy Coffee Shop of Promises...*

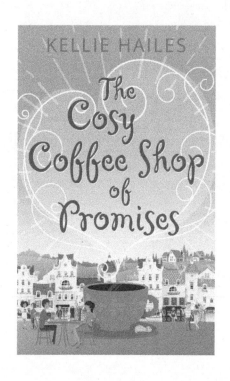

CHAPTER ONE

'Wine. Now. And don't get mouthy with me.'

Mel watched Tony's sea-blue eyes light up as his lips parted slightly...

'What's got your knick...'

'I'm serious,' she cut in, before he had a chance to be the second person to grind her gears that day. 'I'm in no mood for your cheek. And I can tell by that twitchy jaw of yours that you're contemplating still trying to give me some.' Mel took off her navy peacoat and shuddered as wintry air wrapped its way around her thin form. She promptly buttoned up again and tugged her scarf tighter around her neck. 'All I want from you is for you to do your job, pour me a glass of pinot gris and leave me to drink it, alone, and in peace. And why is it so cold in here? It's freezing out. It shouldn't be freezing in.' She shook her head. 'No matter. I don't care. The wine will warm me up.'

'Bu...'

'No. No buts. No whys. No questions.' She pointed to the glass-doored fridge. 'Just get the bottle, get a glass, and pour.' Mel gave Tony her best glare, hoping to get past his notoriously thick skin.

She watched the muscles in his jaw continue to work, as if

debating whether to ignore her order to be left in peace or do that clichéd 'had a bad day, tell me about it' barman patter. Sensibility must have won, because he turned and bent over to grab a bottle of pinot gris from the chiller, giving her a fantastic view of his toned and rounded rear. A view she'd usually take a moment to appreciate, but not right now, not after the unexpected, and not in a good way, phone call she'd just received from her mother.

Tony sloshed the wine into a tired-looking, age-speckled glass, pushed it in her direction, then punched at the card machine. 'Here you go,' he said, proffering the handset.

Mel squinted at the numbers on the screen. 'Tony, um, that's not right. You've overcharged me.'

'No, that's the price.' Tony nodded, but kept his eyes firmly on the bar. 'Since the beginning of this week.'

'Really? You can't tell me a bottle of wine rose in price by almost double in the space of seven days?'

'You're right, it hasn't.' He glanced up. 'But the hole in my muffler is yelling at me to put the prices up. And I haven't in years, so...'

'Oh. Okay. Sorry.' Mel handed over her bank card, embarrassed to have questioned the price rise. She'd heard the village gossip. Tony's business wasn't doing so well. Apparently hadn't been for years, but had got worse since his dad passed away the year before. Not that she knew much about that. She'd been new to town, and didn't want to get a reputation as a gossip, so had only heard the odd conversation here and there over the coffee cups in her café, nothing more.

'So, are you going to just stare into that glass of wine or are you going to drink it? Because I don't have a funnel to pour it back into the bottle. Although reselling it would make my mechanic happier faster. And if you buy two glasses I might even be able to afford to put the heating on.'

Mel shot Tony a grateful smile. Despite his infamous reputation as a ladies' man, he was also known about the small farming town of Rabbits Leap as being something of a gentleman and had quite the knack of making you feel at ease, which, considering her current heightened state of irritation, was quite a feat.

'You're still not taking a sip, or a slug. And, well, it sounds like you needed a slug.'

Mel narrowed her eyes at Tony, hoping to scare him into shutting up with a stern look. 'What did I say about getting mouthy? And teasing for that matter?'

'I'm not teasing. You look pale. Paler than usual, and you know you're pretty pale, so you're almost translucent right now. Even the bright streaks of pink in your hair are looking a little less hot.'

'You pay attention to my hair colour?' Mel's hand unconsciously went to her hair and tucked a stray lock behind her ears. Tony looked at her hair? Since when? She'd always assumed he'd seen her as nothing more than a regular customer, a friendly acquaintance, not someone to take notice of. Sure, they got along well enough, would chat for a moment or two if they passed each other on the street, or if it was quiet in the pub, but that was the extent of their relationship.

'Well, you're about the most exciting thing to happen in this place for the last ten years…'

'Me? Exciting?' A tingle of pleasure stirred within her.

Tony winked and turned that tingle into a zing. Since her last boyfriend, the local vet, had taken off to care for animals overseas, Mel hadn't had any action, let alone a compliment, from a man. And apparently, if that unexpected zing frenzy that had zipped through her body was anything to go by, she'd been craving it.

'Yeah, exciting.' Tony's glance lingered on her face, as if drinking her in. 'And pretty, too.'

She rolled her eyes, trying to ignore the way her body reacted to the words of approval. She picked up her glass and took the suggested slug. She was being stupid. Tony wasn't calling *her* exciting, just her hair. And the only reason he was calling her pretty was because that's what he did; he called women pretty, he charmed them, he took them to bed, and that was that. And she'd had enough of her love life – heck, her life in general – ending with 'that was that' to be interested in someone who'd pretty much created the phrase.

'Feel better?' His eyes, usually dancing with humour, were crinkled at the corners with concern.

'Not really.'

'Have another slug.'

As she lifted the glass she glanced around the bar, taking in the bar leaners with their tired, ring-stained, laminated tops and obsolete ashtrays in their centres. The tall stools next to them looked rickety from decades of propping up farmers, the pool table needed a resurface, and as for the dartboard… it was covered in so many tiny pin holes it was amazing a dart could stay wedged in it. The village chatter was right, Tony was doing it tough…

Her eyes fell on a machine sitting at the far end of the bar. All shiny and silvery and gleaming with newness. That shouldn't be there.

Her blood heated up, and not in an 'oh swoon, a man just complimented me' kind of way.

'What is that?' Mel seethed through gritted teeth.

She couldn't believe what she was seeing. What was he thinking? Did he have it in for her, too? Was it 'Let's Piss Off Mel Day'? She'd moved to Rabbits Leap just over a year ago to try and create a sense of security for herself. A place she could settle down in, call home, maybe even meet a nice, normal guy she could fall in love with. And in one day what little security she'd carefully built was in danger of being blown apart. First her mother calling to tell her she was coming to town and bringing her special brand of crazy with her, and now this?

'What's what?' The crinkles of concern further deepened.

'That.' She pointed to the cause of her ire.

218

'The coffee machine?'

'Yeah, the coffee machine. The coffee machine that should not be in your bar, because I have a coffee machine. In my café. The only café in the village. You remember that? The one place a person can get a good cup of coffee? The place that just happens to be my livelihood, and you want to screw with it?'

Tony took a step back as if he'd been hit with a barrage of arrows. *Good.* His eyebrows gathered in a frown. But he didn't look sorry. Why didn't he look sorry? And why had he straightened up and stopped looking stricken?

'It's just business, Mel.'

'And it's just a small village, Tony.'

She looked at her wine and considered throwing the contents of it over him, then remembered how much it had cost. Taking the glass she brought it to her mouth and tipped it back, swallowing the lot in one long gulp.

She set the glass back on the bar, gently, so he wouldn't see how shaken she was. 'There's only enough room in this village for one coffee machine.' She mentally slapped herself as the words came out with a wobble, not as the threat she'd intended.

'And what does that mean?' Tony folded his arms and leant in towards her, his eyebrow raised.

Mel gulped. He wanted her to throw down the gauntlet? Fine then. 'It means you can try to make coffee. You can spend hours trying to get it right, make thousands of cups, whatever. But your coffee will never be as good as mine and all you'll have is a big hunk of expensive metal sitting unloved at the end of your bar.'

'Sounds like you're challenging me to a coffee-off.'

How could Tony be so cavalier? So unfazed by the truth? He'd spent a ton of money on something he'd only end up regretting.

Mel took a deep breath, picked up her wallet and walked to the door. She spun round to face her adversary.

'There's no challenge here. All you're good for is pulling a pint or three. Coffee? That's for the adults. You leave coffee to me.'

She leant into the old pub door, pushed it with all her might and lurched over the threshold into the watery, late-winter sun and shivered. Could today get any worse?

***

Had he done the wrong thing? Was buying that ridiculous monstrosity and installing it in the pub a stupid idea? He'd spent the last decent chunk of money he had to get it. What if it didn't fly? What would happen next? He couldn't keep the place open on the smell of a beer-soaked carpet, but he couldn't fail either. It was all he had left to remind him of his family. The Bullion had been his dad's baby. The one thing that had kept his dad sane after his mother had passed away. More than that, it was where what few solid memories he had of his mother were. Her smiling at him as he sat at the kitchen table munching on a biscuit while she cooked in the pub's kitchen. The violet scent of her perfume as she'd pulled his four-year-old self into a cuddle after he'd fallen from a bar stool while on an ambitious mountaineering expedition.

Then there was the promise he'd made to his father, the final words they'd shared as his father breathed his last. His vow to preserve The Bullion's history, to keep her alive. Dread tugged at his heart. What if he couldn't keep that promise?

God, why couldn't his father have been more open, more honest with him about their financial situation? Why couldn't he have put away his pride for one second and seen a bank manager, cap in hand, asked for a… Tony shoved the idea away. No. That wasn't an option. Not then. Not now. The McArthurs don't ask for help. That was his dad's number-one rule. A rule his father had also drilled into him. No, he wasn't going cap in hand to a bank manager. He didn't even own a cap, anyway. He just had to come up with some new ideas to breathe life into the old girl. The coffee machine had been one of them, and he'd spent the last of his personal savings buying it.

But what if Mel was right? What if he couldn't make a good coffee? Heck, what if she stole into the pub in the middle of the night and tampered with it so he couldn't?

Tony shook his head. The potential for poverty was turning him paranoid. Besides, the coffee machine was a great idea. Lorry drivers were always stopping in looking for a late-night cup, and who knew? Maybe the locals would like a cup of herbal tea or something before heading home after a big night.

Buy herbal tea. He added the item to his mental grocery list, along with bread, bananas and milk. Maybe he'd see if there was any of that new-age herbal tea stuff that made you sleep. Normally he'd do what his dad had always done and have a cup of hot milk with a dash of malt to send him off. But lately it hadn't done the trick and he'd spent more hours tossing and turning than he had actually sleeping, his mind ticking over with mounting bills, mounting problems and not a hell of a lot of solutions. Heck, he was so bone-tired he wasn't even all that interested in girls. Maybe that was the problem? Maybe he needed to tire himself out …

'Hey, baby brother!'

'Might be. But I'm still taller than you.' Tony grinned at his sister and two nephews as they piled into the pub. 'How you doing, you little scallywags?'

'Scallywags?!'

Tony laughed as the boys feigned insult and horror in perfect unison.

'You heard me. Now come and give your old uncle a hug.'

The boys flew at him, nearly knocking him over as they hurled themselves into his outstretched arms. He drew them in and held them, breathing in the heady mix of mud and cinnamon scent that he was pretty sure they'd been born with.

'Have we cuddled you long enough? Can we have a lemonade now?' Tyler peered up at him with a hopeful eye.

'And a bag of crisps?' asked Jordan, his voice filled with anticipation, and just a hint of cheek.

'Each?' They pleaded in perfect unison.

Two peas in a pod those boys were. And the loves of Jody's life. Since the day she'd found out she'd fallen pregnant to a man she'd met during a shift at the pub, a random, a one-nighter, she'd sworn off all men until the boys were old enough to fend for themselves.

Tony watched as the boys grabbed a bag of crisps each and poured two glasses of lemonade and wondered at what point Jody would decide they were old enough, because at nine they looked pretty well sorted, and he was pretty sure he spotted flashes of loneliness in her eyes when she saw couples holding hands over the bar's leaners.

'So what's with the shiny new toy?' Jody jerked her head down towards the end of the bar.

'It's what's going to save this place.'

Jody snorted and took a sip of Tyler's lemonade, ignoring his wail of displeasure. 'It's going to take a whole lot more than coffee to save this dump.'

Tony bristled. Just because this place wasn't the love of her life it didn't mean it wasn't the love of his, and just as she wouldn't hear a bad word said about her boys, he didn't like a bad word said…

'And don't get all grumpy on me, Tony McArthur. I know you love this joint, but it needs more than one person running it. You need to …'

'If you say settle down, I'll turn the soda dispenser on you.'

'Oooh, soda water, colour me scared.'

'Not soda, dear sister. Raspberry fizzy. Sweet, sticky and staining.'

Jody stuck her tongue out. 'But you should, you know, settle down. It'll do you good having a partner in crime.'

'You're one to talk.'

'I'm well settled down and I've got two partners in crime, right, boys?'

Tony laughed again as the boys rolled their eyes, then took off upstairs to his quarters where his old gaming console lay gathering dust.

'Besides, you're only going to piss off the café girl with that machine in here. You're treading on her turf, and frankly it's not a particularly gentlemanly thing to do.'

Heat washed over Tony's face. Even though he had a reputation for liking the ladies he always tried to treat them well. But that was pleasure, and this was business. Not just business, it was life and death. Actually, it was livelihood or death. And he intended to keep on kicking for as long as possible. Without the bar he was nothing. No one.

'Well, I can see by the flaming shame on your face that she's seen it.'

'Yep,' he sighed. The more he looked at the hunk of metal the worse he felt about what he'd done. There was an unspoken rule among the business people of Rabbits Leap that they didn't poach customers. It was akin to stealing. Yet he'd done just that in a bid to save The Bullion. What was worse, he'd done it to a member of the community he actually respected and always had time for.

'Tony, you've got to apologise, and then take the machine back. Do something. It's a small town and the last thing you need is to be bad-mouthed or to lose customers. Find a way to make it work.'

***

Ting-a-ling.

Mel looked up from arranging a fresh batch of scones on a rose-printed vintage cake stand to see who'd walked in, her customer-ready smile fading as she saw her tall, broad-shouldered, blond, wavy-haired nemesis.

'Get out.' Her words were cool and calm, the opposite of the fire burning in her veins, in her heart. No one was taking away her café, her chance at a stable life, especially not a pretty boy who was used to getting what he wanted with a smile and a wink.

'Is that any way to treat a customer?'

'You're not a customer. You never have been. I've not seen you step foot in here since I opened up – not once.' Mel pointed to the door. 'So get out.'

'Well, maybe it's time I decided to change that. And besides…'

She watched Tony take in the quiet café. Empty, bar her two regulars, Mr Muir and Mrs Wellbelove, who were enjoying their cups of tea and crosswords in separate silence.

'…It looks like you need the business.'

Mel rankled at the words as they hit home. She'd hoped setting up in Rabbits Leap would be a good, solid investment, that it would give her security. But that 'security' was looking as tenuous as her bank balance. The locals weren't joking when they said it was 'the town that tourism forgot'. In summer the odd tourist ambled through, lost, on their way to Torquay. But, on seeing there was nothing more than farms and hills, they quickly ambled out again. As for winter? You could've lain down all day in the middle of the street without threat of being run over. And this winter had been worse, what with farmers shutting up shop due to milk prices falling even further.

'Really? I need the business?' She raised an eyebrow, hoping the small act of defiance would annoy him as much as he'd annoyed her. 'I'm not the one putting prices up. Unlike someone else standing before me…'

Tony threw his hands up in the air as if warding the words off.

Good, she'd got to him.

'Look, Mel, I'm not here to fight.'

'Then what are you here for?'

'Coffee. A flat white. And a scone. They look good.'

'They are good.'

'Then I'll take one.' Tony rubbed his chin. 'Actually, make that two.'

Mel faked ringing up the purchase on the vintage cash register she'd found after scouring auction sites for weeks and weeks. 'That'll be on the house.'

'That's a bit cheap, isn't it?' Tony's lips lifted in a half-smile.

'It's on me. A man desperate enough to install a coffee machine in a pub clearly needs a bit of charity.' Yes, Tony was trying to take business away from her, but really, how much of a threat would he be to her business anyway? It wasn't like he could actually make a decent cup of coffee.

'So, are you going to stand there staring at me like I'm God's gift or are you going to give me my free scones?'

Mel blushed.

'Sorry, I wasn't staring. Just…'

'Imagining me kissing you. Yeah, yeah, I know. Don't worry, you're not the first woman.'

'I wasn't.' Mel sputtered, horrified. 'I wouldn't.'

'I know. I'm teasing. Relax.'

The word had the opposite effect. Mel's body coiled up, ready to attack at the next thing he said that irritated her.

Why was he having this effect on her? Usually nothing ruffled her feathers, or her multicoloured hair. She'd weathered so much change in her life that something as small as someone making an attempt to kill off her coffee business should be laughable. But as she looked into his handsome and openly amused face she wanted to take up her tongs, grab his earlobe in its metal claws, give it a good twist, then drag him to the door and shove him out of it. Instead she picked up the tongs, fished two scones out onto a plate, added a pat of butter and passed the plate to him.

'Can you just… sit. I'll bring your coffee to you.'

With a wink and a grin Tony did exactly as she asked, leaving

225

her to make his coffee in peace. The familiar ritual of grinding the beans, tamping them down, smelling the rich aroma of the coffee as it dripped into a cup while she heated the milk relaxed her, so much more than a man telling her to relax ever would. Maybe the problem wasn't that he was trying to ruin her business; maybe it was that he was trying to take away the most stability she'd had in years.

After her café in Leeds had shown the first signs of bottoming out, Mel had sold while the going was better than worse and decided to search out a new spot to move to. She'd had two rules in mind. One, the place had to have little to no competition. Two, after moving around for so many years, she finally wanted to find a place she would come to call home. So she'd packed up her life, headed south, and stumbled across Rabbits Leap after getting lost and motoring about inland Devon with a perilously low tank of petrol.

The moment she'd seen the pretty village filled with blooming flower boxes, kids meandering down the main street licking ice creams without parents helicoptering about them, and a store smack bang in the middle with a 'for rent' sign stuck to the door, a little part of her heart had burst into song. The plan had been to settle down, set up shop and make enough to save and survive. But, as she watched Tony flick through a fashion magazine, she could see her plans to make Rabbits Leap her forever home go the way of coffee dregs, down the gurgler.

She picked up the coffee and walked it over to Tony's table where he was stuffing his face.

'Your coffee.'

'Thish shcone is amazing.' Tony swallowed and brushed crumbs from his lips and chin.

Full lips, strong angular chin, Mel noted, before mentally swatting herself. She wasn't meant to be perving at the enemy. 'Well, it's my grandma's secret recipe, so it should be.'

'Can I have the recipe?'

'What part of secret do you not understand?' She set the cup down with a clank.

'Sit.' Tony pushed out the chair opposite him with his foot.

'I've things to do.'

'Sit.'

Mel huffed, then did as she was told.

'So how are things?' Tony picked up the cup and took a sip, giving a small grunt of appreciation.

'That's how good yours are going to have to be.' Mel folded her arms across her chest and tipped her head to the side. A small show of arrogance, but for all the things she wasn't great at, she knew she could cook and she could make a damn good cup of coffee.

'It's good to know the benchmark.' Tony's voice was strong but she was sure a hint of panic flashed through those blue sparklers of his. 'Anyway, this isn't about me. How are you? I haven't seen you in the pub with that vet of yours for a while now.'

Mel narrowed her eyes in suspicion. 'Have you been staking me out? Figuring all the ways you can try and horn in on my bit of business?'

'Rabbits Leap makes a habit of knowing Rabbits Leap. We keep an eye on our own. We take care of our own…' A tightening of those lush lips. A moment of regret? No matter. He'd given her ammunition.

'You take care of your own by taking over parts of their businesses? My, how civically minded you are.'

'I know you're annoyed about the machine, Mel, but you don't have to be sarcastic about it. Can't we deal with the situation like adults?'

Mel's grip around herself tightened as her irritation soared. 'I can be whatever I want in my café. And I can say whatever I want, however I want, especially when dealing with a coffee thief. What's next? You'll be calling my beans supplier? Good luck with that. They know what loyalty means.'

Tony's lips thinned out more. Good. She was getting to him. Giving him something to think about.

'As for the vet? Not that it's any of your business but we're over. He decided small-town veterinary work wasn't for him and headed over to Africa to work with wildebeest or something like that.'

'Thought he would.'

'Really?' Mel's chin lifted in surprise. She'd never thought Tony was the kind of guy who delved below the surface of anything. With that easy smile and light laugh, he seemed… well, about as shallow as one of the puddles that amassed on the main street after a spring shower.

'Yeah, he had that look about him, the "this place will do for now" look. I've seen it before. I knew it was only a matter of time before he left.' Tony picked up his coffee and took a sip. 'God, this really is good. Is everything you do this good?'

Mel's ears prickled hot. Was she imagining it or was that a double entendre? She met his blue eyes and saw not a hint of sparkle or tease. Nope, no double entendre; he wasn't trying to pick her up.

'I guess that means I was "this girl will do for now",' she said out loud, more to herself than to Tony.

'Then he was a fool. A man would be lucky to have a pink-haired barista and amazing cook loving him, cooking for him and making his morning coffee.'

'That sounds more like a slave-master relationship than a real, true-love one…'

'I'm sure the man would repay you in other ways.'

This time the sparkle was definitely in his eyes.

'I'd make sure he did.' The words came out before she could stop them, along with a wink. *Traitor.* She dipped her head to hide the flush creeping up over her cheeks. How dare her body flirt so easily with the enemy, even though, with his kind words, he was acting more like a friend. Or someone who might be

228

angling for something more than that. Not that she'd ever sleep with the enemy. Uh-uh. No way.

Taking a long, slow, cooling breath she looked up into Tony's eyes. Something flashed through them. Something quick, hot, fierce. A heck of a lot like desire. Had he been thinking about her… with him? Mel shook the thought clear. Nope, that'd never happen. They were chalk and cheese. Besides, there was no way she was playing around with the local lothario. He didn't tick any of her boxes. Well, not all of them. Hot. Yes. Fun. Yes. But he couldn't commit. She'd heard the village gossip. He was a one-man band. No woman lasted more than a night. Anyway, he was hardly boyfriend material. He only loved himself, and he was obviously careless with money, which meant careless with security, and that was the one thing Mel was always careful about.

'So why did you come here, Tony?'

'I need to apologise and then we need to have a conversation.'

Mel sat up straighter in her chair. An apology? She hadn't seen that coming. 'So, apologise.'

'I'm sorry I bought the coffee machine. Actually, I'm not. But I'm sorry you had to find out about it like that.'

'Not much of an apologiser, are you?'

He at least had the good grace to look slightly ashamed.

'Well, I'm hoping we can come to an arrangement about it.'

'Really? How about I arrange for it to be removed and you go back to bartending?'

'How about you teach me how to use it… and maybe even teach me how to cook?'

Mel couldn't believe what she was hearing. Was Tony mentally deficient?

'Cook? What are you on?'

'That smell, what is it?'

Mel sniffed the air and remembered she had lamb shanks slow-cooking in a tomato balsamic jus in the back kitchen.

'That's my dinner.'

'It smells amazing.'

'Don't try and distract me.' She waved her hand in impatience. 'Why would I teach you my whole trade? Coffee and baking? I'd be out of business within weeks.'

'No, I don't want to know how to bake. I'm talking about learning to cook real food, like whatever it is you've got going back there.' Tony's eyes sparkled with excitement.

Mel could almost see the ideas forming in his head. His whole demeanour was changing in front of her eyes, energy fair sparking off his disturbingly muscular body.

'You've seen the food we do at The Bullion. It's all deep-fried and artery-clogging. I need to get with the times, update the menu, make it appealing, *maybe* even get entertainment in on special nights, see if I can't pull in a few more punters. Turn the place into a tourist attraction, or something. Which would be good for your business, too...'

Tony leaned forward and placed his hand over hers.

Pull away.

But she couldn't. Tony's fingers tightened around the outer edges of her fist, warm, strong, capable. Hands that knew how to work. Weren't afraid of getting dirty...

Did he work out, she mused, as her eyes travelled up the length of his legs and settled on his stomach. Was there a six-pack hiding beneath that grey T-shirt? Strongly defined, hard thighs underneath those denims? Biceps made for picking a woman up and pinning her to a wall...

Get it together, girl! She squeezed her eyes shut, hoping not seeing Tony would stop those unneeded images forming in her head. It didn't work. Was this the effect he had on women? Is that why he was known for having a string of them? Was he truly irresistible?

'So are you going to help me? Or are you too busy meditating over there?'

Mel tugged her hand out from under his and rubbed her face

wearily. It had been a long day. Between her mother's announcement sending her stomach into free-fall and the revelation that the man sitting opposite her had decided to pit himself against her in the business stakes, she was ready to go to bed. Alone.

'What's in it for me?' Mel opened her eyes to see Tony giving her a charming smile.

'The pleasure of my company?'

'I'm not seeing anything pleasurable about your company.' The lie came quick and easy.

'Well, maybe it's time you did.' Tony's teasing tone was back. 'Look, how about this for a deal. You help me create a dinner menu, maybe show me how to make a decent coffee…'

Mel's eyebrows shot up, her hackles rising.

'…and I promise to not serve the java until your café closes at…'

'Three.'

'Three it is.'

'I still don't feel like it's a good enough deal for me to give you this much help…'

'Any wine you drink at the pub will be free for the duration of your help?'

The teasing tone was tinged with desperation. Tony had alluded to things not going great, things needing fixing, but maybe he was in deeper than he was willing to let on? And maybe – an idea flitted about her mind – he could help her with her latest drama, the drama that was about to blow into town any day now…

'Okay. I'm insane for doing this, I'll probably regret it with every fibre of my being, but okay. I'll help you… but you've got to do one more thing for me.'

'Anything. Just name it.'

Mel screwed up her courage and forced the words out before she could talk herself out of them. 'I need you to be my fiancé.'

If you enjoyed *The Little Bookshop at Herring Cove*
then why not try another delightfully uplifting
romance from HQ Digital?

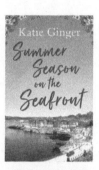